NOT YOURS TO KEEP

NOT YOURS TRILOGY
BOOK 1

ELLA JACOBS

NOT YOURS TO KEEP

This book is a work of fiction. Names, characters, businesses, organizations, places, events and incidents either are the product of the author's imagination or are used fictitiously. Any resemblance to actual persons, living or dead, events, or locales is entirely coincidental.

http://www.ellajacobs.com

ISBN 978-87-974182-1-5

First Edition: October 2022

SHA-256 hash: eff8c6be56491aeb046e5218c
22a6ffdf56fe74f7432cefd2d3c399022fea41b

— FOREWORD —

Dear reader

This is a BDSM romance, but it's not meant to show you how an ideal BDSM relationship is supposed to work. Rather, it will take you on an emotional rollercoaster journey and show you what happens when intense emotions get in the way of proper aftercare and communication, and the lines of consent blur. It will show you how instinctive and all-consuming the need to submit can be when faced with the right—or maybe wrong—Dom.

After many years in the BDSM-lifestyle myself, I've experienced both the highs and lows. The highs can make you soar like nothing else, but the lows can bring you to your knees and make you feel utterly wretched. I guess this is how the world works; the higher you fly, the harder you can drop. But with the right Dom to catch you, the fall will hurt less.

This book, and especially Grigory, will take you through all the emotions. You will hate Grigory and curse at him, but when he shows his tender side, you'll adore him and crave more—just like Clara does. Give him a chance despite all his flaws, and I hope you'll come to love him as much as I do.

Thank you for picking this book up. I hope you'll love reading it as much as I've loved writing it.

Ella

— CHAPTER 1 —

I set off in a sprint up the stairs from the metro and blink as the bright sun greets me at the top. Half an hour underground on a day like this seems like a waste of good weather. Luckily, it's supposed to last the whole summer, so I won't miss out on anything. Besides, my milky skin would burn if I were to spend even half a day under this sun.

The treetops provide a pleasant shade as I turn onto *Unter den Linden*—Under the Linden Trees. It's a fitting name for the boulevard that stretches through the middle of Berlin. Long rows of Linden Trees form a thick canopy above the busy promenade, creating a green haven amidst the city's chaos.

I can't help smiling. And why wouldn't I? Two weeks ago, I handed in my last exam, and now I'm going to spend the rest of the summer here in Berlin with Markus, doing absolutely nothing. Though, absolutely nothing tends to get me restless. I think that's why Markus asked me to come watch his rehearsal today. Or maybe because he knows I love going to work with him, seeing all the backstage preparations it takes to produce an opera.

As the line of trees end, the large building I'm headed for comes into view. Even amongst the other old, majestic buildings here, the opera stands out with its massive size, tall pillars, and sculptures. It's just as intimidating as it is mesmerizing.

My smile widens when I see Markus standing by the front entrance. He appears tiny in front of the ginormous building, but as I approach him, I'm quickly reminded I'm the only tiny creature here. Standing well over six feet tall, he easily dwarfs me and my petite frame, and I have to crane my neck to meet his eyes when I stop in front of him.

"Hi," I say, already feeling that tingling sensation he so easily evokes—a pleasant mix of excitement and fluttering nervousness.

"You look sexy as hell with that smile, Clara." He leans down to give me a deep kiss, robbing me of both air and orientation. His hand travels up my back and into my hair, fisting a handful to keep me in place. Then he intensifies the kiss into a passionate claim of possession, and the bustling city dims into a distant blur as my world zeroes in on him.

I'm panting when he finally releases me, and it takes me a moment to remember where we are. *The smile.* "You don't look too shabby yourself," I say, almost leaning up for another kiss as I take in the broad smile lines behind his day-old scruff and the crinkles at the corners of his eyes. He is utterly charming. His smile could easily part gray clouds on a gloomy day and make any woman go soft in her knees. Especially me.

Markus presses a hand to the small of my back and I follow him into an impressive lobby. Chandeliers, stone floors, and golden moldings give the place an air of grandeur. My mouth falls open as I take it all in. I've been to many places like this with Markus, but these old opera houses never cease to amaze me.

As Markus leads me deeper into the building, I understand why he insisted on meeting me outside. The place is a maze of winding halls and stairwells, and I quickly lose all sense of direction.

"How do you find your way around here?" I say, scanning my surroundings. There aren't even any signs to point you in the right direction.

Markus slips his hand farther around my waist to steer me left, down a new long hallway. "I know how these buildings work."

I guess it makes sense. Markus has been at a new opera house every month—sometimes every two weeks—for the last half year. I've been with him to many of them, and I must say The Berlin State Opera takes the prize, both in terms of size and prestige. "I know, but seriously? This is like a whole new level. The grand monster of them all."

Markus chuckles and leans in to whisper like he's telling me a secret. "I cheated a bit. I had Grigory give me some directions before I came here."

A small shiver runs down my arm at the mention of the intimidating conductor, who's Markus's best friend and the head of this house. I've only met him once and it didn't exactly go great. Like with the building, it wasn't the first time I met a famous musician, but it was the first time I met one with such an overbearing authority, and it rendered me all but speechless.

Feeling a bit unnerved at the prospect of seeing him again

today, I say, "Are you sure it's okay I'm here?" It's only the third day in a six-week period leading up to the premiere in late August, and usually these early, small rehearsals are closed to outsiders. They are quite intimate with only the conductor, his assistant, and a couple of the primary singers going over the music, and a pianist to accompany the singers.

"Of course. Otherwise, I wouldn't bring you." He gives me a reassuring smile as he grabs the handle on a door. "This is one of the benefits of being friends with the conductor." Markus winks and pushes the door open for me. "Plus, Lucia already knows you. And you know how she is. She doesn't mind an audience."

Said woman comes rushing up to me with outstretched arms as soon as we enter the large rehearsal space, the click of her thin heels echoing under the tall ceiling. "Clara, good to see you," she says with a lyrical lilt to her voice. She's playing the lead role in the opera *Tosca* and is every bit the diva as her character—but also friendly and warm if you don't get in her way.

I hug her back and engage in the typical small talk—how have you been, what have you been up to—before asking, "Are you excited to play Tosca again?" It's one of her signature roles, and she's sung it in all the big houses all over the world.

"Of course. This role is perfect for me," she says, tossing back her long auburn hair. "Tosca and I are so alike. One should think Puccini wrote the role for me."

No shit, I want to say, but keep the words to myself. Markus, though, is blunter.

"It's good you're able to see it yourself." Markus grins and gives her a friendly pat on the shoulder. "That is, unless you've misunderstood the role."

Markus and I share an amused look, and Lucia rolls her eyes, then keeps blabbering about how the role fits her. For the next few minutes, she goes on like this, the unchanging topic being herself.

Quickly losing interest, I let her talk without paying much attention. I just smile and nod at her—instead of smiling and waving like the penguins in the *Madagascar* movie would say. I *do* think she'd notice my disinterest if I started waving mindlessly.

My lips curl up with new amusement at the idea, and I don't even think Lucia sees it.

But someone else does.

Feeling the weight of Markus's attention on me, I glance up to find his smile gone, replaced by something purposeful that makes me suck in a long breath. Suddenly, he's gone into full-on dominant mode, and instantly the submissive in me sparks.

He doesn't hear a word Lucia says, doesn't notice a hair on her head. All his focus is amassed on me, and it sucks the strength straight out of my legs and covers my head in fluffy clouds. I go pliant, ready to bend to his will and accept his dominance. His lips twitch with a hint of a smile. He knows the exact effect he has on me. It's really not fair of him to do it here in public, but Lucia is so consumed by herself she probably doesn't notice anyway.

My eyes flutter. I can barely maintain contact, yet I'm unable to see anything else. The room is sucked into a vacuum. The air too.

Breathe, Markus mouths, the corners of his lips lifting into that charming smile of his. He's every bit the classic tenor with his good looks and brilliant charm—but with plenty of male confidence to balance it out.

Warmth spreads through my chest, and my lips twitch, a huge smile threatening to break free. I need to submit. Or let my smile blossom. Maybe both.

The smile wins, bursting across my face as my eyes dart to the floor, finding a moment's reprieve in the wooden floorboards. Taking a deep breath, I look back up and find his gaze alight with triumph.

He loves when I succumb to his will, and I love when he wields his dominance in a single look.

"How's the piano playing going?" Lucia pulls me out of the heady dynamic, and it takes me a second to shrug it off and find my way back to the room.

"It's going great," I say, smiling at her and hoping the heat in my cheeks has faded. "Well, a bit stagnant since I handed in my last exam. I think I need to get back into a routine."

"I know the feeling. Try to find a new, exciting project. It usually helps me."

"Well, I have been considering delving into Liszt lately, but I'm a bit intimidated by his hand size." I hold out my small hand which is better suited for Bach and Mozart, yet I keep insisting on playing music by romantic composers—which is *not* suited for small hands. Especially not Liszt.

Lucia waves off my concern. "Don't let it stop you. I know several concert pianists with small hands who play Liszt and

Rachmaninoff without a problem."

"Really?"

"Oh yes. You just need to know how to roll the big chords and maybe cut out a note here or there." Lucia points to Markus. "Ask him to set you up for a lesson with Grigory. He can surely show you all the tricks—though, God knows Grigory doesn't need them himself with those big hands."

I glance up at Markus and notice a weird smirk on his face. I frown a little but don't think further about it as Lucia brings my attention back to our conversation.

"Seriously, he's a really good teacher despite his gruff façade," she says.

A lesson with the famous conductor would be like a dream, but one of those nerve-racking ones you prefer to stay in your head. Since Markus and Grigory have been good friends for many years, it's not unrealistic per se, but the man is as intimidating as conductors come, and I'm so far from his level I wouldn't be comfortable with it.

I'm about to tell Lucia I'm sure my piano teacher back home can help me when the door opens and I turn to see who's coming.

Speak of the devil.

Hard soles click against the floor as Grigory Volkov enters. He takes the room like he owns it—which he basically does, being the newly appointed chief conductor here at the Berlin state opera. He walks straight up to his music stand, prompting everyone to take their places.

Lucia walks to the middle of the big room, and Markus presses a quick kiss to my lips before following her. I go to take a chair at the side with a sudden need to get out of the way in a hurry.

"From mark 37, 'Mia Gelosa,'" Grigory says and lifts his arms.

The pianist plays the short intro and Markus starts the love duet with a tender "mia gelosa." Lucia chimes in with her own lines as Markus keeps singing about how jealous she is, and their voices blend into perfect harmony, a mix of dueling lines and high moments of shared passion.

Shivers shoot down my arms. It sounds so effortless and deep-felt. They are both amazing singers and actors—the latter not to be taken for granted in the world of opera. If I hadn't seen them together offstage, I would be worried about their sizzling chemistry.

But there's no need to worry. If not because I trust Markus, then because Lucia is the last person he'd fall for. The two would make for an explosion of nuclear proportions if they were more than friends. Her constant rambling and need for control would make him haul her over his knee and give her the spanking of the year, and then she would flip out and give him the raging diva-outburst of the year.

I'd love for him to drag me over his knee, though, and smack my butt until it turns blue. Like he did last night—except for the color. He rarely hits me hard enough to leave bruises. I shift in my seat to see if the soreness, at least, has lingered, but I'm not that lucky.

Heat gathers between my legs as I remember the delicious sting and Markus's arm pinning me in place. I can't help squeezing my thighs together as I watch him. God, I need something else to look at or I'll start wiggling my hips.

I let my eyes drift over the room, and they fall to the conductor instead. He oozes control and perfection with his clean-shaven jaw and formal attire. He's wearing pressed charcoal slacks, black leather shoes, and a white dress shirt with the two top buttons open. There's not a single wrinkle to be found, not a speck of dust on his shiny shoes.

His hair is the only thing not adhering to the strict regimen. It was neatly combed back when he came in, but now it's a haphazard mess, strands falling onto his forehead. Once in a while, he makes a quick brush of his hand to shove it away, but it always falls back, refusing to stay in place. It's a perfect deep brown with only a few streaks of gray at the temples, revealing he's close to fifty.

The furrow between his thick bushy brows deepens as the music intensifies, and my heart beats a little faster at the sight. He looked serious before, and now he appears downright threatening. It doesn't help when he stops the music and speaks with a deep Russian accent before starting the music anew with a quick hand motion.

He's a force field of contrasts, danger, and confidence as he moves his arms with broad strokes, guiding the singers like he was born to do so. He doesn't miss a cue, knowing exactly what he wants and how to get it with no more than a flick of his wrist or a change of expression.

It must be heady being under his musical direction. But also secure. There's no doubt or hesitation, only steady leadership.

I remember the same energy from a few weeks back when Markus took me to see him conduct Rimsky-Korsakov's *Scheherazade* at the Berlin Philharmonic. It seemed he was playing the orchestra and not the orchestra playing the music.

I was in a trance from start to end, pulled into the mesmerizing universe of *1001 Nights* told in notes instead of words. I've always loved Rimsky-Korsakov's *Scheherazade*—the contrasts, the depth, and the dramatic atmosphere. But Grigory Volkov lent an entirely new intensity to it, making the pureness of the violin solos even sweeter and the bombastic brass theme more brutal.

Now he's doing the same with *Tosca,* breathing life into every single note, correcting and adjusting the smallest of details. The magic is clear when they repeat the duet. If I thought it was good before, there are no words for it now.

When Markus took me backstage to meet him after the symphony a few weeks ago, I was a bundle of nerves. I had prepared what to say, and it helped somewhat seeing the friendly way he greeted Markus. But when Grigory's intent gaze landed on me, I went blank. All I could manage was a timid "Hi," as I took his proffered hand.

His palm felt enormous around my slender hand and his eyes bored into me with a directness all too personal for a first-time introduction. It was like he saw something I wasn't aware of myself. Some deep secret part of me no one else could uncover. Like he'd caught me red-handed, fingers deep in the cookie jar.

I shudder at the thought, relieved those eyes don't fall on me today—maybe a bit disappointed he hasn't even acknowledged my presence, but relieved nonetheless.

I force my gaze away, not daring to continue watching. At some point, his eyes are bound to drift my way, and I don't want him to catch me staring like some starry-eyed teenager.

So I move my focus back to the singers.

"Lucia," Markus stops her mid-singing. "It sounds much better when you hold back on the high notes."

"No, no, just listen." She starts singing again without a cue from Grigory.

"Save the climax until I come in; it's too much if you keep going like this the whole way through," Markus says.

Lucia keeps singing like the diva she is, unheeding any input that doesn't fit her personal vision of how the performance should be.

Markus, calm as ever, lets her sing it out, and it's hard not to marvel at his never-ending patience. Not many things can throw him off-kilter, not even a stubborn diva.

The corners of my lips curl up as I watch him watching her. Only his slightly knitted brows reveal his skepticism.

Then something happens. The hairs on my neck stand on end and my skin prickles as I feel someone watching me.

I turn my head and look straight into Grigory's eyes. Dark and intent. His eyes shoot past my defenses, taking me in with a perceptiveness that should only be allowed in intimate relations.

Unease churns in my stomach, and I wring my hands as I try not to cast my eyes down.

He keeps watching me like it's his right to tear past my walls and peer into my most private inner core—where my submission resides.

His gaze is too imposing, and I only last a few seconds before my eyes fall to the floor.

When I chance a glance back up, Grigory lowers his chin in a silent command, forcing me to maintain eye contact.

My blood surges in my veins and my body jitters with the need to turn my gaze away, but I can't.

He's impossible to read. At first glance, I would say he's strict, impatient maybe—doesn't like me being here? But there seems to be no tightness in his features. So maybe he's just curious or bored, needing something else to look at?

His gaze glides down to my fumbling hands, and I think he actually huffs, his chest making this slight jump. When his eyes come back up to meet mine, they narrow with dark intent.

My heart leaps in my chest like it's trying to escape an axe murderer. I stare at the floor—like you're supposed to when facing a dangerous animal—and keep my gaze there for several seconds until I think it's safe to lift my eyes again.

But it isn't. He's still watching.

The ominous undercurrent is gone though. His eyes seem to soften as his mouth makes a small twitch resembling a smile. And then he's gone, his focus back on the singers. My eyes fall to my clenched hands, staring at them with dumbfounded confusion as I try to make sense of what just happened.

"Soft high notes!"

I jump from the sudden force of the rumbling command, but when I look up at Grigory, there's no sign of anger or impatience. His stance is calm, hands resting on the music stand; only his rough features reflect the gravity of his words.

Lucia stops singing immediately, as shocked as I. She swings her long hair and keeps her chin high like she's trying to save face. But when Grigory starts the music from the top, she keeps the high notes soft.

From then on, I try not to stare at Grigory too obviously, but I can't help it. A strange mix of fascination and apprehension draws me to him, and my eyes keep fluttering back. Luckily, he doesn't catch me. I don't think I could bear the weight of those intense eyes again. Something inside me would implode.

* * *

After two hours of rehearsal—me spending half the time reading—Markus stalks toward me with a mischievous smile playing on his lips.

He looks gorgeous in jeans and a marine blue sweater which enhances his blue eyes. Brown leather shoes add a masculine elegance to his casual outfit, and his almost black hair curls with a length that beckons to be ruffled to an unruly mess.

"Good timing." I stand and lean up to get a kiss. Rising on my toes and craning my neck isn't even enough to reach him, so Markus leans down to complete the kiss.

"How so?" he asks against my lips.

"I was starting to get bored." I gather my hands behind me and sway my hips, matching his playful smile with one of my own.

"Good thing I've got something for you then."

"Ooh," I say through rounded lips. "And what is that?" I

really hope he means what I think he does. It's not easy to keep my hips from arching up against him.

Picking up on my thoughts, Markus chuckles. "Not yet, sweetie. I've got other plans for you."

"Do tell." He definitely has my interest piqued. That cocky smile usually means something sexy, and if sexy isn't it, I have no clue what he's up to.

"Grigory has promised to give you a piano lesson."

"What? Really?" Excitement and disbelief clash inside me. We just talked about that. Was that why he looked so self-satisfied?

"Really," Markus confirms, still grinning.

I still can't figure out the smile he's giving me. The mischief doesn't match his words.

I ascribe it to the joy of surprising me though.

He really has surprised me. I have to clench my jaw so it won't drop as I gawk at him. This is every pianist's dream. Only the best of the best get to be taught by the likes of Grigory Volkov—if they are lucky, that is. I'm nowhere near the best. I consider myself a skilled pianist compared to my fellow music students at the university. But that's the university. If you want to truly excel at your instrument, you need to study at the music conservatory.

"I'll come get you in an hour." Markus pulls me from my nervous thoughts, and I follow his line of sight to the exit.

Grigory stands by the door, watching us. His eyes are imposing. Too perceptive. Like he sees every jittering nerve in my body.

All courage leaves me with a swoosh. Turning my head back to Markus, I whisper urgently, "I can't."

Markus's smile widens. He clearly finds my anxiousness cute. *Typical dominant.* "Of course, you can."

Unable to see how I'll be able to play with this man beside me, I shake my head and search for an excuse to get out of the lesson. "I... I haven't got my sheet music."

"Sure, you do." With mischief dancing in his eyes, Markus pulls my flowery elastic folder from his bag and hands it to me.

I aim for a glare as I take the folder, but I don't think I quite manage.

Markus's face turns serious as he takes my upper arms and looks me straight in the eyes. It's the same expression he gives me when he prepares to deliver an order I won't like.

Fuck. What now?

"Look at me," he orders.

I focus my eyes on him, and the rest of the room fades.

"I've known Grigory for a long time, and I fully trust him." Markus leans closer as to underline the next words, "You're in good hands. Nothing I haven't approved will happen."

I gape at him. Didn't he say a piano lesson? Neither the grin nor his sudden dominance adds up with a simple lesson.

"Do you hear me?"

I manage a nod, but my words are stuck in my throat.

"What is your safeword, sweetie?" Markus pushes a thumb under my chin to level my eyes with his.

"Shrek," I say, gulping. "Why would I...?"

"Good," he cuts me off, his smile returning. "Don't worry,

Grigory won't bite." With a wink, he bends to kiss me and gives me a nudge on my back.

My feet carry me over the floorboards on autopilot.

Why do I feel like he's sending me off with a pack of wolves? And why mention the safeword? It's just a simple piano lesson. Right? It doesn't make sense.

Lifting my gaze, I see the man waiting for me. *One wolf,* I correct myself.

His eyes are dark and direct, boring their way straight past my personal sphere. His presence is a palpable power that makes me lower my chin with instinctive submission.

It feels wrong. I don't like it when I become shy like this. I thought I had shaken the tendency when I met Markus and learned to direct my submission to him alone.

I stop next to the door and watch Grigory's large hand rest on the handle. It lingers there, and I shudder as I feel his eyes on me. They are like lasers this close.

When he finally opens the door, I cast a last glance at Markus. No help there. Markus urges me on with a nod, and I step into the hall and lose sight of him.

Fancy leather shoes click against the floor, and the door gives a thud as it falls shut, leaving me alone with the intimidating conductor. My nerves rattle and my heart pounds as I recall Markus's words. *Nothing I haven't approved will happen.*

— CHAPTER 2 —

I follow Grigory Volkov through the winding halls, up through a stairwell, and down more white halls.

Before I met him, I thought he was as tall as Markus. Whenever I've seen videos of him towering over the orchestra from his podium, he looked tall and mighty. But as I walk here behind him, I'm reminded he's of average height.

It doesn't make him any less intimidating. He carries himself with the confident authority of a king. Straight spine, long strides, and a firmness to his step that would make a crowd part. His shoulders are broad and well-defined beneath his white dress shirt. He looks strong. And not the kind of strength you get in a fitness center. It's a more natural kind with thick bones and discreetly toned muscle mass, and I remember seeing the same strength in those perceptive eyes.

I gulp past a nervous knot in my throat. Not even the distance when he watched me today could lessen the imposing feeling of his eyes. How am I to handle an entire hour under his scrutinizing attention?

I'm screwed. Plain and simple.

Removing a key from his pocket, Grigory opens a door and

invites me to enter with a chivalrous hand gesture. Hugging my folder with both arms, I step past him, catching a whiff of an earthy cologne on the way. I feel his eyes follow me, and I grow acutely self-aware, stopping in the middle of the room, not knowing what to do with myself.

The small room reminds me of the rehearsal rooms at the university back in Aarhus. A grand piano, a couple of chairs, and a table. That's it. Nothing to distract while practicing. I can spend hours in those rooms, closed off from the world with nothing but a piano and the music seeping from my fingers.

But right now, it's too small—claustrophobic even. My nerves jitter, and when the door falls shut behind me, the walls close in. There isn't enough room here to be trapped with a human force field like Grigory Volkov.

"Have a seat," he says, pointing his conductor's baton to the bench.

Perching on the padded bench, I take in the familiar pattern of black and white keys—two black, three black, two black, three black, three black... I shake my head and glance back to the last group. No, just two. The pattern doesn't fail me. Of course it doesn't.

But my mind does, and I don't know how I'll get through this if I can't figure out simple things like the key pattern.

Usually, I love playing the piano, and if I hadn't wasted years with the violin before changing instruments, I would have gone all-in on getting into the music conservatory. But right now, I fear touching the keys. Since my practice has staggered after I turned in my last exam two weeks ago, I'm out of practice—*and* a big bundle of nerves.

Grigory moves a chair up and sits beside me, blocking the small space between the piano and the wall. If I want to get out, I either have to leap over him or crawl under the instrument.

My heart pounds as I stare at the monochrome pattern in front of me, unable to look at the man blocking my escape route.

"Begin with an E major scale—four octaves." The Russian accent lends the innocent words an ominous ring as Grigory waves his baton at the keys. I glance at the long thin metal stick. It's as intimidating as his accent. I wonder if it has become an ingrained part of making music to him since he uses it for a simple piano lesson.

I try to ignore it and focus on his words.

I can do this. E major has four sharps—black keys—and I can clearly visualize the pattern.

Here we go. I lift my hands, but my resolve falters when I see my fingers trembling. I try to take a deep breath but only manage a shallow one, and my fingers start tripping before I reach the second octave.

"Slowly," Grigory says and taps a rhythm on the side of the piano, half the tempo of what I just played. "There's no hurry."

I hold back a sigh. I can do better than a slow scale. But I obey anyway and get through the four octaves with an even flow.

Grigory takes my elastic folder from the music stand and taps a slightly faster rhythm. "Again."

I play the scale in the new tempo while he flips through my sheet music. When I'm done, he taps a bit faster yet, and thus, he gradually gets me into an acceptable tempo.

When I'm nearing my tempo limit, he stops me with a hand gesture and points to the sheet on top of the pile. "How much of this have you learned?"

It's Tchaikovsky's "Barcarolle" from *The Seasons*—a piece I've practiced a lot, but still lacks a lot of details. Since I'm out of practice, I fear I can't manage my usual fluency.

"I've played it all. But..."

"Good." He cuts me off before I get a chance to talk myself out of it.

I suppress my protest as he sets the five pages up in front of me. Because no matter what he pulls out of my folder, I doubt I'll be able to play it well with him at my side.

The notes look like ants crawling all over the pages, and my hands start shaking again. I squeeze my eyes shut and curl my fingers, then put them to the keys and play.

It's a wobbly mess from the start, and I curse Markus inwardly. He could've at least made sure I got some practice in this morning. But oh no, he drops me straight into this without as much as a warning.

I barely make it through the first page before Grigory stops me. "Do you have it memorized?"

"Not the last page," I say.

He removes the first four pages and goes to stand at the other end of the room, outside my field of vision.

"Take a couple of deep breaths and give it another go." His dark accent clashes with his calm tone. "Pretend I'm not here."

Easier said than done. But he doesn't seem to be the kind of teacher who gets frustrated with nervous students and their inability to perform. So I close my eyes and take a deep breath. It's easier when he's not right beside me.

I place my hands over the keys. And then I play. It's far from perfect, but I manage to bring out more details this time, and my fingers are steadier.

"Not bad. You already have many fine nuances." Grigory comes back to sit beside me, and his positive remark raises my spirits. Maybe this won't be so bad after all.

"Let's look at the first page." He sets the pages back up on the music stand and points to the first line. "More direction toward the top of the phrase. More legato. Use your arm to lead you." He closes his fingers around my elbow to draw my arm toward him, and my skin sparks alive with acute awareness of his touch.

I instantly regret not having put on a cardigan this morning. It's too intimate, his skin against mine.

Usually, this kind of thing doesn't bother me. It's normal for a piano teacher to adjust the arm, and he's nothing but professional. But I can't shake the vulnerable prickle at the feeling of his strong hand. It's so big and I'm so small.

"Try again," he says, releasing my arm.

My focus went out the window the moment he touched me, so it takes a couple of attempts before I get it right. But when I do, I find the arm movement to work surprisingly well.

We continue working on the first page, line by line. Grigory is calm and patient and seems to be a proficient teacher. His passion for music seeps into everything he says, and I take great joy in it even though I'm still a bundle of nerves.

"The whole page," he says, leaning back in his chair.

With a small sense of achievement, I start from the top. The first two lines go great, but halfway through, I forget some of his corrections and my legato becomes sloppy.

Suddenly, something flicks through the air—a swish and a flash of movement.

Something bites into my skin. "Legato," Grigory reprimands.

I jerk my arm away and press it protectively against myself as I watch Grigory with shock pounding through my system.

He's watching me intently as if gauging my reaction. There's not a flicker of emotion in his features. It's like nothing happened. But the baton in his hand tells a different story.

I snap my eyes away, his gaze too sharp to hold.

Did he just hit me? I can't believe it.

My head churns as I remember what Markus said about my safeword and the promise that Grigory wouldn't bite.

He might not, but his baton sure does.

Did Markus know this would happen? Did he really agree to it? He has never let another man hit me before, so it's hard to believe. But his playful smirk and odd reassurances make sense now.

I jump when a hand comes up to my shoulder. "Take a deep breath," Grigory says.

I try, but the air lodges like a cork in my throat.

"One more time." Grigory's fingers curl around my shoulder, catching my attention. My eyes dart to his hand—his very big hand—then to his face. It's calm and level, his voice the same when he urges, "Deep breath."

He pulls in a long, loud drag of air, and I follow, trapped in his deep gaze as I breathe air into my lungs.

“Good girl,” he says, the corners of his eyes crinkling with the hint of a smile.

Warmth spreads through my system and I avert my gaze, trying to suppress the smile pulling at my lips.

Grigory takes another long breath, and the sound of air rushing past his lips spurs me to do the same.

His hand still lies on my shoulder. Calm and heavy. Just resting there. But its strength is palpable. The hand is huge—much bigger than a normal man’s hand—and much warmer. The heat easily spreads deep into my skin and muscle, soothing the nervous tension away.

But it’s not just his physical strength that is so powerful. It’s also his mere presence. It’s like a warm energy wrapping around me, calming my jittery nerves.

My breathing becomes slow and deep as I fall into the trance of his steady control.

“That’s it,” he says, slowly removing his hand. “Keep breathing and take it one more time from the top. Legato, *all* the way.”

I lift my hands to the keys, take a long breath, and play.

This time, I succeed, keeping a smooth legato all the way.

We continue working on the first page, and it‘s downright scary how many details this man goes into. Every note needs to be perfectly balanced, every harmony polished, and it takes all my focus to keep up.

I had forgotten all about the threat when the baton strikes

again. I yelp and pull my arm away. My skin burns, but what's worse is the feeling of having disappointed him, not having followed through on his instructions. I don't know where it comes from, but I have this strange urge to apologize even though he's the one who has just hit me.

I bite down on my lips and stare into the piano. Suddenly, it's all too much—the stranger hitting me, the intense work, the feeling of letting him down. My chest fills with heavy pressure. I don't think I can do this. I can't live up to his standards, and the baton and his intense dominance... It's too much.

"Clara." Grigory lays his hand on my shoulder blade. "Take a deep breath."

The sound of my name on his lips sends a strange sensation through my veins. I pull in a sharp breath and look at him. There's no rebuke or disappointment in his eyes. Only the command for my attention.

"Good. One more." He takes another deep breath, lifting his chin in a silent command for me to follow. And I do. I pull in air and push it back out. Grigory keeps guiding my breathing while holding my back. It takes me out of my head and into the present, and within a few minutes, I'm ready to go again.

* * *

My world is zeroed in on the music when the door opens. Craning my neck, I see Markus coming toward us, and Grigory gets up to make room for him.

I can't believe an hour has already passed.

Suddenly aware of the burn in my skin, I look down at my

right arm. It feels like it's on fire. Looks like it too. The skin has a rosy hue topped with angry red stripes, and I almost gasp at the sight. I lift my eyes to the man holding the thin metal stick. He studies me with something near curiosity—maybe amusement. I can't quite gauge it.

Markus steps behind me and grabs my shoulders. "I take it everything went well?"

Luckily, he's not talking to me. I don't think I could get a meaningful sentence out right now.

Grigory keeps watching me as he answers. "You have a very fine little sub. Very talented."

Me? Talented? Grigory Volkov saying I'm talented? This can't be real. But the stripes crisscrossing over my milky skin are very real, the tenderness even so when I touch them. And so is the man with the gruff features, whom I've always dreamed of meeting, standing in front of me right this moment.

Markus takes my manhandled arm, and I realize just how strange this is. Not just the famous conductor and the lesson, but the fact that another man has been doling out physical discipline while teaching me, and now my boyfriend is studying the evidence, his fingers prodding and stroking the red marks.

What's even more strange is Markus's reaction. There's amusement in his voice as he says, "I see you had your fun."

"What can I say? It was hard not to." Grigory doesn't bat an eye. Like he's talking about the weather.

I, on the other hand, have gone several different shades of pink and can't sit still. My free hand fumbles with my dress skirt and my eyes flutter up and down. I feel like a rabbit caught between two predators.

Markus releases my arm and tips my head back to study me. "Did you like it?" His expression is alight with a heady mix of dominance and a playfulness I'm too dizzy to comprehend, so I just stare up at him.

Turning to Grigory, Markus says, "I think I'd better get this one home." He pats my arm. "Gather your things."

My legs wobble, and I lean into Markus's hand on my waist as I get up and gather my sheet music.

"Is that all?" Markus asks. "You didn't have your jacket?"

"I don't think so," I say, my head too clouded to remember.

Glancing up, I notice Grigory giving Markus a discreet shake of his head, and it does strange things to me, knowing he's noticed.

Markus leads me into the middle of the room. "Be a good girl and thank Grigory for the lesson."

"Thank you," I say, casting a glance up at the man who's taken the liberty of hitting me every time I missed a note throughout the last hour.

"You're most welcome." His thick brows loom heavily over dark eyes, and his accent lends a dangerous note to his low voice. But there's also something warm and genuine in his expression. The calm sound of his voice clashes with his stern countenance and makes my blood surge in my veins.

I want to keep watching him—solve the riddle, bask in the steady strength of his presence. But I don't dare. And as my eyes flutter away, Markus leads me from the room, through the long corridors, and down to the basement parking garage.

I'm not sure exactly what just transpired, but it's enough to keep my head shrouded in a thick fog the entire way home.

— CHAPTER 3 —

The intoxicating high crashes when we get back to Markus's apartment. I start shaking, and a flood of confusing emotions washes over me, making me feel torn at the edges.

Markus takes my hand and brings me to the living room, dumping the large burgundy pillow onto the floor between his feet. It's the pillow I use for kneeling, and I automatically sink onto it and curl up between his legs.

"I've got you," he reassures, curving one hand over my head and pressing the other to my back.

It feels surreal all that's happened, and yet I feel it, very real, in my body. My right arm is hot, the muscles throbbing beneath my skin, and Grigory's large hand has left a palpable imprint on my shoulder. I can still hear the rumble of his deep voice in my ear as he told me to breathe and still see the sharp focus in his dark gaze.

Grigory Volkov—the famous pianist and conductor I've watched on YouTube countless times—has just given me a piano lesson. A lesson involving discipline and strikes with a baton.

I can't wrap my head around it.

Yet, my whole body prickles when I think about it, and

there's a low hum deep in my belly which shouldn't be there—not when I'm thinking about another man.

"How are you feeling?" Markus leans down to kiss the top of my head, stroking my hair gently.

How am I feeling? Aroused. Nervous. Disappointed with myself. I don't know. My head is such a mess even though the fog has dissipated. "Confused," I end up saying.

"About...?" he inquires, tipping my head up with two fingers under my chin.

I stare into his deep blue eyes, full of sympathy and care for me. I love those eyes. They are comfort and safety. Pleasure and pain in the sweetest combination. *I shouldn't be thinking about another man's eyes.*

"Clara," Markus urges, loosening my fingers from his jeans. I didn't even realize I was clutching them.

I straighten and drag a hand across my forehead. "I don't know. Confused about the strange lesson."

When Markus doesn't reply, I look up to find him smirking.

"Did you like it?" he asks.

"I don't know." I lower my head to hide the smile spreading over my face. *I think I did.*

"Clara," Markus entices, nudging my chin.

"Markus," I say in the same slow voice and smile up at him.

"Don't make me ask again." His countenance sobers as he slips his fingers into my hair, twining it into his grip—a subtle hint of dominance.

I bite my lip and pull in a ragged breath. If he wants me to focus, he really shouldn't wield his intoxicating control. But even as my focus moves into my lower body, it also pulls at the submissive strings in me, and I can't not answer. "It feels wrong. You know..."

"What? That another man disciplined you?"

I nod in his grip.

"But you also liked it?" There's that grin again, and I can't stop my own face from slipping into a matching one. "I thought so," he says, reading the answer on my face.

There's no hiding from this man, so I admit it. "Yeah. But it also feels wrong. I shouldn't want anyone else to hit me."

Markus's face flattens. "You never asked for it. You know this, right? I was the one who sent you off to be disciplined."

"I know. But it doesn't mean I should..." I cast my eyes down. "Like it."

"You know what?" Markus leans in to whisper in my ear, his breath a sensual tickle against my skin. "I quite like the idea of Grigory hitting you, so I would be a tad disappointed if you didn't like it." He sits back up, his face lighting up with a playful smile like he's just told me a dirty secret.

"Really? Why?"

Markus shrugs. "You're mine. You do what I tell you."

The truth of his words rolls through me in a warm, settling wave. "I'm yours," I say in a breathy whisper.

"Yes, you are." He releases my hair to stroke his knuckles over my cheek. "So if I want another man to discipline you, you'll let him."

"Yes," I whisper. Struck by an overwhelming need to demonstrate my submission, I sink forward, burying my head against his thigh. "I'm yours," I say, gripping his legs to find purchase in the strong flood of emotion.

"Take out my cock," Markus says in a husky voice.

I reach up and unbutton his jeans. His cock is already bulging beneath the fabric, and when I drag down his pants and boxers, it springs free, standing tall and proud into the air.

He really means it. He likes the idea of letting another man hit me. It's difficult to comprehend. I couldn't stand if he spanked another woman. But I also couldn't stand dominating someone, so maybe it's just another one of those ways we are different as Dom and sub.

Licking my lips, I wrap my fingers around his length, and a surge of heat rushes through me as I feel how hard it is.

"Use your mouth," Markus orders.

I lean in and lick the tip, swirl my tongue around the head a couple of times, lapping up the salty precum. Then I move to the root and drag my tongue all the way up his length like I know he likes it. The shudder rolling through him spurs me on, and I take him into my mouth, sucking and licking while pumping the base.

"God, Clara, that's good," he moans, digging his hands into my hair, fingers working against my scalp as he struggles to let me have this. He knows I like pleasing him. But he also likes having control, and when I push down over his cock, his hand fists in my hair, and I know the playful teasing is over.

Markus stands, holding me on my knees. My scalp stings from his forceful grip as he presses my mouth over his cock. But I don't even flinch. If anything, the pain heightens the pleasure coursing through my veins.

With one slow movement, he presses into my throat. Water streams from my eyes as I struggle to relax my muscles around the intrusion. He pulls back and pushes in again, groaning as he forces my throat open. This time I cough, and my stomach cramps as my gag reflex stutters.

Markus gives me a second to recover. But no more. This is not for me. This is him taking and me accepting because I'm his.

He forces his way down my throat again, and my eyes go blank as I sink into fuzzy submission.

Feeling me give in, Markus picks up the tempo, tugging my hair to drag my head up and down over his cock. His pleasure-filled groans send me deeper into that warm space where nothing but his will matters. I can do nothing but hold on.

But when he thrusts all the way in and holds still, I grapple at his legs. His cock blocks my airflow, and I push against him as the need to breathe becomes urgent. But Markus's hand is locked into my hair, forcing me in place.

I struggle against my gag reflex as my stomach heaves for air.

Markus pulls out, and I cough and gasp, tears seeping down my cheeks. Spittle drips down my chin as his cock slips over my lips.

Before I get a chance to recover, Markus pulls me up and shoves me forward. "Get on the couch."

I fall onto the cushions and grip the back of the sofa. It's all I can do to keep steady in the turmoil of Markus's aggressive lust. But it doesn't matter; I've lost all sense of direction. He keeps me safe even as he takes what he wants.

He hauls my ass into the air, and I whimper when his cock prods at my entrance. I need him inside me—need him to manifest his dominance in the most primal of ways.

"Touch yourself," he orders.

I slip a hand between my legs and shudder as I slide a finger over my sleek, sensitive nub.

"Can you feel how wet you are?" Markus rubs his cock through my soaked folds. "Your cunt is begging for my cock. Isn't it?"

"Yes," I moan, arching my back.

"Be a good girl and beg me, Clara."

His order is not difficult to obey. The word falls over my lips quite automatically. "Please," I whimper, wriggling my hips eagerly.

Fingers digging into my waist is my only warning before he slams into me, all the way to the hilt.

"Fuck," I cry out, bucking against the painful yet oh so pleasurable intrusion.

Markus keeps pounding into me, and the telltale tension gathers in my lower abdomen. I squeeze my inner muscles around his cock, needing a little more to push me over the edge—a little more of... something.

Reaching under me, Markus grabs the arm I use to touch myself, and I grunt in protest. But the sound becomes a moan when he presses his thumb into my sore skin. I look down and see the angry red marks and Markus's thumb dragging all the way across them. Pain shoots into my nerves, mingling with the pleasure, reminding me how it felt when Grigory hit me. I remember his eyes too. His dark, intent stare fixed on me.

Suddenly, I explode, moaning and bucking as blissful fire shoots through my nerves. Markus finds his own release at the same moment. My mind goes into overdrive, swamped by pleasure, and overwhelmed by the clash of the man behind me and the memory of the man who marked me.

— CHAPTER 4 —

Markus and I have had an old-fashioned power dynamic from the beginning. He likes to take the lead, and I like a man who's not afraid to do so—well, so I learned.

We met at his performance of Schubert's *Winterreise* in Aarhus a year ago. *Winterreise* has always been one of my favorite classical works, and I was ecstatic to go see it—especially after reading the concert hall's high praise for Markus Richter, promising a first-class tenor. *An opera star on the rise,* they called him.

And boy, did he deliver. The entire audience was in a trance, pulled into the story of the lonesome wanderer roaming the bleak winter landscape. It was one of the best and most intense concerts I had seen.

As I was coming into the lobby during the intermission, I saw Markus standing to the side, greeting his fans, and I knew I had to go thank him for the touching music. But people kept coming up to him, and I had a hard time gathering my courage—Markus had already reached stardom in my head with his brilliant performance. So I kept pacing back and forth between chatting people and women rushing to make the bathroom before the bell rang. I tried to come up with something interesting to say, but my mind refused to grant me anything but generic phrases he must have heard a hundred times, and whenever my courage peaked, someone else approached him.

Five minutes before the bell rang, I finally gathered the nerve at the right moment and walked up to him.

"Thank you for the wonderful music," I said, ready to move on at an equally generic response.

But there was nothing generic about Markus.

"Do you have a favorite song?" he asked with a pleasant smile.

"A favorite?" I halted mid-step, my feet already about to carry me away.

"In *Winterreise,*" Markus clarified with an amused smile—bright, wide, and warm. He had one of those charming smiles that made his eyes light up and could make the hardiest of women go red. I was no exception. Blood flushed my cheeks as I turned my gaze away and considered his question.

"'Der Lindenbaum,'" I finally said. "That must be my favorite one. But..." I faltered when I met his eyes. The glimmer of his smile lingered, but there was also something willful that made me feel very small. And not just feel. Markus was tall, towering over my petite frame by more than a head, forcing me to crane my neck to meet those brilliant blue eyes.

"Go on," he urged.

"Erm... 'Frühlingstraum' is also beautiful, with its contrasts between lightness and wistful longing. And all the melancholic songs... The restlessness in 'Erstarrung' is absolutely breathtaking, and in 'Einsamkeit,' you can really feel the loneliness..." I stopped myself as I realized I was blabbering. "Well, they're all good."

Markus chuckled—a warm, reverberating sound that made my belly warm and fuzzy. "That wasn't a very nice question now, was it? I don't think I'd be able to choose one either. They are best heard together."

"Exactly." My face lit up as I looked at the fellow Schubert enthusiast in front of me. I might be studying music at the university, but I had never come across anyone who shared my nerdy enthusiasm for classical music—well, except for the professors.

Markus's chest shook with a silent laugh, and a rush of something unknown swooshed through me at the sight of his warm eyes that held mine so easily. He seemed so easygoing, yet with the poise of a powerful business magnate. He had plenty of confidence for the both of us, and I let it rub off and wash away my nervousness.

"Is there a song you'd rather be without then?" I asked, feeling surprisingly talkative.

"Are you trying to catch me saying something bad about Schubert?" Markus's eyes widened with feigned horror. Then he leaned in, murmuring behind his hand. "To be honest, I think 'Die Post' comes off a bit clumsy with its sudden burst of optimism."

Indeed, the song he mentioned was awkward among all the gloom. I gave a playful smile. "Maybe you should just leave it out next time?"

"I've never thought about that." He nodded, considering my

suggestion. "But then again, I just might end up getting booed off the stage. You *have* noticed all the gray heads around us, right?" He nodded toward the crowd, and I chuckled as I followed his line of sight. Even being in his mid-thirties, Markus was half the age of the average concertgoer here and I, in my mid-twenties, was a youngster compared to the gray-headed crowd.

"Maybe they are so absent-minded they won't notice," I suggested.

Eyeing me mischievously, he was about to say something, but the bell interrupted him. Suddenly, his gaze sharpened, and just as abruptly, the room grew hot.

"Have you any plans after the concert?" Markus's unwavering eyes flushed away my ability to speak, and I only managed a slight shake of my head.

"Meet me at the back entrance, then," he said. "Half an hour after I go off stage. I'll buy you a drink somewhere."

It wasn't a question or a suggestion, and he was off so quickly I didn't get a chance to answer.

But a moment later, I felt a hand on my shoulder. "I didn't get your name."

Turning, I gazed straight into Markus's mesmerizing eyes. "Clara," I told him, fluttering my eyes between him and the floor.

"I'll see you later, Clara." It still wasn't a question. It was a statement, like he knew I would show up. And then he was gone again, leaving me with a huge grin, which kept returning throughout the rest of the concert.

My beaming smile was awfully misplaced in the melancholic atmosphere of the concert hall. The woman next to me—an elderly lady of higher class—gave me a couple of sideways stares, but I couldn't bring myself to care. I was going out with Markus Richter. The man standing on the stage, bringing an entire audience into a trance with his beautiful singing.

Nerves danced in my belly, giddy and excited. But when I finally waited by the back entrance, the chilly summer evening air raising goosebumps on my bare legs, anxiety almost got the better part of me. My feet were shuffling, my hands fumbling, and when Markus appeared, my pounding heart begged me to bolt.

I was like a deer in headlights as Markus came toward me with long strides and a charming smile that stirred up millions of butterflies in my stomach.

"Good to see you, Clara." He bowed to kiss my cheek, and I was too baffled to react sensibly. So I just smiled and started moving when he pressed a hand to the small of my back.

I wasn't used to his kind of gentlemanly behavior, and at first, it racked up my nervousness. But his commanding energy was so straightforward and natural it was hard not to accept it. After a few minutes of walking in comfortable silence, I realized there was nothing odd about it. On the contrary, his steady guidance calmed my nerves and made the earth seem stable beneath my feet even as the Friday night crowd was a rowdy chaos around us.

The boisterous noise would normally overwhelm my nervous system and make me jittery, but Markus was like a shield. I found myself gravitating toward him as he snaked his hand around my waist to guide me through a crowded street, and when he opened a door to a café for me, I felt oh so small as I gazed up at my tall new protector.

My eyelashes fluttered like butterfly wings when his lips spread into an amused smile. If his hand on my back wasn't spurring me on, I would have halted then and there.

"Are you submissive, Clara?" he whispered in my ear as we waited for a waitress.

My eyes flew up to his, wide and shocked. I'd heard the term, of course—knew some people were into such kind of power play. But I was not one of them. My sexual preferences were quite standard. The wildest thing I'd tried was sex in a laundry room. So I shook my head, slightly offended by his suggestion.

He leaned in to add, "Oh, but I think you are."

A waitress came to greet us before I got a chance to protest, and when we sat at the table, I was too preoccupied with scouring the menu to think further about it.

Flickering through the drinks pages, I couldn't decide on anything. The number of options was insurmountable. To make matters worse, I didn't feel like drinking—I'd lost the urge several years ago. But Markus had said drinks, and that's what you were supposed to order on a Friday night, right?

"You look like you could use something warm." Markus pulled me from my scrambling thoughts and nodded toward my hands when I looked at him with confusion.

"Oh." I'd been so nervous I hadn't noticed my hands were cold and had a bluish tint.

"Do you prefer tea or coffee?"

"Tea," I said.

Markus raised a hand to summon a waitress. "Which flavor?"

I flickered back to the page with warm drinks. Earl Grey, green tea, and mint. Easy one. "Mint."

"One coffee with a splash of milk and a cup of mint tea," Markus told the waitress and handed off both our menus.

I almost let out a loud sigh. Like with the hand on my back, I'd never had a man order for me, and it was a surprising relief having him make the decision.

"So, how long have you been a Schubert fan?" Markus asked, taking charge of the conversation too. Most men would use the opportunity to jabber about themselves, but Markus was attentive and listening, keeping a fine balance between asking questions and telling me about himself. Soon I fell into the steady current of his control and talked with an ease I could only muster with my closest friends.

It was wonderful to talk to someone who shared my passion for classical music. After a long conversation about Schubert, we eased into a more casual one about my music studies and piano playing and Markus's busy life as an opera singer.

He had an uncanny ability to make me laugh, and it didn't help when we found out we shared the same joy for animation movies. Markus made these crazy imitations of *Shrek* and *Ice Age* characters that would send me into full-on laughing fits.

When he followed me to the bus, I could barely catch my breath because I was laughing so hard.

"Blue flower, red thorns. Blue flower, red thorns," he said agitatedly, impersonating Donkey from *Shrek* with wagging eyebrows and all. "This would be so much easier if I wasn't colorblind!"

My eyes were running as I stopped by one of the bus stops. "This is me," I said between bursts of laughter, drying my wet eyes. "Good thing this night is over. I don't think I can take any more laughing."

Markus's expression shifted from humorous to deadly serious, and for a moment I thought I had said something wrong.

But when he handed me his phone and said, "Your number," I realized it wasn't offense that had sobered his features. It was something else. A willful gravity that gave weight to his command and silenced the confusion in my head.

I punched in my number and handed him the phone, peeking up at him through lowered lashes, once again struck by his intimidating height. But more so, the directness of his gaze. My legs felt like wobbly springs as he lifted his phone to his ear, piercing me with his stern eyes.

I startled at the buzzing in my jacket. My phone flashed a foreign number when I took it out. Glancing back up at Markus, I saw amusement mingling with the command lingering in his expression.

Pocketing his phone, he said, "Good. Now I can let you go." A dark promise flickered over his features. "For tonight."

* * *

The next day, I was still lying in bed when my phone vibrated on the nightstand. Grabbing it, I saw Markus's name flash on the screen, and a surge of excitement rolled through me.

"Hello," I answered, my voice still husky from sleep.

"I know you're supposed to wait a couple of days before

calling, but I'm leaving tonight, and I want to see you before I take off."

A huge grin stretched across my face. I didn't expect to hear from him this soon. After all, he had a busy career, and I was prepared to wait a week or two—that is, if he hadn't lost interest by then.

Too surprised to say anything sensible, I remained silent, and he took the lead once again.

"You don't have any important plans today now, have you?" he asked.

"Not really."

"Great. Meet me at the same café at one o'clock and I'll buy you lunch."

"Okay," I said. My opinion clearly wasn't of consequence. Or maybe he already knew it. Nonetheless, it was surprisingly easy to be told when and where to show up.

The lunch went much like the night before. I started out a bit reserved, but as Markus's easygoing manner rubbed off, I began to relax, and soon the conversation flowed effortlessly.

It was only when the waitress removed our plates that silence stretched between us. With arms crossed over his chest, Markus leaned back in his chair and studied me for an unnerving moment.

"Come here." Keeping his eyes locked on me, he pulled out the chair beside him.

Another minute of nervous silence passed before I got up to take the offered seat.

Slipping an arm across the back of my chair, Markus angled

toward me, and I felt tiny sitting there under his scrutinizing gaze. My fingers fumbled in my lap, in and out of each other. I couldn't handle all that sharp attention on me. Not when he was so close.

I glued my eyes to the tabletop, hoping it would swallow me up. But no such luck. My unease kept ramping up.

A hand on my cheek jerked me from my anxiety. It was warm and gentle, guiding my face to the side.

Markus leaned in and pressed a slow kiss to my lips. Soft and sensual—the opposite of his overbearing demeanor.

I joined the kiss, brushing my lips against his and leaning into his warm palm, and my tension melted away as I fell into the trance.

Gradually, Markus grew more demanding. It happened so slowly I barely noticed.

First, it was a slight nibbling on my lips, his tongue sliding in to dance with mine. Then his hand slipped into my hair, little by little, until he reached the back of my head and grabbed a fistful of my brown tresses.

My scalp smarted from the pull, but I was so lost in the sensations I only moaned, the pain somehow blending perfectly with the warm pleasure.

My moan seemed to flick a switch in Markus. Suddenly, he crushed his lips against mine, invading my mouth with a force that rendered my tongue useless. With his grip on my hair trapping me, all I could do was surrender and let him have his way.

I'd never been kissed with such passion. Not by far. The

brutality was both startling and intoxicating, the combination rendering my head a sluggish mess.

When he finally released me, it took me a moment to recover. Glancing down, I found my hands clutching his gray sweater. Slowly, I uncurled my fingers and peered up at him. His expression held a gentle warmth I couldn't reconcile with the forceful kiss.

My legs felt just as mushy as my brain when he helped me into my jacket and followed me to the bus.

When the bus pulled up, he took me in another mind-boggling kiss and whispered against my lips, "I'll call you tonight."

The words didn't quite register in my fogged-over brain until I sat with my vibrating phone in my hand late in the evening, feeling giddy like a teenager who had just had her first kiss.

And in some sense, Markus's kiss was my first. I'd never felt so head over heels with a guy I couldn't think about anything else. I was in a constant rush of pink hearts and fluttering butterflies for the next week.

Markus called me every day, and we spent hours talking about everything from animation movies and music to hopes and dreams. I told him about my dream of getting into the music conservatory, and he told me about his life-long aspiration of singing at The Metropolitan Opera in New York.

When he called me Thursday afternoon, barely a week after we'd met, he asked about my plans for the weekend.

"Stay home. Practice piano. Maybe go for a walk or two," I told him.

"You'd rather stay home with your piano than go out Friday night," he stated with a chuckle. But it was a warm laugh—like he knew the feeling. There was none of the judgment I'd expect from most other people.

"Yeah, it's much more fun," I admitted openly.

"Do you think you can manage a few days without your piano and come spend the weekend with me in Rome?"

My jaw went slack, my brain halting like a train screeching on tracks before slowly gaining speed again. "I'm not sure," I teased, barely able to rein in my excitement. "I'm afraid it will get lonely."

"And you're not afraid I will?"

"Well, since you mention it, I am getting a little worried." I couldn't believe he was inviting me to Rome. I wanted to bounce up and down on my bed from pure joy. But then I came to think about all the practicalities. "I'm not sure I'll be able to go on such short notice," I said tentatively. Disappointment churned in my stomach as I realized money might be the one thing standing in the way of dating this wonderful man.

Living off a student education grant and a little piano teaching here and there didn't exactly make for an exciting lifestyle. It was hard enough to afford concerts and the occasional outing with a friend, and I didn't have a wealthy family to help ease the economic shortcomings of student life. Just a regular plane ticket would cut severely into my meager savings.

"It's not a problem," Markus said, picking up on my thoughts. "I'll pay for the trip. You just have to pack a bag and be at the airport on time."

Biting my lip, I fought an internal battle. I really wanted to go, but being economically independent meant I wasn't used to accepting such luxuries from others, so it was hard to accept.

"Do you *want* to go?" he asked calmly when I said nothing.

"Of course." The words blurted out of me as I realized he might misinterpret my hesitance.

"Good. End of discussion. I'll send you the ticket, and then I'm looking forward to seeing you tomorrow."

With that, it was decided. I couldn't argue with the subtle command in his tone. If it had been anyone else, I'd have felt trampled on, but I only felt calm when Markus issued an order like this. He did it with respect and with my needs in mind. It allowed me to shut down the internal battle and spend less energy feeling bad about accepting the ticket.

The trip to Rome was long, the flight alone five hours including a layover. I had only flown a few times before, and I wasn't particularly fond of it. Not so much because of the flight itself, but the chaotic airports and large crowds.

Fortunately, I got a nap on the last plane, so I wasn't completely exhausted when Markus met me at the airport in Rome early in the evening.

With only a couple of hours until his concert, we took a cab directly to the concert hall to drop off my luggage, then went out to get something to eat nearby.

When we were finally on our way to the hotel late in the evening, I was ready to jump right into bed and sleep. But then Markus pushed his hand between my legs in the cab, kneading my inner thighs, and a more urgent need took precedence.

We were barely in our room before we were ripping each other's clothes off. I tried to unbutton his shirt, but he was so busy stripping me down I only got halfway before I realized I stood stark naked in front of him.

I barely got a chance to process my sudden nakedness before Markus sat on the bed and yanked me between his knees. He took me in the same possessive kiss he'd done the weekend before, and I was like jelly in his arms.

When he leaned back to look at me, his mouth was curled into a sneaky smile I couldn't quite comprehend.

But I quickly found out what it was all about. With a quick tug on my hips, he threw me over his knee and started kneading my ass.

Thinking he was messing with me, I laughed and tried to push up. But Markus pressed his forearm to my lower back and refused to let me go. I felt awkward lying there with my butt in the air like he was about to discipline me, but it was also oddly exhilarating.

Smack!

I yelped when his open palm landed on my right ass cheek. Before I could react, my left one heated under another smack.

What the fuck? Was this some kind of warped humor?

Two new smacks resounded in the room and stung my skin.

It didn't really hurt, but I sure couldn't see the fun. I tried to wriggle free again, but Markus didn't budge, and I was growing increasingly uncomfortable as I writhed against his arm. "Markus, what are you doing?"

"Just lie still and let me take control." He sounded like he was giving me a massage and not a spanking.

"Seriously?" I scoffed.

Smack! Smack! Smack!

This time it hurt. Pain bloomed in my skin, and I pushed up on my hands, craning my neck to glare at him. "Ouch, that hurt."

I panted with the need to end this when Markus moved his free hand over my back and into my hair. His touch was careful and slow, yet firm enough to press me back into the mattress. "Relax, Clara. I've got you."

His fingers started massaging my scalp, and God, those fingers... I couldn't help the moan that seeped over my lips.

"Do you know what a safeword is?" he asked, continuing the soothing motions.

I nodded.

"Good. Yours is Shrek."

"Shrek?" A small laugh bubbled out of me. Thinking about the green monster while lying here over Markus's knee seemed wholly absurd.

"Yes, Shrek. If you say the word, I'll stop whatever I'm doing immediately." He dragged his hand down along my back, lingering right above my butt. "Now be a good girl for me and lie still while I spank your ass. I think you might like it."

Who talked like that? My reasonable brain half wanted to glare at him and protest, but another part of me arched at his deep croon and angled my head into his skilled touch.

"Can you do that?"

I groaned my consent. But when he moved his hand back to my ass and delivered two rapid smacks, I tensed at the foreign sensation. Again, the pain was bearable, and after a moment it turned into an almost pleasurable warmth. But I couldn't bring myself to enjoy it. After all, I wasn't into that kind of thing.

Trying to give it a chance like I promised, I let him hit me a few more times before turning my head. "I don't like it."

Markus chuckled and slid two fingers between my folds, and I went absolutely rigid, realizing I was soaking wet. "Are you sure? Your pussy doesn't seem to agree with you."

I must have gone beet red. I buried my head into the covers, forcing down a moan as Markus kept fingering me.

"Don't worry. This will stay our little secret." Slowly, Markus pushed a long finger inside me. Embarrassment, disbelief, and raging need crashed inside me and left my brain in a muddled daze, unable to make sense of anything.

Markus pulled out his finger and massaged my ass, making me wag my hips in a silent plea for more.

Smack! Smack! Two more strikes made me squirm on his lap, but I wasn't sure if I moved out of protest or lust.

Markus kept hitting me, dipping his fingers into my wetness between strikes. The pain grew, but so did my need, and the former only seemed to reinforce the latter until I couldn't deny the spanking turned me on. I finally relinquished my silly ideas of who I was supposed to be, yielding my control to Markus like he'd asked me to.

With each smack, my arousal grew. At some point, I was so needy I moaned and groaned and couldn't decide which was worse, when he stopped hitting or stopped fingering me.

"Now I'm going to lift my arm, and you are going to remain

right where I put you." Markus's tone had taken on a commanding edge that went straight to my pussy and made my insides do a strange flip. "Are we clear?"

My "yes" came out on a long moan. I couldn't believe how I reacted to all of this—him taking control, spanking me, and now commanding me like a drill sergeant.

Markus pushed two fingers inside me and used his other hand to rain strikes down over my ass. Within seconds, my inner muscles clamped down as my entire nether region buzzed on the precipice of an orgasm.

"Be a good girl and come for me, Clara." Markus finished his words with four extra hard strikes.

Even as the pain burst into my flesh, pleasure shot through my body and made my toes curl with a staggering orgasm.

"Fuuck," I groaned, as the pleasure kept rolling through me and Markus kept pumping his fingers in and out until I was thrashing from overstimulation.

As soon as he pulled out and started caressing my sore backside, I went limp, sagging over his legs like I'd just sprinted two miles.

"You really liked that, huh?" He ran his hands up and down my back and down my thighs, and all I could manage was a muffled groan. "I did too," he said.

Grabbing me by the hips, he flipped me over and tossed me onto my back on the mattress and crawled up between my legs. Only taking a second to position himself, he pushed inside me with one long thrust that had me bucking with renewed pleasure.

"Touch yourself," he ordered.

"What?" Masturbation was a private matter for me, and I'd never considered doing it in front of someone.

"Touch yourself," he repeated with the same military command as before. His hard tone shut down the few thoughts left in my head and made me reach down to stroke my clit while he drove into me with hard thrusts.

Within minutes, we both came, and when he laid down behind me and pulled me against his naked body, I was so tired I fell asleep instantly.

* * *

To say I was surprised by my reaction to being hauled over Markus's knee was to put it mildly. The next morning, I was so embarrassed I could barely meet his eyes.

It got even worse when he sat on the edge of the bed, asking bluntly, "So, how did you like being spanked?"

My eyes went wide as I pulled the covers over my face.

Markus tugged them back down. "Did you like it?"

I really did, and as I lay there gazing up at his sexy day-old scruff and those deep blue eyes, I wanted him to do it all over again. But it was more than difficult to admit.

He must have read the answer on my traitorous face since he smirked, and it made my façade crumble, a huge smile slowly spreading across my features.

Pulling at the covers, I tried to hide again, but he held onto them, forcing me to meet those smug eyes.

"I've had a feeling you would enjoy a good beating. It's lovely to see I was right."

"What gave you that idea?" I gave the covers an extra tug without luck.

"You like it when I grab your hair." He placed his palm on my cheek, slowly sliding it up into my hair, fingers running in between my strands and grabbing a handful. "You like when I take control. And you like when I give you such a hard look you can't say no."

I grew smaller and smaller as he revealed all those things I thought were my private secrets.

"Am I not right?" he pressed.

The question was rhetorical, but I nodded anyway—as much as I could with his hand lodged in my hair. I had a terrible urge to disappear beneath the covers, but he still wouldn't allow it. Instead, he released my hair and yanked the blankets off, so I lay completely naked in front of him. He ran a hand between my legs, and his smile widened as he felt how wet I was. Even though it was all very embarrassing, I couldn't help tilting my hips up toward his hand.

"You are very submissive, Clara. Did you know that?"

"No," I said on a breathy moan.

With eyes boring into mine, he stated, "You are," like it was a matter of fact.

* * *

During the year we've been together, I've slowly come to realize the full meaning of Markus's words that first morning in Rome.

Not only does his domineering nature and sadistic tendencies turn me on, but I also find a sense of security in submitting to him—both in and outside the bedroom.

The uneven power dynamic has grown rapidly. At first, it was only on a subtle level—Markus taking the lead with his hand on my back, ordering for me at restaurants. But gradually, the dynamic became more pronounced as Markus started making decisions for me and giving me orders even when we were apart.

It helps me put aside some of my habitual worries when he puts his foot down—like when he told me to accept the plane ticket—and I thrive being under his steady control.

He doesn't use his power to bulldoze me or to get his way. He always has an eye on my needs, making decisions that are good for me, and it's easy to accept his control. Whenever he decrees something, I never want to go against him. On the contrary, I wish to please him. On the rare occasion I do something at odds with his orders, the guilt is terrible.

But as his control has worked its way deeper into my life, my need to be with him has also grown, and being apart is becoming increasingly difficult. When we're together and I get to submit to him, I'm calm and thriving. But when we're apart, the stability I get from his dominance wavers, leaving me on shaky ground. I think I've always had this buzzing restlessness inside me; I just never noticed until I met Markus and felt how it was to be without it.

Before this summer, we hadn't spent more than a week together. Mostly, though, our schedules only allowed us a few days at a time. Markus spent a lot of money—me, a lot of time—to fly me out to whatever European city his work brought him to. And whenever he had a few days off, he came to Denmark.

This summer, we've been particularly lucky. All my exams have been written assignments, so I came to Berlin at the end of May, and since Markus has only had a few concerts spread out over a month, he's been here most of the time.

The rest of the summer, Markus will be here in Berlin working on *Tosca.* I'll be enjoying my vacation here until I go home to start the master's program in September.

Three months together. Half the time has already passed, but luckily we still have seven weeks left until I go home.

— CHAPTER 5 —

"You have a piano lesson at three," Markus says Friday morning when I'm still lying in bed.

I rub my sleepy eyes and focus on him. Dressed in a V-neck T-shirt, jeans, and blazer, he looks damn sexy. The mix of casual and elegant suits him well.

"Grigory will meet you in the lobby."

I push up to sit, suddenly wide awake. "It's only been four days."

Markus offers no explanation, just a serious, "If I were you, I'd be there on time." Then he smirks and adds, "Or your arms may not feel so good when you come home."

He leans down to drop a kiss on my forehead, and I wrap my arms around his neck. "Will you come get me?"

"Sure thing. I can't have you staggering around that big building on your own with endorphins rushing through your system." Straightening, Markus winks at me, rubs my hair, and adds, "Don't stay in bed too long."

Then he's on his way.

I waste no time lying around but get up as soon as my legs get the message I'm awake. I need to practice, eat, and bathe. Did

I say practice? Usually you get piano lessons once every one or two weeks. But four days later? It's not enough time to prepare. Not even if you spend hours by the piano like I've done the last couple of days.

But what's worse than the lack of practice is the thought of Grigory—being alone with him and his baton in that small room. My stomach does a nervous flip. And what Markus said about being late... The thought alone sends shivers crawling down my arms. So much I'm in the lobby fifteen minutes early.

Stress hormones course through my body even though I have plenty of time to spare. I can't stand still; I pace back and forth on the same spot.

This reminds me of waiting for Markus after the concert a year ago. Only, this is worse. With Markus, it was drinks and conversation; this time, it's piano and baton strikes—a combination I have trouble grasping. Plus, it's with a man I can barely utter two words to.

My stomach twists and I consider bolting. I could call Markus and tell him I have a stomachache. It's not far from the truth.

But no. I can't lie to Markus. Not even if it's just a half-lie.

And Markus won't accept nerves as a good enough reason for running off. He might not be the type to dole out punishment for small missteps, but this sure wouldn't count as one. He'd haul me over his knee and beat my ass ten different shades of blue for purposeful disobedience.

Damn, Markus may be easygoing and charming, but if you provoke him, he'll flip like a switch and all hell will rain down.

I'm gnawing at my finger when the sound of a door pulls me

from my thoughts.

Grigory appears at the other end of the large lobby, and I all but scurry across the tiled floor.

He doesn't say anything, just nods and leads the way into the belly of the monstrous building. Humming a melody from *Scheherazade,* he seems quite content with the silence stretching between us. If I only saw this angle of him, his relaxed yet confident posture and the calm humming, I would think him an approachable man. But when I think of those eyes and his stern face... Strict discipline and control are the only words popping into my head.

If Markus can be scary when provoked, I definitely don't want to get on the wrong side of this man.

"Lose the cardigan," he says, once we enter the rehearsal room.

I turn to him, and alarm must be written all over my face. I'd worn the cardigan as a layer of protection, and now he wants me to lose it?

"Go on," he says with a hint of amusement and takes the folder from my hand to set it on the piano. "We don't have all day."

I wriggle out of it, and I feel like a shaken soda bottle as I sink onto the piano bench. Now I'm only wearing a light summer dress with narrow straps that covers even less than the one I wore the first time.

So much for that protection.

I expect him to tell me which scale to begin with, so when he steps up beside me and puts a hand on my shoulder, I jump.

"Deep breaths," he says, drawing out the vowels.

My first breaths are staggered, but Grigory is patient, giving me the time I need to make the fizzing bubbles settle down. So when he finally takes a seat beside me and tells me to play a scale, I actually feel calm, and the warm-up goes much better than I could have hoped.

Throughout the lesson, he makes broad hand movements and hums along to guide me in the right direction. He has an uncanny attention to detail and can spend ten minutes on a single note. I've never had such a demanding piano teacher. But I haven't had one with such an inherent sense of music either, and although it requires a razor-sharp focus, I love delving into the music in such a meticulous manner.

I'm so absorbed I forget about the evil little stick, and when the first strike lands, I'm as shocked as last time, pulling my hands from the piano with a gasp.

And like the first lesson, Grigory places his large palm flat on my back, drawing in an audible breath.

I imitate, but it doesn't help much. The feeling of his hand is too much. His whole palm is pressed directly against my skin. It's too intimate, and my breath goes ragged instead of settling.

"Close your eyes," he says softly.

"What?" I'm on the verge of freaking out. If I close my eyes, it will only become more intimate.

Lowering his voice, he repeats, "Close your eyes."

I shut my eyes because this man is really difficult to disobey.

"Good, now try again. Deep breath."

I pull in a long breath and push the air back out on a ragged exhale that loosens my tight muscles.

"Good girl. One more."

Unable to do anything else, I obey. Once again, my muscles loosen. I start noticing the hand on my shoulder—and not just the invasion of my personal space, but how it *feels.*

It's large and heavy. No, not just large. Enormous. A true pianist's hand. With the strength of a soldier. I feel the power like a dormant energy waiting to be roused.

But most of all, it's warm. So warm it could melt an ice block. And right now, it's melting away my anxious nerves, soothing the chill in my skin.

This man is nothing but contrasts against me. I'm small and cold-skinned; he's large and warm. I'm nervous and shy; he's confident and powerful.

Plus, he's nearly double my age. I'm twenty-five, and he's close to fifty—young and inexperienced against competent and accomplished.

It's an intimidating mix of opposites. Nerve-racking, really. But as I sit here with his warm hand on my shoulder, I realize it's also safe. He's scary as hell with his authoritative demeanor, but his patient control makes me feel like he could carry everything even if the building collapsed around us.

"Are you ready to go again?" he asks.

Opening my eyes, I look at him, and my stomach makes a strange flip as I meet a set of unwavering dark eyes below thick brows. I'm not sure what it is, but something about him draws me in—makes me want to be ready just to please him. Giving a slight nod, I pull my eyes away, a bit shocked at my reaction to... well, all of this.

"Take it from the top."

I quickly forget about my reaction as I delve back into the music, and when the next strike lands, I'm not as shocked as the first time.

Grigory continues this way, teaching and hitting, gradually ramping up the intensity. When I finally think I'm getting used to the evil stick, thinking I can handle one strike without being overwhelmed, Grigory escalates the pain level. I get the feeling he deliberately pushes me. The strikes go from stinging mildly to burning deep in my skin as the lesson progresses, and every time he hits me, I have to take a minute to recover.

He's always there with his hand, ready to help me through it, guiding my breathing. But it messes with my head, constantly being overwhelmed like this, and when Markus comes an hour later, the ground is wobbling beneath me.

* * *

Grigory rises from his chair and puts his hand on my shoulder, "Good job today."

Warmth seeps through my body and a bright smile spreads across my face at his appraisal. I take a moment to get it under control before meeting Markus's eyes.

Markus comes up to me and presses a kiss to my head. "Pack up your things." Then he steps away from the piano to speak to Grigory. "I wanted to talk to you about an offer I got." He rubs his hand over his two-day-old scruff and folds his arms over his chest. "The Hungarian State Opera wants me to sing *La Traviata* in the fall, but I'm in two minds. I'm on tour at the time and would have to cancel two dates."

"Who's conducting and who's directing?" Grigory asks, matching Markus's wide stance and crossed arms.

I have to look away. All this masculine dominance doesn't fit in such a small room, and watching only makes it worse. So I force my attention to the task at hand while the two men weigh the pros and cons.

When I start putting on my cardigan, I can't suppress the urge to explore the red welts across my arm. My skin is tender to the touch, and I wince when I prod at one of the more severe marks. But then I do it again, oddly fascinated with the red stripes, and a small tingling sensation erupts in my belly.

Glancing up, I realize Grigory is watching me, his eyes narrowed as he takes in my red arm and prodding fingers. I quickly push through the sleeve, gather my bag and folder, and walk up to Markus, hoping he will lend me a bit of support since my knees aren't doing a great job of it.

"It sounds like it might be worth canceling the two concerts," Markus says to Grigory, then turns to me. He peruses me for a few seconds before giving his order. "Down."

He says it with *that* tone, and I stare at him with wide eyes. He can't be serious. Does he really want me to kneel when there's someone else here?

He lifts his eyebrows in a silent command, and I sink to the floor, holding his gaze in the hopes he will react to my silent plea.

But he doesn't. There's only the smug dominance alight in his gaze. He knows how much it takes for me to do this in the presence of someone else, and I think he gets off on it, just like he said he liked Grigory hitting me. This is the purest testament to his power over me, and I feel it too as I settle on my knees at his side, a few feet from Grigory.

"Where were you supposed to go?" Grigory asks, and I become hyperaware of his black slacks in my periphery. The proximity is heady, and my pulse hammers away. I might be facing Markus, but it feels like I'm kneeling for them both.

"Rome and Napoli." Markus presses my head against his thigh in a silent way of telling me he's got me. I close my eyes and focus on his touch, trying to block out the other man in the room. But the deep rumble of Grigory's voice makes it impossible.

"Choose Italy." Grigory's verdict is resolute. "The coffee is better there."

Markus laughs. "Is that what it's come to with you nowadays? Choosing concerts based on coffee?"

"I *should* do so," the world-renowned conductor says tersely. "Coffee is important."

"Yeah, yeah," Markus pats my head in time with his words. "So is scotch and chocolate cake, right? Maybe you should just stick to Scotland?"

"No, that wouldn't work. The Scotts can't do coffee."

They continue the banter for some time, and I find myself slowly letting go of my self-consciousness.

There's no awkwardness or tension in the room—no curiosity at my unusual position and obvious display of submission. I guess it makes sense. Markus has once told me

Grigory has been in a Dom/sub relationship before, so he's probably used to seeing a woman kneeling.

So I let myself slip into a submissive headspace and enjoy being at Markus's foot. After all, it's easier being down here than up there where the air is thick with male dominance and I would be expected to participate in the conversation.

"Clara," Markus drags my attention back to the room as he takes a step back and nudges my chin up. "Can you be a good girl and show Grigory what I taught you last night?"

Blood swooshes through my veins and gathers in my cheeks. No, no, no. He can't be serious. Not here. In front of *him.* Isn't it enough the man gets to discipline me?

I grow acutely aware of Grigory, feeling his large figure looming next to me, his eyes boring into me.

Markus steps behind me, and I reach for him, needing the shield of his body between the intimidating man and me. But Markus turns me by the shoulders, forcing me to kneel right before Grigory.

My hands fist and unclench on my thighs, my whole body thrumming from the adrenaline spike.

Please don't, I want to beg, but I can't make myself say anything. I have no idea how Markus will demonstrate this—if he'll whip out his cock and shove it into my throat, or worse, ask the conductor to do it.

Panic is rising in my chest when Markus grabs my hair and tugs my head back, demanding I stay with him.

I give a small shake of my head, hoping Grigory won't see. But of course, he does. I feel his eyes on me like lasers and I know how perceptive they are. I couldn't twitch an eye without him knowing.

Markus's lips tip up in a cheeky smile. "Oh yes," he says, answering my silent plea. "Open your mouth."

Clenching my jaw, I stare up at him with wide, frightened eyes.

"Was that a question?" Markus tugs my head farther back, straining the front of my neck.

"No." My answer is barely audible.

"Then open your mouth. I want Grigory to see what a good girl you are." Markus's features edge into a stern expression that forces his words straight past my embarrassment and into the core of my submissive soul.

There's nothing I can do. My lips fall apart, and I feel my autonomy slipping out of my hands.

Markus's eyes light up with appraisal, and it shoots straight into that same submissive place and spreads warmth into my bones. "Good girl," he says. "Now, a little more."

I open a smidgen farther, and Markus keeps urging me on until my mouth is wide agape.

"That's it. Keep it like that." Nudging my head into its normal position, he turns his attention to Grigory and says soberly, "We were practicing gag reflex control last night."

"Sounds useful." The conductor seems just as unabashed by the topic, and my hands quiver as I look at his legs. They are all I see, right there in front of me. I'd have to lean my head far back to meet his dark eyes. "How did you go about it?"

I feel tiny, caught here between the two tall men. Their

power is a palpable energy around me, and I can almost feel how my helplessness feeds it—making their voices a bit deeper, their postures a bit prouder. I think they both get off on this, having me at their mercy, bending to their will. And fuck, I really do too.

Markus lifts a finger to the corner of my mouth, caressing the sensitive spot, making me acutely aware of how open my mouth is. His voice takes on a gruff note as I feel him watching me—it's the same sound as when he tells me to get on my knees and suck his cock. "I tied her to a chair, told her to keep her mouth open," his finger travels over my bottom lip, "and pressed a dildo to the back of her throat."

"And how did she do?" Grigory asks.

"Go ahead, see for yourself," Markus invites, and my heart rate spikes as he tugs my hair back, forcing me to look up at the conductor.

His brows are set in two thick lines, and the furrow between them makes him look alarmingly intense. I shift my hips, unable to sit still beneath the unwavering command in his eyes. I imagine this is what it must feel like being a small mouse in an open field with a hawk watching from the only tree.

Grigory lifts his thumb to my lips, and I start panting. The movement is slow yet purposeful as he presses the pad against my bottom lip. My mouth twitches with the need to close, and I think he sees it because his eyes light up, just for a moment—a small flash before the dark intent is back.

Slowly, he pushes his thumb over my lip and into my mouth. I feel it hovering above my tongue right before it presses down. My hips jerk involuntarily, and I furrow my brows as helplessness seeps into my bones.

His thumb makes a slow journey across my tongue, and the intrusion is stark. He could have pressed his cock into my mouth and I'd have felt less invaded. At least then, I would have had my eyes to myself. But this slow invasion of both my mouth and eyes makes it feel like he's reaching into my very core, accessing the most secret corners of my soul.

A slow panic creeps across my arms as he makes his way to the back of my tongue. It only gets worse when my eyes flutter down and I notice the big bulge in his pants. I press my head back and try to move it from side to side to eject the intruding finger. *This is so wrong.*

"Easy, sweetie." Markus tightens his grip on my hair, reminding me I'm doing this because he wants me to. It's oddly reassuring, and I stop struggling.

My eyes flicker back up, and I look straight into Grigory's forceful gaze that demands my full attention on him. His eyes narrow as he reaches the spot right at the edge of my gag reflex. He knows exactly what he's doing. Stopping for a second, he gives the smallest tug of his lips—a smug smile—then he presses into the spot that should trigger my gag reflex.

I fight to subdue the reflex, bunching my shoulders up and fisting my hands as I struggle to relax my throat like Markus has taught me.

"Very good," Grigory says, sounding pleased as he turns his eyes to Markus.

There seems to be this strange camaraderie between the two men, like it's quite natural for them to team up on me, exposing me in this very sexual manner together. Most men would be uncomfortable getting a boner in the company of a friend, but there's no awkwardness or uncertainty here. They're just having fun, like two guys having a beer after work.

"She made a whole minute last night." Markus strokes his free hand along my cheek like he's proud of me.

A minute. I sure won't last so long today. I can't take it much longer, sitting here on the floor, trapped between the two men—a stranger's thumb pressed against the back of my throat. Two seconds more and I'll be dry heaving.

My pounding heart becomes too loud, and my stomach contracts with the need to cough. I twitch my head against Markus's grip, but he only tightens it, making the roots of my hair sting.

My tongue starts struggling against the length of Grigory's finger, and I make a few strangled noises. Water streams from the corners of my eyes as the urge to gag rises in my throat, and I'm not sure a few of the tears aren't from the intense vulnerability I feel staring up at the powerful man above me.

"Relax your tongue." Grigory's eyes are back on me, matching the strictness of his tone. There's no compromise or leniency. It's a firm command. And it works.

It knocks the struggle straight out of me. My shoulders fall into place, my hands unclench, and my tongue relaxes as I fall into the spell of Grigory's demanding stare.

"Good girl," he praises, slowly dragging his thumb back across my tongue and over my bottom lip.

I don't dare to close my mouth. Not even when I feel the

trickle of spit slip from the corner.

Grigory grazes a knuckle down the side of my mouth, catching the embarrassing moisture, and I feel so utterly exposed. Helpless.

"You may close your mouth," Grigory says in a gentle voice that pulls me deeper under his spell, and I slowly close my jaw as I stare into the steady calm of his eyes.

The loss of Markus's grip on my hair knocks me out of the trance, and I scramble around and bury my face into his legs, needing the safety.

"Good girl," Markus praises, patting my hair. "You did so well."

Warmth blossoms in my chest, mingling with the weight of their control which has settled like an overwhelming yet stabilizing energy in me.

"When would you like her back?" Markus asks Grigory as he sinks to his haunches and wraps me up in a hug.

I sink into him, soaking up the safety of his warm arms as I listen to Grigory's deep voice.

"Wednesday. I've got orchestra rehearsals until two, so a quarter past. I'll come get her in the lobby."

It's five days from now. I clench my hand around Markus's shirt as nervousness and excitement speed through my veins.

"She'll be there." Draping an arm around my waist, Markus guides me to my feet, then splays a hand on my cheek to catch my attention. "Now, thank Grigory for the lesson, sweetie."

"Thank you," I say, dropping my eyes to the floor, my cheeks heating. I'm too embarrassed to look straight at him, yet my eyes can't stay down, and they flicker back up to notice he's watching me way too closely.

His gaze sharpens, pupils expanding and brows lowering, and I feel the startling intensity of his focus honing in on me. My pulse quickens, and my eyes dart up and down, unable to keep contact and unable to stay away.

Minutes seem to go by this way, but it's probably only long seconds.

"You're welcome," he finally says, breaking the harrowing silence. His accent sounds thicker than usual, and my blood swooshes through my veins, making me wonder if the suspended silence actually was better.

Markus puts his hand on my back and guides me along. My feet only move out of muscle memory as my brain is rendered mush after what just happened.

Even as thoughts filter back in, my head is no clearer. All I can think about is the conductor's finger in my mouth and the way he watched me, and when Markus asks me something, it takes me eons to compile a sensible answer.

When we get home, Markus plops me down on the sofa and tells me to stay while he prepares dinner.

"That's my responsibility," I protest. It has been ever since I came here six weeks ago, and I hate when I can't live up to it.

"You're in no state to be in a kitchen," he says with a wide grin and curls my fingers around the remote. "Watch some TV."

"But..."

"It's an order," he says, raising his eyebrows at me. And that's it. Done and closed. I turn on the TV and go to Netflix.

After all, this isn't the worst order in the history of mankind. No matter how much I love to demonstrate my submission, I also love Markus's attentive thoughtfulness and his masterly way of reading me.

— CHAPTER 6 —

I spend the next few days rehearsing like crazy. Morning, noon, evening. Only a few hours away from Markus's music room and I'm jittery with the need to go back. The lessons with Grigory have spiked my motivation, but it's not without pressure. Five days between lessons isn't much, but I do my best and hope Grigory will see my effort.

"Good to see your practice is coming along so well," Markus says when I come rushing out from the music room when he comes home. One of Markus's few rules is I come to greet him, first thing, whenever one of us comes home.

"I've already played five hours today and want to keep going." I'm practically bouncing on my feet.

"What have you planned for dinner?"

"Omelet," I say hesitantly and bite my cheek. It's one of my go-to quick-dishes, and I make the best omelet he's ever had—Markus's own words. But after more than a month of French sauces, Indian meals, and home-baked pizza, I would have liked to make something more interesting.

"In a hurry to get back to the piano, huh?"

"Yeah," I say, relaxing at the sight of his warm smile.

Looping an arm around my waist, he pulls me flush against him, making me squeal. "I'll make you a deal," he says. "I'll order some Chinese while you go play, and in return, you'll spend an hour with me on the couch when the food comes?"

"A whole hour?" I say, my mouth agape with feigned indignation.

"All right. Fifty-nine minutes. Can you live with that?" The cocky glimmer in his eyes is impossible to resist.

"All right then." I throw my arms around his neck and push up against him in a deep kiss.

He quickly hijacks the kiss, sliding his hands under my blouse to explore my skin while demanding entrance to my mouth, possessing me with his tongue. His fingers close around the clasp of my bra as he pulls back to watch me with a mischievous glimmer.

"I thought we had a deal," I say, discrediting my resolute words as I press my hips against him.

He lets go of my bra to pull me closer, making his erection press into my stomach. Leaning his head dangerously close to mine, he says in a husky voice, "That deal can easily be revoked if you don't behave."

I bat my eyelids. "I'm as innocent as a lamb."

With a huff, he says, "And my dick is as limp as overcooked spaghetti." He releases me and swats my ass. "Hurry along before I change my mind."

I sprint back to the music room, casting him a sassy look over my shoulder, and I hear his booming laughter fill the hall behind me.

* * *

On Wednesday I get so lost in practicing I lose track of everything else. Suddenly it's well past noon, and I only have half an hour before I need to leave.

The piano bench nearly topples over when I dash up. My pulse hammers as I dart back and forth in the apartment, trying to find the right clothes, applying make-up, and grabbing a quick lunch. If Markus was here, he'd make me take a moment to breathe. But he's not. He's rehearsing at the opera because I've accidentally laid claim to the music room.

Last night, I told him it wasn't necessary—I'd postpone my practice until he was done. But Markus would hear none of it, and when I kept nagging, feeling bad about having taken over his place, he threw me over the kitchen counter and fucked every last ounce of resistance out of me.

I smile at the thought as I push the elevator button with a relieved breath. That was a close call. But I made it—even with five minutes to spare.

I allow myself to walk at a leisurely pace on my way to the metro. The sun is beating down from an open sky, warming my shoulders and brightening my smile. I might feel nervous as hell, but most of all, I'm relieved and happy I diverted the huge catastrophe of being late.

Something feels amiss though. Like I've forgotten something. It keeps nagging at me until I'm a block from the metro.

Then it hits me. My flowery elastic folder. There's no room for it in my bag, and I forgot to grab it when I rushed out the door. Without my sheet music, I can't play what I've been working on, and if I go back for it, there's no way I'll make it on time—not without the Greek gods, Thor, Odin, and Buddha all bestowing me a miracle at the same time.

I grab my phone and check the time. If I'm fast and lucky, I can catch the next metro and arrive on the dot.

I make a quick decision, spin around, and set off in a run, nearly slamming into a man who curses at me.

"*Entschuldigung.*" I fling the German apology over my shoulder as I sprint on. No time for embarrassment.

I'm panting and heaving when I'm back at the metro station, clutching my flowery folder in one hand, ten minutes later. I keep up the tempo down the stairs as I hear the train pull up to the platform. Reaching the bottom of the stairs, I see the open doors and think I'm going to make it. But just as I run up to a yellow car, the door closes. Right in front of me. I push the button frantically, but it's no use. The cars squeal against the tracks and start moving.

I damn near curse out loud as I grab my head. *This can't be happening. This can't be happening.* Looking frantically around, I find the screen which tells me the next train leaves in ten minutes.

That's ten minutes too late.

The thought of showing up late for an appointment with Grigory Volkov twists my stomach into knots. I can't imagine how he'll react. He's stern and intimidating as is. If it gets any worse, I don't think I'll be able to handle it.

* * *

My lungs are raw when I run up the stairs to the opera, and I can barely catch my breath. Pulling out my phone one last time, I see I'm only six minutes late. That's not too bad. Maybe he'll forgive me when I explain I forgot my folder. Or maybe he's late.

Hope blooms in my chest but dies a quick death when I push through the doors and find Grigory sitting on one of the benches, arms crossed, features set in stone.

"You're late," he says, pushing to his feet.

I hurry to him—like getting there two seconds quicker will help anything. "I'm so sorry. I forgot my folder, and I didn't want to show up without it. And then..."

Grigory grabs my arm. It's not bruising, but it's hard enough to shut me up.

My entire system quivers as he drags me down the halls. My panting reverberates off the empty walls, and my pulse is as loud as a jackhammer. Grigory, though, doesn't say a word. He's completely impassive, his features stern and rough, and I can't tell if he's mad or it's just his usual expression. It drives my nerves through the roof.

"Take a seat," he says when we enter the rehearsal room.

I sink onto the piano bench and stare into the keys before me, clutching my folder and bag in my lap. The door falls shut, and Grigory's measured steps echo ominously as they approach me.

I'm not sure what I expect, but him gently taking my folder and bag is not it. He puts them aside and steps behind me, wrapping his hands around my shoulders.

First, it speeds up my pulse. But he doesn't do anything. He just holds me, and when I realize nothing else will happen, my breathing finally begins to calm down. It takes several minutes before it's back to a level rhythm, but Grigory remains patient as usual, and only when I'm completely calm does he speak.

"So, do you want to start with your punishment or save it for later?" His voice is unperturbed, like he's asking whether I want ice cream of pudding for dessert.

My shoulders immediately tense, and Grigory gives them a squeeze, urging them back down.

"It's your choice." He brushes his thumbs over my arms. "We can get it over with now, or we can wait and let Markus watch. I'm sure he'd enjoy that."

Fuck. I don't know. Why does he even give me this choice? It only makes everything harder. And how will he punish me? Spank me like Markus does?

My insides twist. I can't let a stranger pull down my pants and haul me over his knee.

I start breathing hard again. Maybe it would be best to wait until Markus is here. He'll lend me some much-needed support.

But then I think about the hour that will pass in between—how my anxiety will ramp up as I sit here imagining Grigory punishing me.

God no. Then I'd rather get it over with.

My answer is a barely audible mutter. "Now."

"What's that?" Grigory squeezes my arms as they once again bunch up toward my ears.

"Now," I repeat, a little louder.

"Very well." Grigory takes hold of the collar of my cardigan to pull it off. My skin heats where his fingers graze it, and my nape prickles nervously as I realize how close he is.

I watch his large hand reach over me and close the lid on the piano. "Put your right arm on the lid, underside up."

I do as he says, and a heavy rock lands with a thud in the pit of my stomach as I put my arm on the cool surface. It's only my arm, but I feel utterly exposed, holding it out like this, knowing what's coming.

"Five strikes for being late," he says and holds his baton over my bare skin.

The first strike lands with an angry swish, and I yelp and pull my arm back as fire bursts into my skin. It's much harder than when I play. Or maybe my skin is more sensitive on the underside. Or he hasn't worked me up to this level yet. I don't know. It hurts like hell.

"Keep your arm on the lid," he orders in a dangerous tone.

I throw my arm back out and grab onto my right bicep as I pant through the lingering pain.

Grigory nudges my hand away. It's gentle and slow, unlike his order from a few seconds ago. "Hold onto the bench."

I reach down and grab the edge of the bench and brace for the next strike.

It's as hard as the first, and I clutch the wood, using all my will to keep my burning arm in place.

A third strike, and I'm heaving for air. It really hurts.

"Breathe," Grigory says, a slow long word to soothe me. His hand is still on my left arm, rubbing up and down in between strikes.

I take a deep breath, and just as I push the air back out, Grigory strikes again.

I yelp and squeeze my eyes shut. *Please stop now. Please stop now.*

I push air in and out through my lips, panic building in my chest. I can handle Markus punishing me because I'm his. But a stranger wielding a cruel metal stick to discipline me for something I've done wrong... that I can't take. My safeword hovers right at the tip of my tongue, and I think I'm going to say it.

Grigory tightens his hand on my shoulder like he's trying to calm me even as he hurts me. And damn him, it helps. The large hand is so insisting I can't refuse the comfort.

"Can you be a good girl and take the last one?"

I press my lips together and nod. My safeword vanishes as quickly as it came because how can I refuse when he says it like this?

Grigory hovers the slim metal stick over my arm, and I squeeze my eyes shut.

Swish!

The stick cuts into my arm, and I bend forward as searing pain bursts into my flesh. I rub my left hand on my thigh, trying to process the pain, still not daring to remove my right arm from the piano. With Markus, I'd scream and yell, writhe and struggle, grab his arm or his leg. But with this man, I don't dare to, and I'm about to combust from the overload that I can't find a release for.

Grigory eases my arm into my lap. "Sh, sh, shh," he soothes.

"It's all over now. You did very well."

He rubs my arms with both hands. Up and down. Up and down. All the way from my shoulders to my elbows. His touch is so firm it demands my attention, chases away the tension in my muscles, and lets me focus on something other than the pain.

When Markus caresses me, it's warm and comfortable. This is firm and demanding. Yet, his touch holds a startling gentleness. It's a heady package that draws my attention, levels my focus like he does with the baton when teaching me, and I find myself leaning into him, my breathing calming.

I don't know what it is about this man. He has a frightening way of directing my focus just where he wants it.

"Good girl," he says as the tension leaves my arms. The praise goes straight to that warm place inside me that craves to please and obey under a steady hand.

I don't know how long we stay like this—him rubbing my arms and me sinking deeper into submission. When he finally lets me go, I'm loose in every muscle, calm and settled, yet my mind feels fragile, like it's undergone huge strain and can't even consider the smallest of things.

"Let's play something." Grigory pulls out my sheet music for the piece we're working on and sits beside me.

My pulse cranks up as I glance from the sheet music and to the baton in his hand.

Grigory puts the stick on the piano and splays a large hand on my back. "I won't hit you anymore today. We're just going to play a little until Markus comes."

Glancing up at the clock, I'm relieved to see there are only twenty minutes left. But also a bit disappointed as I feel the intense warmth of Grigory's hand and his calming presence. I don't want to lose it so soon.

Grigory makes me take a couple of slow scales and play through the piece I'm working on, one hand at a time. It takes all my focus doing these small things, and when Markus comes, I feel disoriented and exhausted.

"Everything okay?" Markus asks when we make eye contact.

Grigory stands up and puts a hand on my shoulder. "We had an unfortunate incident today." He gives me a small squeeze, and it feels oddly protective. Though I'm not sure it's not just my fuzzy brain reading something into it. "The young lady was late."

Markus takes the chair beside us and leans in to stroke my cheek. "Oh, sweetie, I told you not to be late."

I bite the inside of my cheek, embarrassment flushing my skin.

Markus keeps stroking my cheek as he looks up at Grigory. "What was the consequence?"

Grigory lifts my right arm, holding the underside up for Markus to see five perfectly aligned red welts. I feel like a museum object up for assessment. But to my surprise, there's nothing humiliating about it. At least not in a bad way. Rather, it warms my insides and pulls me deeper into the silent haze.

"Such pretty marks," Markus says, stroking the stripes. "Well done with the symmetry."

"We didn't get time for much piano, so she'd better come back in a day or two." Grigory's fingers tighten around my shoulder, and this time his grip is more demanding, making my heart flutter.

"Let's give her a day to recover, shall we, and I'll have her back here Friday?" Markus gets up and takes my hand to make me follow.

"Sounds great." Grigory levels me with a firm look that makes me lean into Markus—both for safety and support as my legs become jelly.

Markus wraps an arm around my shoulders and leans down. "Thank Grigory for teaching you a lesson."

I freeze in his firm hold and give the slightest shake of my head. *Please no.*

"Do it," Markus orders in a low voice.

My eyes flicker up and down between Grigory and the floor and finally settle on the ground as I mutter, "Thank you for teaching me a lesson."

"What's that?" Grigory says, and my cheeks become burning hot. I know he heard.

"Speak up." Markus's voice is low and growly, revealing his dominant mood.

I raise my voice just above a whisper. "Thank you for teaching me a lesson."

I don't look at Grigory, but I can feel the smug dominance radiating off him.

"I'll make sure this doesn't happen again," Markus assures Grigory.

"Don't do it on my account," Grigory says, and when my eyes flicker up, I catch a glimpse of the satisfied smugness in his eyes.

Markus leads me toward the door, and I cling to him, the ground feeling like it's resting on springs, my head swirling from what just happened.

Did Grigory enjoy that? Punishing me?

* * *

When we're in the car and the worst of my dizziness has settled, I ask Markus, "Does Grigory like to dole out punishment?" The thought unnerves me. Markus likes the power play of punishments, but he doesn't enjoy hurting me. He'd rather hit me for pleasure.

"Oh yes. He's a real sadist." Markus turns to me as he stops at a red light. "I would be more careful not to be late. Next time, he might not go so easy on you."

"Was that easy?" I say incredulously. I do believe the marks on my arm prove otherwise.

"Don't worry, sweetie." Markus rubs my thigh and sets the car into gear. "He won't haul you over his knee and whip your ass when I'm not there."

Alarm must show on my face, but Markus seems to revel in it.

"We've agreed he won't hit anything but your arms. But that metal stick..." he pulls air through his teeth and inclines his head. "You should have seen the flutist who screwed up the intro to 'Recondita Armonia' a few months ago."

I gape at him with horrified eyes, and Markus breaks out laughing.

Pulling in a loud breath, I swat at him. "Damn you." He can

be so convincing. And cruel conductors aren't unheard of.

When Markus has finished laughing, I say, "Has Grigory ever done this to someone else? I mean, discipline someone in a lesson?"

Markus smirks. "You're his first victim. And I daresay he enjoys it quite a bit."

This information both scares and excites me, and I'm quiet for the rest of the ride.

When we get back to Markus's place, he brings me to the living room and asks, "What's for dinner?"

I freeze in the middle of the room. *Fuck, fuck, fuck.* Dinner has been my responsibility since I came here six weeks ago, and not once have I forgotten. Until now.

Markus doesn't expect me to serve home-cooked meals every day. He just wants me to have a plan, and if I have a busy day, pizza from the Italian place around the corner is as good a plan as any. But I've been so caught up in practice and trying not to be late that dinner hasn't even crossed my mind.

I lower my head and gather my hands in front of me. "I'm sorry," I say. "I forgot. I was so busy getting ready that..." I stop myself, knowing Markus doesn't like poor excuses.

I see his feet pass me in my periphery and hear him settle on the couch. "Come here." His voice is low and serious, and there's no doubting what comes next.

I hesitate a second before I move to stand in front of him.

"This is not acceptable, Clara." He unbuttons my pants and pulls down the zipper. "Dinner is your responsibility. If you can't handle it, come tell me. Don't ever neglect an order I've given you in favor of something else." He pulls my pants down, and I swallow against the tight knot in my throat.

"I'm sorry. I didn't mean to."

"I know you didn't. But it doesn't change the fact that you didn't obey." He tugs my pants off as I lift one foot at a time. "Get over my knee."

I hate when he makes me do this myself. It's much easier when he hauls me down and forces me in place. Like this, the shame becomes much starker, and I can really feel the regret gnawing at me as I get in place to take my punishment.

Markus circles one hand on my ass cheeks and presses the other to my back, pinning me to the couch. "Now, you've already had one punishment today, and I know it couldn't have been easy, so you'll only get ten strikes."

"Thank you." My mumble doesn't sound grateful, but I truly am. Sometimes he'll give me thirty—even forty when he's really disappointed—so ten is mild.

Markus lifts his hand and slams it down on my ass. Pain bursts into my skin, and I yelp and dig my hands into the space between two sofa cushions, fighting the need to struggle. The stress of the day hits me like a train, and suddenly ten strikes seem unbearable.

"Please," I whimper, tensing my muscles as I brace for the next one.

Slam!

Tears gather in my eyes, and I fumble behind me to get hold of Markus, needing to feel he's still got me despite being disappointed with me. He takes my hand and holds it in a tight, yet reassuring grip on my back as he hits me again.

Slam!

I whimper through the pain and clamp onto Markus's hand. I hate disappointing him, and the guilt is almost as bad as the fire bursting into my flesh.

The next strike has my tears flowing, and through the last six smacks, I'm weeping and shaking, grabbing onto Markus's hand and the sofa cushion.

After the tenth smack, Markus gathers me in his arms and kisses my head. "It's over now. I've got you, sweetie." He holds me like this for a long while. "Don't forget it again," he adds.

"I won't," I whimper between quiet sobs. "I promise."

Markus takes my shoulders and holds me out to watch me. "Two punishments in one day, huh? That's a first."

I wipe at my wet cheeks. "Yeah."

"And by two different men."

God, I have no capacity to handle such information now, and I fall forward, pressing the top of my head into his shoulder.

Markus chuckles and wraps his hand gently around my nape. "Let's hope you've learned your lesson so we don't have to repeat this."

— CHAPTER 7 —

During the next couple of weeks, I make sure not to repeat the incident of two punishments in one day. Actually, I do my darndest to avoid any punishment at all.

I start getting up early in the mornings. Well, at least to me, seven thirty is early. I've never been a morning person and never will be. But it's late enough for me to get my eight hours of sleep and early enough to give me enough time for both practice and dinner preparations before going to a piano lesson in the afternoon.

Two times a week, I get lessons with Grigory, but I keep up the routine the other days too—except for the weekends, which I spend with Markus. My newfound structure gives me motivation and energy, and I even sleep better at night. Markus sees the change as well.

"I'm glad it turned out so well with the lessons," he says on a Friday when he walks me to the lobby at the opera after we've met up for lunch. "You have this cute spring to your step and radiate this lively energy I haven't seen since you started on those damn exams."

"Really?" I light up.

"Yeah. Playing the piano is good for you." Markus leans in to give me a soft kiss, then winks at me as he pulls away. "And the discipline too."

I reach out to take his hand and watch his fingers interlace with mine. I really do love this man. But this thing with sending me off to be dominated by another man is confusing, and I hope he's not just keeping it going for my sake.

"Are you really okay with all of this? The lessons. Grigory and his baton." I flutter my eyes back and forth between Markus and our hands. "You know..."

"Of course, sweetie. I think it's quite fun sharing you with Grigory." He reaches a hand up to stroke my cheek. "You don't have to worry about me. If I'm unhappy with anything, I'll say so."

"Okay." I tighten my grip on his hand. I hate that he has to go. Nervousness is already crawling in my stomach at the prospect of meeting Grigory here alone. Having done this twice a week for three weeks hasn't made it any easier. I'm a nervous mess every time he comes to get me, and it's taxing, to tell the truth.

Before I can say anything to Markus about it, he takes his phone out to check the clock. "I really gotta go." He gives me a cheeky smile. "Got a dirty date with my language coach."

I shake my head and huff a laugh. There's nothing sexy about that man—plus, he's a man. But he's good at what he does.

Taking me by the shoulders, Markus asks, "Are you okay?"

I give him my best smile and nod even though it's hard to let go of him. I don't want him to be late because of me.

He studies me for a moment then seems to accept my response. "I'll see you in an hour." With a hand on my nape, he claims me in a deep kiss.

I watch him cross the large space, and with each step he takes, the lump of anxiety in my belly grows. When he disappears through the staff entrance, my throat is tight, and I have to subdue the need to run after him.

I'm not usually this emotional, but normally I've had a good night's sleep before a lesson. It's just because I'm tired. I barely slept last night, having had one of those restless nights of endless tossing and turning I have every so often. They are fewer when I have a good daily routine and regular sleep pattern, but they will sneak in here and there no matter what I do.

As I wait, I try to focus on the positive, needing to get myself under control before Grigory shows up. Markus is right. The piano lessons are good for me. Grigory's detailed approach to music is inspiring, and my piano playing is rapidly improving these days. Taking lessons with Grigory may be intense, and the emotions of submitting to two men are a mess at times, but in the end, I thrive with playing this much, and Grigory... My stomach makes a little flip that says it all.

Five minutes later, the man himself appears, proud and mighty, a force to be reckoned with.

I feel minuscule beneath his perceptive stare as I walk to him. My eyes dart back and forth, wanting to look at him but not daring to. His features are stern and unreadable as usual, and my nerves are a mess of flayed ends and taut knots as I follow him through the halls.

When we're finally at the piano, I quickly become calmer. It helps to have something to focus on, and when I just listen to him without looking, it's an entirely different experience. Whereas his hard features make him appear serious and stern, his voice has a deep, resonant quality that soothes me. Combined with his steady command, I'm quickly lulled into a sense of security.

There's this clarity about his instructions that puts me at ease. He may not be the nicest teacher, but that's not what I need. I've had too many of those teachers who throw you an *excellent* at every turn. You can never tell when they actually mean it. With Grigory, I always know what he wants and what he means. He doesn't sugar-coat anything. If I do something wrong, I get a verbal reprimand or a strike with the baton. But he also lets me know when I succeed. His praise is subtle—a nod of approval or a *well done*—but I can tell he means it, and each time it makes me beam with pride.

When he takes out his baton, though, things become more complicated. The first strike always takes me aback; however, today it's worse than usual. I nearly start hyperventilating, tension crackling through my body.

"Easy now." Grigory puts his hand on my shoulder. "Breathe through it."

It takes some time to get my breath to settle, but Grigory is patient as ever with an uncanny ability to know when I'm ready. Actually, the uncanniness extends to reading me in general. As the lesson proceeds, Grigory doesn't ramp up the pain as usual. I think he must sense I'm in a strange place today and adjusts the intensity as not to overwhelm me too much. He even seems to lessen his musical demands.

I'm genuinely relieved and end up feeling decidedly calm.

But suddenly, it all snaps. Grigory accidentally hits the same spot twice in a row, and the pain from the first doesn't recede before a new burn erupts on top of it.

"Ouch," I yelp, jerking my arm to me. I don't think the pain is nearly as bad as the worst Grigory has doled out in previous lessons, but it jars my whole system, and it feels like fire licking my skin.

I shut myself off as an onslaught of emotion crashes through me. This is wrong, being here with another man when I belong to Markus. It's too much, all of it—the pain, the intense focus, giving up control to a stranger.

The urge to cry becomes a tight knot in my throat, and my muscles constrict.

I thought I was okay with all of this, but I'm not.

My feet rise up on the balls, preparing to bolt. I have no idea where to; I just need to get out of here—get away from the man who acts like it's his right to demand my submission.

But before I gather the courage to go through with it, Grigory gets up behind me and puts both hands on my shoulders. They are large and heavy, keeping me in place with their sheer weight.

"Clara, what's going on with you?" Grigory's voice is calm and steady, but there's a dark note somewhere in there that unmistakably demands an answer.

"Please, can I leave?" I say.

"You sure can't. Not when you're on the brink of a

breakdown. Now tell me what happened."

A few tears drip from my eyes and I hurriedly brush my sleeves over my cheeks. "I don't know. It's just too much."

Grigory starts kneading my arms, up and down in gentle motions. "What is too much?"

"All of this." I throw my hands into the air, my despondency turning into agitation. "You hitting me. Acting like you have every right to do so."

"Well, haven't I?" he asks calmly, completely unaffected by my little outburst.

"What?" My tone is tense as I curl my hands together in my lap.

"You belong to Markus, and he has allowed me to hit you. So I do think I have the right to do so."

His answer throws me completely off. It's incredibly arrogant, yet his touch is attentive and caring, and I don't know which one to latch on to.

I want to be offended, but how can I be when his large fingers curl around my arm, demanding all my attention with a startling gentleness?

How can I when he's right?

Markus did allow him to hit me. And I belong to Markus. Thus Grigory has every right to hit and dominate me.

The realization sinks in, fogging over the chaos in my mind and loosening my rigid limbs.

This is not wrong. I'm exactly where Markus wants me. And even more so, I do want this—the safety of these strong hands and Grigory's unwavering command.

"Good girl," Grigory croons, sensing the exact moment I give in.

The approving rumble hits straight into some fundamental part of me, right at my core. A part that craves his approval with fierce intensity and wants nothing more than to submit to him. And not just because Markus has sent me here. Grigory's overbearing authority balances the imbalance in me.

His warm hands seem to emphasize his words as they stroke up and down along my skin, easing the nervous cold.

I imagine how it would feel to be engulfed by the warmth. Feel it against my back, wrapped around me in a safe embrace. I wonder if his chest would feel as strong as his hands—if his arms would band around me like steel. Could I even handle the extreme vulnerability I would feel?

The thought is unsettling yet settling, and my breath becomes deeper yet more labored as the idea swirls in my mind.

The power imbalance is heavy and palpable in the air as Grigory squeezes my arms. The large pads of his fingers dig into my muscle. It hurts. But the pain feeds my submission, and I let out a small whimper of surrender as I let go of the lingering resistance.

He gives a low growl in response, digging his fingers a bit deeper.

I don't know what happens. My head goes blank, and all that exists is Grigory and his impossible power. I feel small. Nonexistent. Swallowed up by him. But it's not a loss. It's calm.

We stay like this for a minute. Two. Maybe Three.

Our breathing falls into the same rhythm, syncing with each

other, and I have a deep sense of something falling into place—a piece of a puzzle finding its place, a golf ball rolling on the edge and finally dropping into the hole.

Grigory's fingers loosen. Slowly. Almost reluctantly. And I'm just as reluctant, wanting to reach up and press his hands back to my arms.

But then he's gone, back to the chair beside me. Too far away. I hover for a moment, adrift in a restless void, before I can regain my footing on solid ground.

But it's not the same ground as the one he took me from. Something has changed. Some essential part of me has been nudged out of place—or maybe farther into place. I don't know.

Grigory puts his baton away and leans back in the chair. "Play for me, Clara." His voice is soft and warm. It sounds so intimate, and when I put my fingers to the keys, it is. I'm not playing for my piano teacher. Not for a random onlooker. The music is something personal—something special—that I give to *him,* and it feels like the most vulnerable act I've ever done.

"That was beautiful," Grigory says when the last note has rung out, and his voice is full of a strange kind of reverence. "Do it again."

He doesn't correct me or strike me even though I make several mistakes. He just lets me play the piece in its entirety several times.

I play with everything I have, imbuing every little note with deep-felt emotion, and when Markus comes in and breaks our bubble, I feel raw and exposed, all my feelings hanging on the outside.

When Markus asks me to thank Grigory for the lesson, it's even harder than usual to meet his eye. I feel like I've given him something deeply personal, and for the next few days I wage an inner battle as I try to decide whether I gave him too much or just enough.

— CHAPTER 8 —

After the weekend, Grigory is extra severe with his mean, little stick. It's almost like he's compensating for going easy on me Friday. He hits me more and harder, and my arm is a constant burn, my mind overwhelmed and blurry. But what's more, are my emotions. The vulnerability from the last lesson still lingers—the entrance he forged to my submission still wide ajar.

When he starts hitting me, I'm uneasy, trying to shut the door and keep him out to protect myself. But as Grigory keeps going, all I can do is try to stay afloat in the whirlwind of his command.

Somehow, I manage to keep my balance. I don't know how. Every time the baton strikes, I whimper at the searing pain, but Grigory doesn't give me time to overthink or panic. He forces my attention back to the music or my breathing, and I'm helpless to do anything but go along.

"Deep breaths," he urges when my mind is about to combust from the overload of pain, and when he pulls in a loud breath, I automatically imitate. There's no room to think. Just follow and obey.

"One more," he orders, splaying his hand on my back where

my dress dips into a deep V, leaving my skin bare. His warm palm sends tingling shivers into my skin like ripples in water, and I suck in a shuddering breath at the intimacy.

I let myself get lost in it, closing my eyes and listening to his deep voice, soaking up the warmth. But even though that single hand is warm enough to set my skin ablaze, it's not enough. I want more. I want to feel the strength in his hands as they curl all the way around my arms. I want to feel how small I am under his all-consuming power.

I whimper when Grigory removes his hand. I actually whimper. Mortification makes a rapid crawl toward my cheeks, but Grigory stops it with a harsh "Play." And with that, my mind is wiped clean, and all that exists is the music.

Until his baton bites into my skin. Harder than ever before.

The pain is sharp, making me hiss. It burns through my flesh and into my muscle. But after a second, it becomes a deep and soothing warmth that seeps through my body, dragging my mind deeper into a floaty sensation.

It's like being high while wrapped in a warm cocoon of safety.

Please hit me again. The words hover on my lips. But I forget them the moment his warm palm presses against my back, and instead, I want to beg him never to remove his hand.

For a long while, he keeps it there. Longer than he's done before. He just sits with his hand on my back, anchoring me so I won't sink into my head. Though, I'm not even sure there's much to sink into. It all seems so mushy up there.

"Start packing up your things," he finally says.

My eyes dart to him, confused and groggy.

His thumb moves over my skin in a slow stroke that has a gust of air rushing in through my lips. "You've had enough for one day," he says.

I skim the room, trying to grasp what's going on. When I notice the clock, I'm surprised to see it's a quarter past four. More than an hour has passed.

Where's Markus?

"Take your time. No hurry." Grigory gently removes his hand and gets up, leaving my side.

It feels cold without him here, and I stare after him, silently begging him to return, but he's looking at his phone.

I gather my sheet music in my folder, unable to go anything but slow. A wave of dizziness hits me when I stand up, causing me to grab onto the piano. I blink my eyes. The whole room is blurry, my mind the same. If I didn't know better, I'd think someone had drugged me.

Taking a minute to adjust, my sight slowly clears up, and I scan the room again.

My attention lands on the intimidating man in the white button-up shirt, who stands in the middle of the room, typing away on his phone. His thick brows are low and serious. I can't tell whether he's in a grave mood or just relaxing his face, but the vision has my stomach quivering. Or maybe fluttering?

That's when it hits me. I'm alone with Grigory. Without the piano to distract me.

I suddenly don't know what to do with myself, and I clench and unclench my hand on the piano edge, flitting my eyes back and forth.

That's right. My bag and cardigan on the floor. I'm supposed to pack up.

I stare at my things for a long second before finally bowing to pick them up.

It seems like too much of a hassle to put the cardigan on, so I gather it in my arms along with my bag and folder. It's clumsy and inelegant, like carrying a heap of groceries when you've forgotten a bag, but I can't seem to manage anything else.

When I glance up again, I realize Grigory is watching me, having witnessed my blundering attempt at packing up. Suddenly, the latent mortification of the last hour washes over me.

Blood surges to my cheeks. Maybe I should just leave. I take a hesitant step forward and stop mid-step.

Shouldn't Markus be here?

Grigory answers my unspoken question. "Markus is running late. You are to meet him in C3."

That's the cue I needed. I force my legs back to work and walk toward the door.

With three long steps, Grigory reaches it before me, gripping the handle. "Can you find C3 on your own?" he inquires, and I don't miss the amusement in his voice.

Mortification morphs into anger and back. Why wouldn't I be able to find it on my own? I'm not some child who can't navigate a building.

"Of course," I say, reaching for the handle with a sudden urge to get out of here. I'll push his hand away if I have to.

Before I can find out whether I can make myself shove at his large hand, he opens the door.

I quickly slip into the hall without looking at him. Relieved to have escaped, I glance around. The hall splits into three corridors, and my eyes jump back and forth between them as I try to process the information Grigory gave me. *C3,* he said. I have no idea where that is.

Turning around to see this room's number, I realize Grigory is still in the doorway, watching me. But he's not just watching. A wide grin is plastered across his face, directed straight at me.

I'm so perplexed I start walking, not caring whether it's the right direction. I just have to get away from him.

I can't believe he would laugh at me. I'd expect annoyance or frustration. Maybe even mockery. But never would I ever expect this perpetually stern man to grin at my dazed confusion.

It hurts more than I care to admit.

I barely register footfalls coming up behind me, and I jump, nearly dropping everything I'm carrying, when a large hand wraps around my arm.

Grigory gathers my shoulder bag and cardigan in one large hand and turns me in the opposite direction.

His grip is like steel as he drags me down the hall. I want to pull away or tell him to let me go, but his grip is so insistent it snuffs out my resistance.

For a moment, I sink back into the hazy place where I can't focus on anything but his dominance, but as we veer down a corridor with people, embarrassment rises anew.

This man really has no shame. He nods to the people like

there's nothing odd about dragging a much younger woman along by the arm.

I, on the other hand, can't bear to lift my gaze. I feel like a disobedient schoolgirl on her way to the headmaster's office.

Is that how he sees me? A young woman who can't hold her own? With the age difference and my insecure behavior around him, it doesn't seem unlikely. I even told him I knew the way then went in the wrong direction.

I shudder at the embarrassing thought. God, how stupid. I should have just told him I didn't know where it was.

Grigory leads me down a stairwell and down one more long corridor, and it's only when we reach the door marked C3 he releases me.

He takes my bag and hangs it on his arm before folding out my cardigan behind me. Reluctantly, I push my arms through the sleeves, and I feel tiny when he pushes the fabric in place over my shoulders and adjusts it. It's only his hands touching me, but his wide and tall size is palpable, dwarfing me even though I can't see it.

A few days ago, maybe even a few minutes, I would have reveled in the power difference, but right now I only feel inferior and naive.

He hangs my bag over my shoulder, then curls his hands around my arms like he did last Friday by the piano. A flood of emotion washes over me—longing, want, sadness. I've been yearning for this since I came here today—actually, since I left Friday.

I can't stop myself from leaning into it. My knees go weak

and my chin lowers as my body submits to his touch. I shouldn't react this way. Not with the way he just treated me, laughing at my confusion and dragging me along by the arm.

But I can't help it—It's purely instinctive.

It makes me feel like the starstruck girl I think he sees me as. I don't think I'm much more than a fun little experiment to him. He's doing Markus a favor by teaching me while having a little fun with his baton. That's surely all. And here I am, falling for the famous conductor who's twice my age. My boyfriend's best friend.

Grigory rubs his hands up and down my arms a few times and gives me a long, almost tender squeeze.

"I'll see you in a couple of days," he says, opening the door to C3.

I cast a final glance at him. His eyes seem to flicker with something warm, but all I see is the lingering grin.

The feeling of being the joke of the day is so bad that I want to dig myself a deep hole and stay there. Usually, I can carry myself with a worthy posture and speak whole sentences without my tongue tying into knots, but with Grigory, it all goes south, rendering me an incoherent mess.

I don't tell Markus about the episode. Instead, I bury it in that deep hole I wish I could bury myself in.

— CHAPTER 9 —

Grigory's grin keeps popping up in my head like a mocking banner commercial the next day, and I can't shake the feeling of being handled like a little girl. Nothing I do will make me forget it. TV, piano, books, warm baths, music. I try it all, but the feeling remains.

Who does he think he is, dragging me along like that?

He might be twice my age and tenfold as important, but it doesn't give him the right to treat me like some errant child who'd run off as soon as he let me loose.

Maybe it's my own fault though. I did go off in the wrong direction after telling him I knew the way. Why couldn't I just have asked him for directions like a normal person?

I press the heel of my hand to my forehead. It seems so simple now that I sit here at home, but yesterday my brain was so fogged over I'm not sure I could have managed two coherent words. This seems to be the case more often than not when I'm around Grigory—I stagger and flounder, unable to find my words or balance.

I'm not sure why it suddenly bothers me this much. It's been this way since the first time I met him.

But then again, Grigory hasn't shown amusement at my expense before.

That grin...

I grunt, burying my face into the nearest pillow. *Someone just shoot me now.*

I need to get out of here and find something to get my mind off his stupid grin.

Maybe I should head into the city center? I haven't done much exploring here, and there is loads to see.

Wasting no time, I change my clothes, apply some make-up, and head to the metro. When sitting in one of the yellow cars, I shoot Markus a quick text, letting him know I'm going out.

Five minutes later, his response pings in.

Have a good time. I want you home by five. You don't have to worry about dinner.

He's probably planned to take me out, which is more than fine by me. I love eating out with him, plus it will be a welcome distraction.

I get off near Gendarmenmarkt to watch the impressive buildings, then venture down the streets to browse the stores. The inner city isn't too packed on a Tuesday afternoon like today, but it's never possible to avoid crowds here—especially not in the tourist season.

I prefer my hometown, Aarhus, where you can stroll through the city on a Tuesday without having to zig-zag to avoid bumping into people. But the boisterous life provides a needed distraction that helps keeping the cringe-worthy thoughts at a distance.

I spend several hours here, admiring the old buildings and

monuments, browsing a bookstore with a large music section, and reading at a café.

My timing is perfect. Ten minutes before my deadline, I step into the apartment.

Setting my strappy sandals beside Markus's brown leather shoes, I smile. *He's already home.*

But my smile fades when I see a pair of shiny black leather shoes and hear the complicated notes of piano music and singing from the music room. Markus doesn't play the piano that well. And he's not so meticulous with his shoe polishing.

It can't be.

My stomach twists. I've spent the whole day trying to forget Grigory, and now he's here?

Taking off my summer jacket, I consider disregarding Markus's rule about greeting him when I get home.

He sure wouldn't like that. And the thought of disobeying him makes my stomach churn.

So I step up to the closed door and squeeze my eyes shut, knocking two times. There's no response. I carefully open, and instantly an emotional, restless energy hits me. It's "Erstarrung," the fourth song in Schubert's *Winterreise.* I know the two men like to play together, but I haven't heard it before. Actually, I haven't heard Grigory play live outside brief demonstrations in our lessons.

The intensity takes me aback, and I halt mid-step, staring at the scene in front of me.

Grigory is sitting by the piano, fingers moving in swift, rolling movements, and Markus stands next to the instrument, deeply immersed in the music.

Not missing a note, Grigory looks up at me, his eyes ablaze with the same intensity quivering in the music.

The air lodges in my throat. There's never enough oxygen when that man fixates on me. I want to break the contact but remain frozen in place, unable to do anything but accept the intrusion of his eyes.

Only a moment passes, but it feels like minutes, and when he releases me, the air snaps back into my lungs with a loud gasp.

Markus turns to me and points at the sofa.

I'm not comfortable being here. It feels like I'm intruding on something private, and I can't handle being near Grigory today. I perch stiffly on the sofa and try not to look at him despite feeling his eyes on me. Instead, I watch the red oriental carpet, the paintings on the walls, the stacks of books on the side table.

Most opera singers couldn't afford the luxury of a big rehearsal space like this in their home. It's only because Markus has inherited a large sum of money from his dad that he's been able to buy an apartment like this and have such a wonderful space.

This is my favorite room in Markus's apartment. It's like stepping into a different world when you come from the white and black tones, steel and clean lines of the rest of his home. Personally, I find the modern, masculine style somewhat cold. The music room, however, I could easily have chosen for myself with its warm, welcoming atmosphere, old furniture, and brown and red color schemes.

The far wall is lined with old bookshelves full of sheet music and books about music. In front of them, the grand piano dominates the room with its impressive size. It's nothing like the small rehearsal room Grigory teaches me in, where the instrument takes up half the space. Here, there's plenty of room around it. There are side tables, a desk, and the antique mahogany sofa with red velvet which I'm sitting on.

Markus has intentionally decorated the room differently, so you can sink into a bubble far from the rest of the world, just you and the music. And it works. He spends long days in here when rehearsing new roles—singing and reading background material.

I can spend hours in here myself, lying on the large oriental rug while writing my exams, reading books, or listening to music. There's something stabilizing about being on the floor, feeling solid ground below you, that has always calmed me.

But today is not one of those days, and when Markus sings the last line and snaps his fingers toward the floor, I shake my head. I can't handle being in such a vulnerable position when Grigory is here—not after what happened yesterday.

Grigory plays the outro as I silently beg Markus for reprieve. But as usual I can't refuse his dominant authority, so I glide onto the carpet.

He probably thinks it will be easier for me to kneel this time since I've done it in Grigory's presence once before. But it's not. If anything, it's harder.

When I meet Grigory's eyes, I find them alight with something resembling triumph—maybe amusement. I might be seeing something that isn't there after what happened yesterday, but even rational thinking won't shut down the feeling of being an amusement to him.

I pull my legs up to my chest and wrap my arms around them in an ineffective shield.

Grigory turns back to the sheet music and eases into the gentle intro of "Der Lindenbaum," his fingers moving rapidly yet effortlessly, mimicking the sound of rustling leaves.

Leaning my forehead against my knees, I inhale deeply. It doesn't matter how I feel or what happens around me; those notes always hit me the same way. Serene peace washes over me, loosening my tense shoulders and deepening my breath. And when Markus starts singing, a tinge of mournful yearning weaves into the calm, making the thuds of my heart heavier.

I've heard this music so many times—through headphones, speakers, in a concert hall. But not this close, alive and breathing, the vibrations in the air, the intensity seeping from the men like a palpable energy. And what a depth of expression. Even in the world of professionals it's rare to come across such profound feelings.

It's so moving my chest wells up with unrestrained emotion, my eyes filling with moisture. Lifting my head, I wipe at my damp eyes. A prickling awareness makes me look up to find Grigory watching me. His hands are still moving over the keys, but all his attention is on me.

His features are soft, the line between his brows less deep, his eyes full of something tender—maybe compassion? It's startling to see such gentle emotions on the always stern man, and it crushes my defenses. I want to hide my head again, protect the vulnerability painted over my face, but I can't look away.

Grigory moves into the agitated middle part, and we stare at each other as he effortlessly fires off the rapid notes by heart.

When he finally releases me, I feel robbed. I'm not sure of what exactly, but it's something personal—too personal to give to a man I barely know. But it doesn't matter. When he captures my eyes again, he holds me afloat with a silent demand that mingles with a gentleness pulling at my heart. I fall deeper under his power, and the music works its magic like a spell, binding me closer to him.

The two men play through the first half of *Winterreise,* and I fall deep into a trance. My breath follows the ups and downs of the music, my chest rising in sudden jerks at the tense peaks, and a steady calm settles over me when the music finds a restful flow.

It's a wide spectrum of emotion that leaves me vulnerable and exposed, and Grigory sees it all—takes it all.

When the final chord rings out, the two men take a moment for themselves, letting the intensity die down. Then they nod at each other and step back into the real world. Grigory gets up and puts the sheet music back on the shelf, and Markus turns to me with a smile.

But I can't shake off the charged energy as easily, and I feel adrift as I lose Grigory and the music, which both have anchored me through the emotional rollercoaster of the last twenty minutes.

"Are you okay?" Markus asks, helping me up on my feet.

The room spins around me like it did yesterday when I got up from the piano bench. I reach out for Markus who lends me some stability with a hand on my waist. But then my eyes flit over the room and fall into the trap of Grigory's gaze. He watches me like he's privy to some deep secret, and that's when it hits me. I've put all my most private, intimate feelings out there for him to inspect and scrutinize. And I just let him take it all. I feel naked and horribly exposed under his gaze.

Forcing my eyes away, I step closer to Markus, seeking shelter behind his tall frame.

He puts a hand on my cheek and kisses the top of my head. "We are going to get something to eat, the three of us. Go put on your shoes and jacket."

I'm happy to oblige, needing to get away from Grigory. But as I take a hasty step, I lose my balance.

Markus is quick to grab my waist. "Easy now. Go slow."

My eyes drift by Grigory, and my stomach sinks when I see the same grin as yesterday plastered to his face. Wide and amused.

Unheeding Markus's words, I scramble toward the hall, again desperate to get away from Grigory. Why can't I pull it together when he's around? And why do my legs need to fail me right when he's watching?

I thought we just had a connection—thought the way he pulled me into the music and compelled my submission meant something. But maybe he just enjoyed lording his immense power. Maybe he thinks it's fun toying with me, making me stagger and act like a helpless girl.

Fuck, it hurts.

I start putting on my jacket, and that's when I realize what Markus said. *The three of us.* My throat works to swallow, but the lump won't go away, and adrenaline spikes in my blood, making my heart pump hard.

Sticking a foot into my sandal, I pause. Maybe I should tell Markus I don't want to come. He won't need an elaborate explanation. My troubled eyes will be enough. I just need to get him alone since I can't say it in front of Grigory.

I'm working up my resolve, about to go find Markus, when the man I try to avoid comes into the hall. His authority pervades the room, making it shrink to a claustrophobic box with six solid surfaces and no air.

Panic messes with my focus, and my balance is off as I lift my leg behind me to strap the sandal. It takes too long, so I move to set my foot down so I won't trip.

But somehow, the buckle gets stuck on my sleeve, and I fall forward, face first.

I brace for the mortifying collision, but it never comes. Instead of crashing to the floor, I crash back into a wide chest as a large arm comes around my shoulders. The air leaves me with a loud gush, and the impact sets a dormant wave of emotions rolling. Shock, confusion, and overwhelming vulnerability clash together, and suddenly I'm breathing hard as moisture gathers in my eyes.

"Shh, sh, shh. I've got you," Grigory whispers, his arm still wrapped around me. "I've got you, little girl."

Those last two words confirm everything I fear about the way he sees me, yet they hold no belittlement. He says it with such startling tenderness it sucks the air straight out of me. All resistance goes *swoosh,* and I sink back into him, letting his arms hold me steady with the promise of safety.

"I've got you," he reassures, tightening his arm around my chest, squeezing my arm with his big hand. "No falling on my watch."

I've thought about this so many times—a furtive wish in the hidden corners of my mind. To feel his body pressed against mine. It's everything and more than I could have imagined. His power is everywhere—in his firm hold, his strong chest, in the very air around us. It's in the immense warmth covering my back and in the depth of his voice right next to my ear. I can't breathe, and yet the air runs deeper and calmer into my lungs.

It swallows all my thoughts, all my insecurities and doubt, and for a moment, the safe cocoon of his grip is the only thing that exists.

"Can you stand on your own?" he asks gently.

I give a small nod, and slowly he pulls his arm away, giving me time to find my footing before releasing me completely. Then he sinks onto his haunches in front of me, and I make quick work of wiping the moisture from my cheeks, hoping he doesn't notice.

I watch in stunned silence as he closes the clasp on my ankle and picks up my other sandal. "Hold onto my shoulder," he says.

Tentatively, I reach a hand out. I haven't touched him before, and it's almost like kissing someone for the first time, sending a thrill through my veins as I press my hand to his shoulder.

He might be the one on the floor, but I feel small and fragile as I sense the dormant strength beneath the padding in his suit jacket.

Curving his hand around my ankle, he lifts my foot and

slides the shoe on. His touch has my heart beating wildly, and I lean into him, needing the support.

I feel like a child as I watch him buckle the strap, but it's not in the belittling sense like earlier. This time, I feel cared for—warm and fuzzy. It's confusing as hell, and when he gives my ankle a squeeze and gets up, my head starts swirling again.

Luckily, Markus comes a moment later, saying something to Grigory in an upbeat tone. I don't notice the words, too focused on seeking his support as I slip up to him and sink into his arms. Markus accepts me without pause like he always does, and I breathe a sigh of relief as his arms close around me. But it's not without an underlying wish it was someone else holding me.

— CHAPTER 10 —

We go to a small French restaurant nearby. Markus guides me to the seat by the wall and sits beside me with Grigory across from him. I feel trapped here in the corner, but I'm grateful for having Markus at my side, nonetheless.

The two men chat about the selections while I try to make my still blurry mind focus on the wealth of options in the leather-bound menu.

When the waiter comes to take our orders, I haven't come to a decision yet. Markus and Grigory each order a steak along with a bottle of red wine to share. I'm inclined to take the easy route and say I'll have the same, but my stomach is too unsettled for meat and I don't like wine.

I fumble with the menu as I feel all attention turn to me. The waiter does nothing to hide his irritation, but Markus is a well of patience, leaning his arm across the back of my chair, saying, "What are you considering?"

Relieved he comes to my aid, I show him the three contestants in the menu.

"This one." He points to the dish with halibut, lemon butter, spinach, and potatoes.

I look up at the waiter. "I'd like the..." Feeling Grigory's eyes on me, my tongue curls around itself, and I forget what I was saying. Luckily, Markus takes charge, informing the waiter I'll have the halibut and a Coke.

"Dessert?" the snooty waiter asks.

Markus takes a look at the menu and says to Grigory, "I take it you'd like the chocolate cake?"

"Of course," Grigory says, and Markus orders chocolate cake for all of us.

"Three chocolate cakes," the waiter confirms and gathers our menus, giving me a blatantly unimpressed once-over as I hand him mine.

I'm not impressed with myself either, and it's hard not to bury my face in my hands now that I don't have the large menu to hide behind.

What must Grigory think of me? First, my legs fail me, then my tongue and my decision-making—not to mention my ability to handle a normal social situation. I feel so inferior around him. He's in control of everything, and I'm in control of nothing.

I decide it's best to stay out of the conversation, knowing my tongue won't cooperate if I try to speak.

The men sample their wine, twirling it in the glasses and sipping it while discussing its bouquet. Markus loves good wine, and Grigory appears to share the interest as they launch into a conversation about grape types and wine districts.

In my world, four types of grapes exist—green and red ones, with or without seeds. I couldn't contribute even if I liked wine. I've tried it a few times, but it's one of those bitter "adult drinks"

I've never learned to appreciate. The same goes for coffee, beer, and shots. I'm more of a colorful drinks kind of girl, preferring not to taste the alcohol. Actually, nowadays I'd rather not have any alcohol at all.

I had my alcohol-swamped years of drinking as a teenager, but unlike most of my peers, I lost the taste years ago. I've found my own way to get a buzz now. Remembering how Markus spanked me into a pleasant wooziness a couple nights ago, I gaze up at him with a small smile tugging on my lips. He gives me one of his wide, charming ones in return, and it settles some of my unease.

The waiter returns with plates of beautifully presented food. It looks absolutely delicious, and on any other night, I would dig in with great gusto, but with the strain and confusion of the day twisting in my stomach, I don't have much appetite. I start eating anyway, needing the distraction.

The conversation shifts to *Winterreise*, and the two men have different interpretations of the story about the lonely wanderer who ventures out into the ruthless winter after his lover has left him for another man.

"Throughout the whole work, we have these small glimmers of youthful rebellion that hint he will pull through in the end," Grigory says.

"I don't think he ever fully recovers from the blow," Markus counters. "The music in 'Der Leiermann' is too bleak to insinuate any light at the end of the tunnel." He speaks of the final song, which concludes the story with a somber atmosphere.

"You can't sing, *sind wir selber Götter,* so close to the end if you have given up all hope," Grigory argues, referring to the third last song, 'Mut,' which holds a breath of hope amidst all the gloom.

I try to keep my eyes away from Grigory, but like a child and a cookie jar, I always dwell longer than intended on him. He seems pleasant and approachable, his hand gestures open and free as he leans back in his chair, debating with passion and interest. I'm close to saying something to him several times, but then he catches me looking, and his eyes narrow into an unreadable expression that kills my resolve.

"It was actually during a conversation about *Winterreise* I fell for this one," Markus says, sending a smile my way, giving my thigh a squeeze.

"Is that so?" Grigory asks curiously.

"She came up to me during the intermission to thank me for the music. She was clearly too shy to stay and talk, but I didn't let her go so easily." Markus winks at me, and I give him a tentative smile.

"I asked which song she liked the most," Markus continues, "And it turned out she had all kinds of interesting thoughts and opinions, and I was smitten right then and there."

Casting a glance at Grigory, I discover he's watching me with a curious gaze. "So, what's your take on our discussion?"

It's time I prove there's more to me than the shy girl with downcast eyes, so I straighten my spine and keep my gaze on him. "There will always be these small glimmers of light, even in the darkest of places. I think 'Mut' is one final desperate attempt at finding hope. But in the end, the wanderer is unable to move past the defeat. Our faiths are largely determined by the people we choose to be around, and he chooses a lousy fiddler without shoes. There's no hope in that."

"Interesting angle." Grigory nods, seeming to consider my argument. "Maybe the wanderer can be seen as a parallel to Schubert himself. He died only a year after finishing *Winterreise*, and according to his friends, it wore him down so much it seems to have hurried along his untimely death."

Leaning forward on his elbows, Markus breaks off the conductor's musings. "Grigory, I know you like to share your immense knowledge of composers and their fascinating lives. But right now, no one's learning anything new. Clara already knows all of this, and you only risk falling off your high horse when she tells you something new."

My jaw drops, shock widening my eyes as I stare up at Markus. I would never expect him to speak to Grigory like this. I prepare myself for heavy tension and irritable looks, but instead, I hear a deep chuckle from across the table.

"You may have a point. I'd better keep quiet, then." Grigory shakes his head and takes a sip of his wine, studying me over the rim of the glass. "I see someone has done their homework," he says with a glimmer in his eyes, and I don't know whether to smile or dive beneath the table.

I go with the first.

Luckily, he doesn't put my knowledge to the test. I might have spent a lot of time studying Schubert and his music, but my knowledge can't possibly compete with a man who has made a living out of playing classical music for thirty years.

The two men keep talking a while before Grigory turns to me again. "Do you like studying music at the university?"

"A lot," I say, relieved how stable my voice is. "I love that there are so many practical classes, unlike many other university studies."

"You don't like the academic work?" he asks, cutting a chunk off his steak.

I openly tell him about my studies, all the while keeping my back straight and maintaining eye contact for more than two seconds at a time.

I tell him I'm happy to learn the academic approach, though I prefer the practical classes—especially the piano lessons. Those are by far my favorites. And the small rehearsal rooms with grand pianos are one of the best things about studying there. "I can spend hours in those rooms, just me and the piano," I tell him with a smile.

"Have you ever considered the music conservatory?" Grigory asks, and I must say I'm a bit surprised. The conservatory is the most prestigious place to study music, and he knows how much it takes to get in, and I don't have it.

"Yeah, but I started playing too late and don't have the technique," I say.

"The conservatory isn't all about technique, you know. At least not here in Berlin. They tend to look more for inherent musicality. Technique can always be taught. The other not so much."

I twirl my fork nervously, uncomfortable with the direction of the conversation. The conservatory has always been my dream, but I know it's not a realistic one, and talking about it makes me wistful. "Yeah, but I'm happy with the university, and now I'm starting the master's program in the fall." My plan is already laid out. Two more years and I have my degree.

"How much piano is there on the master's program?"

"There are no piano classes." I swallow hard as I sense his disapproval at these words. "If I wanted the practical master's program, I had to stay on with my supplementary subject—which is English—for another half year, and I needed to get back to music." Being away from music to study a secondary subject for the better part of a year sucked the soul right out of me. "So I'll have to settle for the academic approach."

"So no piano, huh?"

"Well, no piano classes. But I'll still have access to the practice facilities. And I won't have many classes, so I'll have plenty of room to prioritize it."

Grigory gathers his utensils at the side of his plate, dabs his mouth with his napkin, and leans back in his seat with his arms crossed over his chest. "The master's program is not the right thing for you."

I immediately drop my eyes, anger and hurt warring in my chest.

It's none of his business whether I've chosen right or wrong. I've talked this over with Markus a hundred times, and we both agree this is better than me continuing on with my supplementary subject and being miserable for another six months just so I can get a few practical classes. Now, Grigory has the gall to tell me it's the wrong choice. He doesn't even know the circumstances.

But even as I'm fuming and want to hate him, sadness wells up in my chest and tightens my throat. The way he glared at me and told me straight out I'd made a wrong decision hurt. If not for the way he did it, then because I can't control my need to please him.

Soon, the feeling of having disappointed him burns at my submissive core, searing away the anger, leaving only strained sadness.

I gather my own utensils, even though I'm only halfway done, and stare into the tabletop.

Markus and Grigory pick up a new conversation, but this time I barely listen. All I can think is I need to stop seeing Grigory. I have to ask Markus to put an end to the piano lessons. It's quickly becoming too complicated—too painful. My emotions are rattling like a stone in a tin can, back and forth, up and down, a constant confusing noise I can't put an end to until I get distance from the man who has provoked it.

The waiter comes to ask if we are done and when we want the chocolate cakes.

"We'll take them right away," Grigory replies, and I feel him studying me as the waiter gathers our plates. When the waiter leans in to take my half-full one, Grigory stops him with a raised hand. "Leave hers until you bring the dessert."

Could he treat me any more belittling? First, he lectures me on my studies, and now he wants the waiter to leave my plate like I can't make the decision myself. Next, he'll probably order me to eat up.

Markus beats him to the latter. Leaning in with a hand on my back, he says discreetly, "You should eat some more, sweetie."

Reluctantly, I pick up my fork and take another bite. Silence stretches across the table, and defeat settles like a pile of bricks on my chest as I feel both men's attention on me.

I had finally gained some control over myself and stabilized the self-assurance that always wavers like a flag in the wind in Grigory's presence. But one small blow and I'm back on unsteady ground.

Markus keeps his hand on my back as the two men start speaking in subdued voices. I know they keep the conversation down because of me—some kind of respect as they sense my tense mood—but I'd rather they'd ignore me and speak loudly and laugh. This way, I feel like I'm ruining the dinner, and the tension is painful.

I manage a couple more forkfuls of food, but my appetite has vanished, and when the dessert comes, I only take two bites before pushing the plate away. The chocolate is too dark for my taste, anyway.

Grigory, on the other hand, is over the moon with the cake. Pointing his fork to it, eyes wide, he says, "This cake sure is something."

Markus laughs at Grigory's continued appraisal, and the tension dissipates—at least on their side of the table.

If I hadn't been so disheartened, I'd have laughed too at the sight of the perpetually controlled man showing such enthusiasm over cake.

When Grigory is done, he points his fork to my plate. "Aren't you going to eat that?"

I shake my head.

"Then we'll trade." He switches our plates and quickly finishes my portion. Then he signals to the waiter that we want to pay and stands up to put his jacket on. "I think you need to get your sub home, Markus." He gives me a worried, almost sympathetic look, but I only notice his words.

I clench my jaw. Is it really so hard to address me like an equal adult?

Anger and hurt eat at me, but most of all, I feel tired and defeated. It doesn't matter how much I seethe at his way of speaking about me. The man is right. I do need to get home—away from him.

* * *

The chilly summer night air clears my head, bringing back my determination to make one last attempt at proving myself as an adult to Grigory. "Have a nice evening," I say, stretching out my hand.

The determination is short-lived. The moment I see my hand hovering in the air between us, I regret it. I don't know what I'm doing. I never shake his hand. I'm so busy proving I'm a grown woman that I forget to think. A simple "see you soon" would have been more than enough.

Grigory's massive hand folds around mine—swallowing it up—and a slow smile spreads across his face.

Great. I've given him one more thing to laugh at. *Just great.* I can't even show some normal politeness without amusing him?

My blood boils, and I try to pull my hand back, not caring it's rude.

But Grigory tightens his grip.

I gape, shocked at his audacity, and his smile widens.

Panic seizes me, making me blurt out, "I had a great time," just to make this end.

But Grigory won't put me out of my misery. He puts his other hand on top of our gathered ones, regarding me with an intensity that makes me feel stripped to the bone.

"Did you?" His tone is doubtful. He knows I didn't. But there's no mockery or amusement behind his words, only concern, and it takes me aback as much as his grin did.

I stare into the pavement, all courage knocked out of me in one blow. My hand goes limp in his, and his grip turns softer, less forceful. His thumb makes a few strokes across the back of my hand. It's startling. The gentleness is so at odds with the mocking laugh and his strict authority.

"I'll be in Vienna for a week, so I won't see you until next Wednesday." From the corner of my eye, I sense him inclining his head, seeking my attention.

I let my eyes glide back up to his, and I find a strange gentleness there that pulls at me. But my self-conscious mind won't see anything but the belittling smile from a minute ago.

"While I'm away, I want you to practice four hours a day as a minimum." His deep voice matches the calmness of his eyes but clashes with his powerful stance and the severe lines of his face.

A tight "okay" is all I manage. My head spins and my pulse pounds, distorting everything in a confusing blur.

"Good." He holds onto my hand a minute longer, regarding me silently. "I enjoyed how sweetly you reacted to the music today." For a beat, his features seem milder, the line between his brows smaller.

Then he releases me.

I'm left baffled as the two men say goodbye. I have no idea what to make of what just happened. Grigory's signals are so mixed that my head is about to burst.

Grigory gets into the back of the black Mercedes waiting at the curb, and Markus takes my hand, and I follow him on autopilot.

"What's wrong, sweetie?" he asks, once we get a little farther down the street.

I try to write off his concern with a shrug and a half-hearted smile. But I can't hide from him.

"I can almost hear the gears turning in your head." His brows furrow. "And don't think I didn't notice how uncomfortable you suddenly were at the restaurant."

I let out a heavy sigh. I'd rather not talk about this, but Markus will pry it from me if need be, so I might as well tell him. "I can't figure Grigory out," I say. "One minute he seems attentive and caring, the next he's talking down to me."

"What do you mean?" Markus asks calmly.

"When we finished eating, he said you had to take me home like I was some little girl who needed to get to bed."

"Ooh, sweetie, that's not talking down to you." Markus pulls me to his side, holding me there as we walk. "You know, Grigory might not show it in a conventional way, but he's quite protective of you. He could see how uncomfortable you were."

"That's not all," I say, frustration growing in my voice. "He keeps laughing at me like he thinks I'm funny, and it really hurts."

"Why do you think he laughs at you?" Markus asks, taken aback.

"Because I can never manage to act coherently around him. Today when you helped me up from the floor and I almost fell, he had a huge grin on his face, and when I offered him my hand, back at the restaurant, he seemed to find it amusing." My voice rises to a strained pitch. "He treats me like a child, goddammit. He wouldn't even let me put on my own shoes today."

At the time, helping with my shoes seemed protective, but in light of everything else, it seems like yet another way of demonstrating his superiority.

I look up to see Markus is also laughing at me now, his lips curved up in an amused grin.

"It's not funny," I say, my gaze dropping to the large slabs of the pavement which move like a conveyor belt beneath my feet.

Markus halts by a traffic light with a green Ampelmann and takes my shoulders in his hands. "It *is* a little funny."

I shake my head in confusion. He's usually sympathetic, listening to my worries no matter how trivial.

"Do you remember how shy you often got when we met?"

I nod. He gave me such intrusive looks I couldn't find my words. Now, it takes a bit more to get me there, but the reaction is still the same—when he grabs me by the throat, pressing me up against the wall in a deep kiss, or when he forces me to my knees with a single nod of his chin.

"You could barely stand on your own two legs if I looked a bit too directly at you," he says with an affectionate expression.

"That's different." I belong to Markus, and we are both aware of the dynamic between us.

Taking my head between his hands, he leans closer. "Sweetheart, you are very submissive, and Grigory is very dominating. It would be strange if you weren't affected by him." He moves his hands down to rub my arms. "Especially with all the hitting he does to your arm."

"Why does he laugh at me, then? Doesn't he just see me as an immature little girl?"

Markus's expression turns serious, his hands going still on my arms. "He doesn't laugh at you. He knows why you get so shy and lose your balance." The corner of his mouth tips up. "If I'm not wrong, I think he quite purposefully tries to stir that reaction. He smiles because he thinks you're cute."

"Like a little girl?"

Markus rolls his eyes. "God, Clara, will you get out of that head of yours? Grigory really likes you."

"How do you know?"

"Well, if it wasn't goddamn obvious, I know because he's told me."

"Really?" I can hardly believe it, yet I grow full of hope.

"Yes," he confirms, his deep blue eyes warming. "He found you utterly charming when you staggered out of the rehearsal room yesterday, thinking you could find your own way with your head all foggy."

"He told you *that?*" I ask, mouth agape.

"Of course. You should have seen his expression. He was completely infatuated."

"It was so embarrassing," I say, fiddling with the buttons on his jacket.

"You were halfway in subspace. Nothing embarrassing about that." Markus strokes his knuckles over my cheek, and the traffic light starts beeping, letting us know we have a green light again, but we both ignore it.

"Maybe he didn't know it," I say.

"You know, Grigory has been in this lifestyle much longer than I have. If anyone knows when a sub is going under, it's him. I'm honestly not sure I'd have noticed if he hadn't texted, saying you were in subspace."

I give him a slow smile. "You would have. You always do."

Markus's lips curve up. "Yeah. You're right." He leans in to kiss my forehead, then adds, "Plus, it's quite obvious. You become all googly eyed." He crosses his eyes, making a funny face.

I shake my head and snicker. "It's not that bad."

"Maybe not. But it sure is cute. I must agree with Grigory on that."

Red gathers in my cheeks. "Does he really find me cute?"

"Sure does."

My smile widens uncontrollably, my eyes lighting up with shy elation. It takes me a moment to realize how inappropriate it is and hurry to ask, "Are you really okay with me reacting like that?"

"Of course. Otherwise, I wouldn't keep sending you back for

him to hit you."

Markus sure knows how to make a girl blush, and I bite my lips, swaying my hips gently.

"I think it's cute seeing how he affects you. And who knows? One day I might let him do more than hit you with his baton." He winks at me and leads me across the crosswalk, which once more has a green light.

— CHAPTER 11 —

The following week, I'm a mess of mixed emotions. One minute, I'm jumping with excitement, and the next I'm pacing and fidgeting.

I no longer know what to think about Grigory and the piano lessons. The conversation with Markus has helped ease my worries somewhat, but I'm still not convinced Grigory doesn't see me as a young woman who can't hold her own. After all, my befuddled behavior around him is so bad it can't possibly be charming all the time. I still want to flee my own head when I think about my horrible attempt at ordering food.

Regardless of how I feel, the urge to impress Grigory remains—strong as ever. I spend hours by the piano every day, often exceeding the four hours he prescribed. Well, except for Saturday. Markus has the day off, and he takes me to see the TV tower followed by a visit to Häagen-Dazs—his favorite ice cream place.

The weather is amazing. The sun beats down from a clear sky, and every so often, a gentle breeze drifts by, taking the top of the heat. I strut around in a cherry red dress with white flowers and a lively skirt, feeling perky and happy.

"You are bursting with summer and life," Markus says, stopping at the square in front of the TV tower, lust glimmering in his eyes.

"Thanks." I flash him a bright smile, wriggling my hips to set the skirt alive.

Looping an arm around me, he dips me back in a deep kiss among all the people. A couple of whistles erupt from the crowd, and my cheeks heat as I sling my arms around his neck for support. When he pulls me back up, I'm hot and flustered, peeking up at him with shy admiration as he takes my hand and heads toward the metro, bringing us to our next stop.

At the café, we each get our own waffle with several scoops of ice cream, topped with caramel sauce and whipped cream. It's hard work consuming it all, and we are both exhausted when we get home.

I collapse beside Markus on the sofa, and we spend a whole hour there, talking, making fun, and enjoying each other's company.

It's late afternoon when we finally get up from the couch. I've only spent an hour in the music room, and we are going to the movies tonight. There's no way I'll make all four hours Grigory has prescribed. However, I *have* achieved six hours both Thursday and Friday. It must make up for the missed hours, right?

* * *

Wednesday morning, Markus tells me Grigory will come after dinner to have our lesson here.

If I was jittery before, I'm not sure what this makes me. An absolute nervous wreck? I can barely focus on anything all day. Ten minutes by the piano and I'm already distracted and playing sloppily.

It's much more personal having a lesson here, and I'm not comfortable with anything becoming more personal with Grigory. It's hard enough keeping him inside the piano teacher box as is. Of course, he doesn't belong entirely in that box—never has. But I need to keep him there as much as possible to preserve my sanity, and the professional surroundings at the opera help me uphold the illusion.

I'm already struggling to deal with his shifting moods and unreadable expressions. I don't think I'll be able to handle blurry lines and confusing emotions as well.

I pace through the apartment in the afternoon, my hands quivering as I go through my clothes, trying to decide what to wear. A simple change of location shouldn't make me this nervous.

But that's not all there is to it.

The prospect of seeing Grigory again—feeling his calm authority and having his sharp gaze bore into me—has me on edge.

But I also miss it. I've struggled with the realization as it has grown over the past week, and I'm afraid it has filled me so much it'll spill over and he'll see it.

I don't want to embarrass myself further by having feelings for him I shouldn't have—feelings that aren't reciprocated and never will be. He may find me cute, but this is only fun and games, since I belong to another man. So I do my best to deny how much seeing him again means to me.

"Why is he coming here?" I ask Markus at dinner.

"He hasn't been at the opera today, and he's too busy tomorrow," Markus explains.

"Why not wait until Friday, then?" My fingers tap nervously on the table as I twirl pasta on my fork without eating it.

"You don't want him to come tonight?" Markus lifts an incredulous brow.

I exhale loudly, releasing my fork so it clanks against the plate. "Erm... I guess I do..."

Markus chuckles. "I thought so." Getting up with our plates in his hands, he bends to give me a kiss, and that's when the bell rings. "Go open the door."

"Can't you do it?" I all but beg, nervously biting my finger.

"No." He gives me that dominant expression that leaves no room to argue.

With a loud sigh, I pad to the hallway and check myself in the mirror. Black form-fitting pants enhance my delicate hourglass figure, and the dusty rose top with a lace lining gives me a sweet look. I check my teeth and tug a stray lock of my brown hair back into my side ponytail on my shoulder, then open the door.

The moment I see Grigory, my eyes dart to the ground. But I quickly pull myself together, squaring my shoulders and lifting my eyes to his.

"Hi," I say, stepping to the side.

"Good evening," he replies with an amiable tone at odds with his stern features.

The hallway shrinks to a fourth of its size when he enters. I gather my hands in front of me, rocking back and forth on the balls of my feet, considering whether to stay or go back to Markus. The latter would ease my nerves, but it would also be rude. So I stay.

Stepping out of his black leather shoes, Grigory scans me from my restless feet and up to my face. The sides of his mouth curl up, and I have to remind myself what Markus said. He's not laughing at me; he finds me cute.

My own lips curve up, and the smile keeps unfurling, trying to spread across my entire face like a bright beaming ray of sunshine. I try to fight it off, and when I don't quite succeed, I lower my head, my restless feet growing still more unruly.

Fortunately, Markus comes and redirects Grigory's attention. "How did the concerts go?" he asks as they shake hands, patting each other on the back in a typical man hug.

"Good. World-class singers and, as always, an impeccable orchestra."

"Good to hear they benefited from a new chief conductor," Markus says with a cocky grin, insinuating Grigory's departure after ten years as the head of the orchestra has done them good.

"Hardly. They've already started slipping." Grigory pulls his lips into a tight line, but his eyes reveal the underlying humor.

I can't help laughing, and he gives me a wry expression, huffing a tsk-sound as he shakes his head. There's no derision. Only dry humor. And it sets a flutter to my stomach, warming my cheeks, even as I'm surprised to find my feet have settled.

"How about a glass of scotch to help ease the disappointment?" Markus suggests. "I have a twelve-year-old Bowmore collecting dust in my cabinet."

"Twelve-year Bowmore." Grigory gives an approving nod. "It would be a shame to let it go to waste."

Markus turns to me. "Go warm up in the music room while we have a drink."

I give him an acquiescent nod and remain in place as he goes to the living room, waiting for Grigory to pass me before crossing the hall.

When he passes me, his hand comes up to my arm, giving it a quick squeeze. Sizzles shoot down my skin, and my eyes dart up to him. But he's already on his way, his back to me.

I suck in a deep breath and inadvertently inhale a whiff of his earthy cologne lingering in the air. My stomach flutters and my skin suddenly feels hot and tingly.

He shouldn't affect me this way.

Reminding my feet to move, I go into the music room and start playing. It's a good thing the warm-up exercises are embedded into my muscle memory because my head still refuses to leave the hallway and the squeeze on my arm.

It was only a simple gesture which meant nothing, I try telling myself. Yet, my insides go mushy every time I remember the almost reflexive way he touched me. I can hardly wait for him to come and hit me with his evil stick, just so I can feel his warm hand afterward.

When he comes in fifteen minutes later, I manage to smile openly despite the tingling in my bones.

Bringing a chair up, he then takes a seat beside me. Calm and confident as usual, he sits with his arms crossed, baton resting between his fingers. My eyes rest a bit too long on the thin metal stick, and when I look back up, his eyes glimmer darkly, making my throat work to swallow.

"How much have you played since the last time I saw you?" he asks.

I straighten and push back my shoulders, remembering his order, which has been hovering at the front of my mind for a week. "I've played at least four hours a day. Well, except for Saturday. However, I got six hours in several other days." I smile proudly.

"How much did you play Saturday?" His hard features are unreadable as ever, his downturned brows lending him a serious expression, which I know doesn't always match his disposition. But for a moment, I think it does. He seems more grave than usual. But then again, it might be the effect of not having seen him for a while.

"Two hours," I say, my smile fading as I shift nervously in my seat.

Grigory gives a tight nod, and I don't know whether it's approval or acknowledgment of my answer.

"Give me a C minor scale," he says, and as we go through my technique exercises, I forget his scowl and curt response.

Whenever my head is about to drift back to it, I get a sharp bite with the baton, and soon there's nothing but the music and Grigory's steady command; the pain in my arm and the warmth of his hand on my shoulder. Our surroundings slip from my consciousness as well. It doesn't matter we're in Markus's apartment. We could be sitting in an open field or an abandoned warehouse. I wouldn't notice as long as Grigory directs my attention.

We work on a Debussy piece I've started on. The "*Arabesque* No 1." Grigory seems pleased with my choice and nudges me off the bench a few times to demonstrate the beautiful rises and falls of the elastic rhythm.

"More hesitance on the first note, hold back on the first bars, then build up. Slowly. And back down again," he instructs while playing the first two lines.

"Have you played it yourself before?" I ask.

"Many years ago. One of my first Debussy pieces."

"Oh." I try to conceal my need to gawk. He's picking the notes off the sheet like he played it yesterday and a hundred times the week before.

Grigory moves back to his chair, and I take the bench, starting the same passage he just played.

"Gently," Grigory urges, holding a hand above mine.

I go again, lingering on the first note, a smile popping to my lips as I hear how beautiful it sounds.

"That's it," Grigory praises. "Now give a bit more. Not too much." He guides me through the music like this, his hand swaying back and forth above mine, making halting gestures and sweeping motions to form the music.

When I finish for the night, I'm enthralled—mesmerized by how the music came to life. All because of Grigory, his inherent sense of music, and steady guidance. I want to play it again, keep practicing until I know the music by heart and can disappear into it without thought.

"Good job on the Debussy piece," Grigory says, getting up. His face gives away no emotion, but when he ends a lesson with a compliment like this, I know he means it.

I beam up at him, pride swelling in my chest. "Thank you," I say, my lashes fluttering.

"Wait here." Pointing his baton to the bench, he leaves and closes the door behind him.

I want to jump up and clap my hands, but I remain seated, not wanting him to see my burst of joy if he suddenly returns. So I settle on clapping my hands soundlessly in my lap before reaching back for the keys, my fingers itching with the need to play.

After fifteen minutes of practice and no sign of Grigory, I start wondering why he wanted me to stay put. But I don't dwell on it and keep playing.

A few minutes later, the door opens, and both Grigory and Markus enter. My first impulse is to smile at Markus, but my smile fades when I see his expression. With his mouth set in a straight line and brows knitted together, I sense an admonishment coming.

"What's going on?" I ask, my voice already strained.

"Get up." Grigory's sharp command makes me startle, spurring me up from the bench. His stern expression matches Markus's, only, on him it looks menacing.

Grigory steps into the middle of the room, hands gathered at his back, shoulders squared, and legs slightly parted. It's a stance that commands attention and respect and instills fear when combined with his grim expression.

Markus is still by the door, keeping in the background, and my eyes dart to him, desperate for some kind of reassurance. But I only get a slight shake of his head. There's no help.

What the hell is going on? Have I done something wrong?

I must have. But for the life of me, I can't think what it might be. The lesson went well, and Grigory seemed more than pleased when he left.

Gathering my hands in front of me, I try to subdue my nervous fingers, but the tips of my feet start tapping instead. I have to clench the muscles in my limbs to be still, and my eyes dart down, seeking refuge on the floor.

The room goes silent—eerily so. I feel the weight of Grigory's eyes like bricks piling up on top of me, growing more unbearable with each second. My chest tightens, and I want to sink to the floor, become as small as possible.

I've known all along this is a man you don't want to upset, and now, somehow, I've done it.

"Look at me." It's Grigory's accented baritone again, and I react instinctively, lifting my chin to meet his hard gaze even though it's the last thing I want to do. His brows *are* lower than normal, like when I told him about my practice.

Could that be it? He's disappointed I missed two hours one day? A knot forms in my throat, and my breath goes ragged.

I have to fight my every instinct to keep my eyes level, and my hands start fidgeting again. It's all I can do to stay upright.

"I'm impressed with your effort," Grigory says, crossing his arms over his chest, making his broad build seem even more intimidating. "For that, I'll give you credit. But you have been disobedient. I told you to play at least four hours *each day.*" He lets his eyes scorch mine for a second before stating with cutting accuracy, "You haven't done so."

Tears prickle behind my eyes. How could I think I could compensate for lost hours another day? How could I disobey him so consciously? I feel so stupid. Sad. Regretful. My chest constricts around my lungs, and I manage to expel a weak, "I'm sorry," my eyes darting back to the ground as the words ring into the room.

"Look at me," he repeats, his voice calm but no less possible to disobey than his stern one. "You've done very well, and I would have gladly given you a day off." The lines in his forehead smooth out for a moment, his eyes almost gentle. But then his features tighten again, his voice turning icy. "But you should *at least* have asked Markus for permission. I won't accept that you take my words into your own hands, construing them to fit your needs."

That's not what I've done. I want to say it out loud. But I don't. Because I know he's right. It wasn't deliberate, but I did construe the meaning of his words, failing to heed them directly.

Moisture wells in my eyes, and a tear falls down my cheek, but I don't dare lift my hand to remove it.

Grigory steps up to me, two long strides closing the distance, making me feel the thrumming energy of his authority all the way to my bones.

Brushing a knuckle over my cheek, he catches the fallen tear.

I feel stark naked, unable to hide my pressing need to shed more. His unforgiving gaze takes it all in, and the weight of it increases tenfold with the proximity.

My eyes fall away again. I can't do this. I can't take his disappointment. It's about to break me.

"You'll receive fifteen strikes for your disobedience. Bare hand."

I can't. I can't. I can't. The words swirl through my head like a broken record, and tears seep from my eyes in a rapid flow. This is nothing like when he punished me for being late. That was only a "fun little punishment" for his enjoyment, I realize now. This time, it's for real.

With a finger under my chin, he lifts my head up to meet his gaze. His gentle touch is a stark contrast to his stern demeanor.

"I'm sorry," I repeat, my voice barely a whisper.

"Markus is here to lend you some support," Grigory says softly. "But since it's my order you failed to obey, I will be the one doling out the punishment."

I shake with the need to pull away—break free from his invasive eyes, spearing straight through my defenses—and hide the vulnerability running down my cheeks, sounding in my ragged breaths.

My knees are about to cave in when Markus steps up to the side of the grand piano and orders, "Come here." I all but run to him. I'll do anything to escape Grigory's scolding stare. Even if it means placing myself in the direct line of another set of disappointed eyes.

"Take off your pants." Markus's uncompromising tone sends

another spear of regret through my chest.

"I can't," I finally say out loud.

"Do it," he orders, tone flat.

Gulping past the knot in my throat, I pull down the long zipper at my hip and drag my pants down, stepping out of them. I slump in defeat, and when Markus grips my waist to hoist my upper body up over the piano, I make no protest.

My legs dangle over the side as Markus holds me in place, and when Grigory comes up behind me, I feel like a naked woman caught in a net. I want to fight, but Markus's grip is too strong and I'm too defeated to make the effort. It would only make everything worse, I'm sure. So I lie stiffly, palms glued to the instrument I usually love, but now seems heartless with its cold surface and the hard edge pressing into my hip.

I startle when Grigory traces my hip bone. Then I hear his steps recede, and my head fights a battle to decide whether I'm more relieved or disappointed. The room is left in silence as he disappears, and my ragged breathing and frantic heartbeats become a claustrophobic cacophony to my ears.

The dull thuds of Grigory's steps return. He's not wearing his leather shoes, and the lack of those clicking heels makes him seem more human somehow. But his disapproving scowl is etched into my mind, and my bared ass is too much of a reminder of what's to come to let me forget he's far from harmless.

Markus lifts me by the waist when Grigory's demanding presence looms over me again, and a soft blanket is pushed under my hips. It's a small mercy I don't deserve, and tears start dripping onto the blank surface with the knowledge that Grigory gave it to me anyway.

A large, heavy hand—Grigory's hand—spreads out on my right cheek, and panic rises in me. "Markus," I plead, knowing he's the one more likely to stop this. "I can't do this. I can't."

Frantically, I dry at my tears, but they keep falling, already forming a small pool on the black lid. "Markus," I repeat, desperation filling my voice.

"Be a good girl and take your punishment, sweetie," he says.

Markus's tender words almost break me, and determination to take the punishment blends with the overwhelming fear.

The fear wins when Grigory's hand lifts and lands with a rapid smack. My body constricts on itself, my heartbeat bursting into a frantic rhythm. The dripping of tears becomes a steady beat on the surface. There's nothing I can do to hold them in.

It's not so much the pain—the pain is tolerable. It's the shame.

Shame is always a part of punishment, but when Markus is the one dealing out the blows, I can take it. He knows me—all of me. My strengths and weaknesses; vulnerabilities and boundaries. I trust him to accept and love it all, and it doesn't matter if he sees me a blubbering mess as I bawl my eyes out or hear me scream in pain and beg for mercy. Because in the end, I'm irrevocably his. He'll hold me through it all and give me a place where I belong.

But a stranger disciplining me like this, ass in the air and tears streaming from my eyes… I can't take it. Especially not when it's a man I so badly want to please.

One more smack on my other cheek, and my muscles become stiff coils, my chest restricting, denying me more than shallow gulps of air.

When the third blow lands, I fall apart. Desperate sobs rise in my throat, and I push my hands against the surface, using all my strength trying to get up. I need to breathe. Get up where there's more air and sit up straight to access it. But only my chest leaves the surface, and soon I must give up the struggle to focus on getting any air at all. It's no use though. Each frantic breath lodges in my throat, and panic makes black spots dance in my vision.

Suddenly, two hands grab my arms, strong and big, and someone powerful leans in, hovering right above my back. At first, it only feeds my panic, confining my world to a tight, entrapped space. But then I realize the hands are just holding me. Gently. There's no threat.

I notice the warmth of the body inches from mine, the hot air of a man's breath on my ear.

"Easy now," Grigory lulls, voice airy and full of sympathy. "Deep breaths." He pulls in a long suck of air, and I follow with a staggered breath, the imitation so ingrained I don't even have to think about it. But I'm unable to follow when he holds the breath, and my air gushes out with a sob.

"One more," he says calmly and pulls in a loud breath for me to follow.

I repeat, feeling my body shake with an oncoming sob as I try to hold onto the air like he does. His reassuring squeeze on my arms helps me hold down the sob, and I push the air out on a long, slow exhale.

It takes a couple of minutes, but finally my crying turns into silent tears, and my chest rising and falling with labored breaths is the only thing moving. The rest of me is still, my clammy palms and wet cheek plastered to the surface and my legs hanging limply toward the floor.

Markus has shifted to make room for Grigory. But he hasn't left me. His one hand still lingers on my hip, letting me know he's here, taking care of me even as he lets another man punish me. And it gives me the courage to let go.

I let go of all the strain holding my muscles taut, going slack in Grigory's grasp. I let go of all my vulnerability, letting it slide to the surface like a balloon underwater, flowing up for everyone to see.

It's far too intimate, but necessary to keep the panic at bay.

"Good girl." Grigory's voice is a low rumble beside my ear. The approval hits straight into my deep-seated need to please him, and somehow, it gives me the final nudge into acceptance.

Grigory straightens again and Markus shifts back to hold me by the waist, his hands both restraining and stabilizing.

When Grigory puts his palm flat on my butt, I inhale sharply, preparing for the next blow. It lands with a loud smack the moment I release the air. The force spreads out in my skin, all the way into my muscles, a heady combination of pain and warmth. I scrunch up my face, but that's as far as my reaction goes.

Another smack hits my other butt cheek with a bit more force. But even this is bearable.

Five down, ten to go. I can do this.

The following swats gradually become harder, and I whimper every time the hand smacks down. But I breathe through the pain, and Grigory gives me enough time in between for the stinging burn to settle into a warm cover on my skin.

Six, seven, eight, nine, I count in my head. Only six more and we're done.

The hand lifts, and I suck in a deep breath.

Slam! Slam! Slam!

Pain rips through my nether region as the hand clashes violently with my flesh, three times in rapid succession, pulling tears back to my eyes.

I don't get time to process before three equally hard blows collide with my other cheek. A new burn shoots into skin and muscle, crashing with the pain already throbbing there. I scream with the full force of my lungs, unable to hold anything in—I scream in pain and scream in despair at being betrayed. First, he gets me to calm down and builds up slowly, making me trust him, then suddenly he rips it all apart, assaulting me with an overload of pain that frays the edges of my mind.

Like a wild animal, I thrash on the piano, helplessly trying to process the onslaught of pain. I bang my fists into the surface, and angry tears flow down my cheeks as my scream renews itself, burning through my throat.

Markus manages to get me up and sit on the edge of the piano while I frantically kick my legs into everything and all they can find—which is mostly air. I shove at him as I keep screaming, filling the room with piercing desperation. I hate him for letting a stranger see me like this. Hate him for allowing a stranger to beat me. Hate him for allowing such humiliation.

I hate him.

I hate Grigory.

I hate Grigory and everything he does to me.

Markus wraps me up in his embrace, trapping my arms between us. I keep thrashing, but all I achieve is exhaustion. I want to keep fighting and hating, but eventually, my screams die down, turning into sobs, and my kicking grows weaker, my writhing stilling to small jerks.

Finally, I'm so drained I give in and huddle against him as I weep. I need him too much to keep hating him, so instead, I desperately cling to him like he's the last oxygen on the bottom of a deep, dark sea.

With a solid hold around me, gentle caresses, and soothing words, Markus manages to calm me down. I stop crying and hang limply in his arms, my body shaking as the adrenaline seeps out.

All too quickly, he pulls away. *He can't leave me already.* I clutch his blouse, staring up at him with desperate eyes. But he easily pries my hands off. And gives them to Grigory.

I watch, horrified, as Grigory's large hands close around my wrists. My breathing turns shallow, my eyes stinging with new tears. I pull at my arms, but it's no use. Nothing is of any use with this man. His grip is like steel. Hard and unbreakable. Even when he gathers my wrists in a single hand, they are trapped with frightening ease.

I give Markus another pleading look, but he has stepped back and gives me a slight shake of his head.

Grigory grabs my chin with his free hand, forcing me to meet his eyes.

I make one last feeble attempt at escape, but he only squeezes my chin between his fingers, keeping his steady gaze trained on me until my energy runs dry. All I can do is sit and cry in his hopeless grip, tears slipping from my cheeks and onto his big hand.

With a lift of his chin, he pulls in a deep breath.

I refuse to do anything this man tells me and attempt a spiteful glare, but I don't think I quite manage it.

His eyes, however, remain calm as ever. Unrelenting. So much so that I falter, my fuming anger slipping through my fingers. And when he raises his brows in silent command, I'm done for. My lips slip apart, and my lungs expand to let in air. He holds me there for a second, and when I imitate his slow exhale, the corners of his mouth tip up in a smile.

I seethe with rage, but it's like a small fire in an airless space, and his steady power snuffs the flame out. And not just the anger. He takes all my carefully built defenses—all my resistance—and squashes it between large hands. Soon, it's only his hold on me that matters, and I go along each time he takes a deep inhale or makes a sharp exhale. My breath becomes his—only working because he wants it to.

"You did well, *devochka.*" His deep, sincere voice pushes me the final inch, over the edge and into complete, helpless submission. All resolve I've ever had disintegrates like snowflakes on a hot stove. The only thing left is my deep-seated need to obey him—a need that burns so hot it hurts.

I've tried to deny the urge for a long time, but now it's pointless. He's broken down all my defenses, making it impossible to hide anything—from him or myself. Every tiny emotion is painted in large strokes in my eyes, my face, and my body, for him to read in capital letters.

"You'll do as I say from here on," he states matter-of-factly, arrogant in his conviction I will.

But how can it be arrogant when it's the truth?

Not a single fiber of my being doubts his words as he bores the meaning into me with his grave eyes.

The words are embedded in the depth of my soul when he releases my chin and circles his arms around me. I sag against him, limp and pliant, as he pulls me to him.

"Everything's okay now, *devochka*," he soothes, repeating the Russian-sounding word that is like a caress to my ears. I have no clue what it means semantically, but his praising tone transmits it clearly.

He moves one hand in circles on my back while the other is an iron band around my waist, holding me up and keeping me safe. I don't know why, but it makes me cry again. The tears seem to have no end tonight. But this time, it's calm, cathartic tears that wash away the strain, panic, and confusion.

"Shh, everything's okay now," he repeats, kissing my hair.

I don't think I've ever felt so safe. And that's despite the man holding me being the same one who ripped me apart, tore me to shreds, and made anger burn hot and livid inside me. And now, I'm desperate for his protection, pressing myself against his chest and gripping the white fabric of his dress shirt in my fists, all inhibitions gone.

How can one man elicit such opposite reactions in such a short span of time?

I shouldn't feel safe here. But I do. I truly do.

The world around me could go up in flames and I wouldn't care as long as I'm here in his arms.

When my tears finally stop falling, leaving the steady beating of his heart the only sound, I pull my legs up under me, shifting to rest my head on his shoulder, my hands gathered at his chest. Grigory loosens his grip to let me settle into the new position. But only for a second. Then he tightens an arm around my waist and covers my cheek with a large hand, pressing me close.

Within minutes, I start dozing off. Voices murmur indecipherable words beside me, and then Markus slips his hands around me while Grigory withdraws. Half sleeping, I grab at Grigory's shirt, clenching the fabric in desperate fists, and his deep chuckle makes his chest vibrate beneath my hands. Markus pries me off, and the irony doesn't escape me—few minutes ago, it was him I refused to let go of.

Markus lifts me up and I'm too exhausted to complain even as my entire being yearns to return to the arms he took me from. He carries me into the living room, lays me on the sofa, and covers me with a blanket.

Several footfalls move somewhere close, maybe far away. When the sofa dips beside me, I'm not sure which man is where, and I'm too tired to lift my heavy eyelids to find out.

I get my answer when a wide palm moves over my hair. Grigory's hand is not to be mistaken.

I wriggle up on the couch to get closer, and like he understands my openness—or rather, explicit need—he grabs me under my arms and drags me up to place my head in his lap. He keeps stroking my hair, and when I fumble to find something to hold onto, he takes my hand, making me feel ever so small as my fingers disappear into his large grip.

"Is she already out?" Markus's voice is a whisper in front of me.

"There's still a bit of life left," Grigory says in a hushed tone.

Blinking my sleepy eyes, I see Markus crouching in front of me in the dim living room.

"There she is." He gives me a warm smile and holds a straw to my mouth.

I manage a small tug on my lips before my eyes slide shut again, and then I slurp orange juice through the straw. Everything in the world is in its place—calm and quiet inside and around me.

Only half an hour ago, I was hanging over the piano, hyperventilating and sobbing. Not long after, I willingly took my punishment. A few more swats, I was screaming and writhing, hating Grigory with intense emotion. Now I lie here, clutching his hand and hoping he'll never let go. I have no idea how he got me through so many emotions in one night and got me out on the other side in one piece—even with a deep calm seated in my chest.

Markus sinks down on the couch by my feet and slides a hand under the blanket to rest it on my legs. The two men carry a low conversation, and I feel fragile here between them. Powerless and helpless. But it's okay. More than okay, in fact. Because they take care of me, and they've got control enough for me to let go of everything.

So I do just that. And while the two deep voices drift above me like a gentle sound effect, my breathing becomes deeper and deeper, and soon I fade into a calm, peaceful sleep.

— CHAPTER 12 —

"How are you feeling today?" Markus asks when I pad into the kitchen in the morning.

He's leaning against the counter, coffee mug in hand, looking relaxed and stylish in a gray T-shirt, dark blue blazer, and jeans. His jaw is covered in a sexy two-day stubble that makes him look incredibly masculine. It's too bad it's like kissing a hedgehog.

Dropping into a chair at the dining table, I send him a sleepy smile. "Fine—I think."

"Good." He takes a final swig of his coffee and empties the rest in the sink. Then he walks to me with long-legged strides and leans a hand on the back of my chair. "Take it easy today and call me if there's anything at all. It's not unusual to have some strong reactions after a night like the one you had."

"I will," I say, lifting a hand to feel his chest.

"I'll get some takeout on my way home." He bends to kiss me. "See you tonight." At that, he leaves.

I grab some breakfast and bring it with me to the living room, where I plop onto the couch and turn on the TV. It doesn't take long for me to understand what Markus meant. Despite being fine on the surface, I feel this strange buzzing restlessness.

A fragileness—like my foundation has been knocked off balance.

It's probably not so strange I'm still affected. Last night was extremely overwhelming. Grigory broke open all my most vulnerable parts. He saw me scream with the full force of my lungs and thrash desperately, and he saw me cry silent tears and cling to him for comfort. In a matter of minutes, he took me from hating him to needing him more than the air in my lungs.

And the way he held me...

The whole world slipped into a vacuum. Nothing could touch me there in his arms. I felt safer than I ever have any other place—and I barely even know him. His willful control was a potent force around us, but instead of being a threat, it was a shield protecting me from the entire world and all its chaos.

My insides go all mushy. If he wanted to repeat the devastating punishment, I'd willingly go along if I knew he'd hold me so protectively again.

Suddenly, a burning need to feel his strong arms grips me.

I bring the comforter into the living room and wrap myself up in it. But it does a lousy job of replacing Grigory's embrace, and the fragileness creeps to the surface.

Deciding to follow Markus's advice about taking it easy, I click into Netflix's animation category and find just the movie I need. *How to Train Your Dragon.* Piano practice can wait. I've got plenty of time to get in the four hours later.

My piano teacher punished me, for God's sake!

The thought shoots into my head like a strike of lightning, making my toes curl. Piano teacher and punishment are two words that don't go together.

But Grigory has never just been my piano teacher. I know that. But the illusion helped keep my emotions in check. With the illusion now crushed, I don't know how I'll cope with all the feelings swirling through my mind, making my heart jump and my stomach flutter. I don't know how to go back to the piano lessons. Should I just act like normal—like nothing happened?

Will Grigory do that? Was last night only a fun scene, getting to hit his friend's submissive, acting out his sadistic tendencies? Or did it mean something more to him, like it did to me?

The idea that he might be unaffected shoots dread through my stomach, and I consider asking Markus to postpone the piano lesson tomorrow. It might be good for me to take some time to get my feelings under control before seeing Grigory again.

But then I think about not seeing Grigory tomorrow, and I can't stand the thought. I need his powerful authority to appease this buzzing unease—to stabilize the wobbling ground beneath my feet. There's no chance in hell I'll ask for a break, no matter how much my logical brain tells me I should.

* * *

Markus comes home early in the evening, and I fall straight into his arms when I go to greet him in the hallway.

"Oh, sweetie. You really needed a hug, huh?" Markus pulls me into him and rains kisses down on my head.

The unease has been coming and going in small gusts throughout the day, but now that he's here, it comes crashing in a huge wave. It's not because Markus instigates it; it's because he gives me the stability I need to finally let go and confront the chaos reigning within me.

"Come." Taking me by the hand, he leads me to the living room where he drops onto the sofa and takes me into his lap.

I curl up against him and hold on for dear life as I start shuddering, tremors rippling through my body. I feel shaken to the core and can't seem to find my footing.

"I'm sorry," I say. "I don't know what's wrong."

"It's the aftereffects from last night," Markus says with a warm voice. "It's quite normal. Just let it happen. I've got you." To emphasize his words, he tightens his arms around me, and I feel small yet safe as I huddle against him, letting his strength hold us both as I shed all of mine.

I keep trembling for a long while, and when the storm finally dies down, we sit in silence, Markus running his hand over my hair in long strokes and me inhaling his familiar scent in deep breaths.

"Grigory might want to spend some time holding you tomorrow too," Markus finally says. "It's always meant a lot to him, being able to take care of a woman after having hurt her."

"Really?" I say against his chest. It's difficult to imagine the gruff, controlled man needing something so gentle as this. But when I remember the way he wrapped his arms around me last night, like I was a fragile thing needing safekeeping, it somehow adds up anyway.

"Of course. Doms need aftercare too. It's not just for your sake I spend so much time holding you."

I nuzzle his neck and take a deep breath that brings me the

fresh notes of his aftershave. "I love how you always hold me. And knowing you want it too makes it so much better."

Markus chuckles—a deep warm sound. "You are so wonderfully submissive, Clara. Always so in tune with me." He rubs my back and rocks me gently. "And tomorrow I want you to let Grigory take care of you, however much he needs. Can you do that?"

I suck in a loud breath, the need to obey surging through me like a warm gush of wind. "Yes, Markus."

"Good girl. I would hate not to give Grigory the opportunity. I know I couldn't stand not being able to take care of you after a severe punishment." He tightens his grip on me and presses his lips against the top of my head. "I won't be picking you up tomorrow, so the two of you can take whatever time you need. Grigory will get you home."

"Thank you," I murmur, wrapping my hands around his waist and burying my head in his shoulder. The memory of Grigory's arms has been haunting me all day, and knowing I'll soon feel it again calms the nervous restlessness still shuddering in my veins.

"Of course, sweetie." Nudging my head up, he presses a long kiss to my lips. "Now, go get the food in the hallway. We both need to eat."

I scurry to the hall and pick up the white plastic bag with takeout. A warm scent of cinnamon and ginger wafts through the air. *Indian food.* A smile springs to my lips. Markus doesn't care much for this cuisine, but he has gotten it anyway because he knows I love it.

"Get plates and utensils too," Markus says when I set the bag on the coffee table. "And your pillow."

When I come back, Markus has turned on the TV. "I see you've been watching *How to Train Your Dragon,*" he says. "Do you want to watch the second one with me?"

With an eager nod, I dump the large burgundy pillow between his feet and sink onto it.

Markus starts the movie and ladles a healthy portion of rice and chicken tikka masala onto a plate. "Eat," he says, handing me the fragrant food.

I dig in at once, feeling much better now that I'm nestled between the safety of his legs, watching one of my favorite movies and eating my favorite food—knowing I'll soon get to feel Grigory's safe embrace again.

When I've cleared every last bit of rice from the plate, Markus gives me another healthy portion with a warm smile.

"What was it Grigory called me last night?" I ask when the memory pops into my head.

"When?"

"By the piano, when he held me. It sounded Russian." Markus has sung in Russian a few times and is familiar with the language, so he might know what it means.

He considers for a moment, then seems to remember. "Oh, you mean *devochka*? It means little girl," he tells me, then adds with a warm gaze, "The Russians like diminutives."

I can't help smiling. My worries about Grigory seeing me as a little girl have subsided—or rather, the worries about him meaning it in a condescending way. It seems to be affectionate, and Markus's explanation only confirms it.

— CHAPTER 13 —

When I enter the large lobby at the opera on Friday, I'm as nervous as usual, but in a different way. Today it's not stomach-churning anxiety that makes my hands quiver. It's more of a fluttery sensation that sends heat to my cheeks and belly.

When Grigory appears by the staff entrance, I get up from the bench, about to go to him. I always come to him. But I pause when he walks toward me. Long, purposeful strides take him across the space, his eyes boring straight into me and refusing to let go.

Shy vulnerability washes over me, pervading my entire posture—my shoulders sink, my eyes flit down, and my hands hug each other. I can't control it. All I can do is remain on my feet and keep the air flowing to my lungs until I see his black leather shoes right in front of me.

Slowly, I let my eyes drift up—over his black slacks, the row of buttons on his white shirt, his strong jaw. My heart beats a little harder with every inch I go, and when I reach his dark eyes, it beats so hard my knees are quivering.

Grigory is unreadable as ever, but as I keep watching him with unrestrained vulnerability written all over my face, something happens. His hard features soften, the faint lines above his brow smoothing out.

He lifts a hand and brushes a stray lock of hair behind my ear. His fingers skim my cheekbone on their way, sending gentle shivers down my neck.

"Pretty Clara," he murmurs, as softly as his touch. His palm curves around my cheek, and I lean into the immense warmth.

His thumb makes a few strokes over my skin, and my eyes fall shut. The tenderness calls upon a well of emotion that floods my senses. But even as I stagger in the overwhelming surge, I'm also calm. Time seems to stop as his hand becomes my entire world.

Suddenly, his touch disappears, leaving a cold spot in its wake.

I snap my eyes open and watch Grigory turn on his heel and walk away. A knot forms in my throat, tears welling in my eyes, and it takes all I have to shake it off and hurry after him.

Everything has changed when we get to the rehearsal room. All tenderness is gone, and Grigory seems closed off—even sterner than usual.

"You know the procedure," he says, waving his baton at my cardigan.

Hurriedly, I slip out of it and put my sheet music on the stand. Confusion has me on edge, and my mind works overtime to figure out what the hell happened.

"Give me a C minor scale." Grigory brings a chair up beside me, and when I wait for him to sit, I get a gruff, "begin."

My hands tremble when I put them on the keys, and I set off

at an uneven tempo.

"Don't run off," he scolds. "You know better."

I squeeze my eyes shut and flex my fingers, unease weighing heavily on my chest. I start at a slow tempo, but I have no control and run off again.

"Clara, tempo!" Grigory's firm reprimand makes me jump. "This is not good enough."

Biting my lips together, I watch him with a feeling of inadequacy. He must see the shock on my face because he blinks once, a flash of surprise flickering over his features. Then he seems to snap out of something and his features soften. It's far from the tender expression in the lobby, but there's a sliver of compassion.

"Just breathe," he says with an underlying current of tension. He places his hand on my back, and his touch is tentative—strained like his voice. His fingers flex on my skin, almost like he's afraid to touch me. But then his hand settles, warm and heavy. He takes a deep breath, and I'm not sure if it's to calm himself or me. "Just breathe," he repeats, now with an even tone.

He guides me through several breaths before I finally manage to shrug off the worst tension and calm my shaky hands.

"Now try again." He's back to his steady self. When my tempo wobbles, he remains patient, saying, "easy now," tapping the beat on the piano.

The rest of the lesson continues as usual. Grigory starts hitting my arm once we get the warm-up over with, guiding me into the music with his calm control.

But I still feel shaken, unable to forget the horrible tension and his abrupt change of mood. What's even harder to forget is the tenderness in the lobby and his comforting touch when he took me in his arms two days ago.

Every time he puts his hand on my back, a bolt of yearning shoots through me. His hand is far from enough. I want to feel his arms, his chest—sink into his embrace and let him carry all my burdens.

All I can do is hope I get to feel it once we get the piano playing over with.

The need to be close to him only grows throughout the lesson. I get a feeling Grigory goes harder on me with his evil stick than usual, and it drives up my need for comfort. But I can't tell if the strikes are actually harder or it just seems so because I'm sensitive.

Nevertheless, I react stronger than normal, hissing through my teeth and even cursing a few times.

When we're finally done, Grigory steps around the piano and presses his palms into the surface, watching me for a minute.

I shrink under his gaze, growing increasingly uncomfortable.

"Gather your things," he finally says. "My driver will take you home."

My stomach sinks. *Is that it? He's sending me home?* What about aftercare?

I put on my cardigan and take my folder and bag, then step into the middle of the room without meeting his eyes. "It's okay, I can take the metro."

Grigory doesn't answer. He grabs my arm like he did a week ago and takes me out of the room.

We walk in tense silence, and when I again try to tell him I'll just take the metro, he tightens his grip and says with a stern edge, "You're taking my car."

So I keep my mouth shut the rest of the way to the basement parking garage.

Grigory opens the back door on the black Mercedes before the driver gets a chance to round the car and do it. I'm about to get in when he grabs both my arms from behind.

I freeze, the urge to cry suddenly tightening my throat. Every fiber, every instinct wants me to lean into him, but I can feel his distance even in his touch—his hands clenching and unclenching around my arms. It's like he's conflicted. Like he can't decide whether to keep me or let me go.

He goes with the latter.

It damn near breaks me when he shoves me into the car and slams the door shut between us.

Leaning down to the open driver's window, he shoots off Markus's address. Then he's gone—leaving without another glance in my direction.

* * *

During the weekend, I disappear into the music room at every chance I get. As a small protest, I start a new piece instead of practicing what I've been working on with Grigory. I pick Rachmaninoff's prelude in D minor. It's supposed to be one of his more manageable pieces, but it's extremely strenuous.

It doesn't matter though. I need the challenge to keep my attention from the constant hurt clawing at my chest, and I need the forceful music to level the turmoil of feelings boiling inside me. But most of all, I'm driven to impress Grigory. If I can learn this piece, I'll definitely accomplish that.

I spend all my time busting my ass by the piano. I don't think I've ever spent so much time practicing before. Especially not on the same piece.

Yet, I'm far from ready to play the prelude on Monday, so I leave the sheet music at home and don't tell Grigory about it.

Since I haven't played a single note of my other pieces, I've made no progress after our last lesson. Shame prickles in my nerves as I play the piece I was supposed to work on, but Grigory doesn't call me out on my lack of preparation before the end of the lesson.

"Have you played four hours *every day?*" His voice takes on a hard edge.

"Yes." I give a slight nod without looking at him. I've played double. If not more.

Grabbing my chin, he turns my head to him. His thick brows furrow as he studies me with incredulity. He clearly doesn't find the signs of lying he's searching for because he only huffs a "hmm" and releases me.

I get why he doubts me, but it still hurts. When I leave the room, I have to clench my jaw to hold in all the hurt and anger swirling within me.

Once again, I have a feeling he was harsher with the baton than usual, and in the evening, I have concrete proof. The welts don't fade into a light pink hue like they normally do. Instead, they become purple bruises that are awfully striking on my white skin.

Wanting to avoid any and all questions about the piano lessons, I put on a long T-shirt so Markus won't notice. But whenever I'm alone by the piano, I pull up the sleeve and stare at my speckled arm, pressing my fingers into the sore marks to feel it tightening beneath my skin. It's the first time Grigory's baton leaves blue marks, and I'm as mesmerized as I'm horrified.

The bruises are like mosquito bites you can't stop scratching, and with each time I do, I miss Grigory's patient comfort more. I need him to put me back together after having ripped me open last week. And if not that, then at least to bring me down from the shock and pain that comes with every strike of his baton.

But he only gave me the bare minimum of comfort—just enough to get me ready to play again—and the emotional turmoil keeps growing.

I keep retreating to the piano room, practicing the Rachmaninoff piece and neglecting everything else. It's the only way to get a reprieve from the chaotic whirlwinds shaking me from the inside. The second my fingers leave the keys, images and sensations swamp my head—my hysterical screams after Grigory ripped me apart; his warm embrace where nothing else in the world mattered; the startling tenderness before our lesson last week.

Everything inside me is on the verge of combusting, and I'm not only tired in the evenings, but depleted.

Wednesday evening, Markus comes into the music room with concern written across his face. "We need to talk."

"Please just let me play," I say, my voice strained.

Markus comes to crouch beside me. "You've said that for six days now, sweetie. I've given you plenty of time to process whatever is going on. No more." He frees one of my hands from my incessant fumbling to hold it. "What happened at the piano lesson on Friday? You shut completely off and become defensive every time I ask about it, and Grigory does the same."

"Nothing," I say. *Absolutely frigging nothing.*

"Nothing?" Markus raises an eyebrow.

"Yeah, nothing." I all but sneer, throwing my free hand into the air.

Markus grips my jaw, and his eyes become dangerously direct. "Clara, I've been patient with you, accepting your pissy attitude and leaving you alone like you've asked me to. But it clearly isn't what you need." His mouth twists, impatience lacing his words. "This is the last time I ask, and if I don't get an acceptable answer, I'll haul you over my knee and smack it out of you."

I can't hold back my snappy bitterness. "We had the piano lesson, and then he dragged me down to his fancy car and ordered his chauffeur to take me home."

Markus remains silent for a moment, and I hold my breath as I wait to see if my answer is good enough. "So, he didn't spend any time holding you? Or talking?"

I shake my head.

"Well, that explains a whole lot—about the both of you." Markus gets up, his mouth set in a grim line. "I'll cancel your lesson tomorrow."

I stare at the sheet music in front of me as he walks toward the door. I had just worked up the courage to play Rachmaninoff for Grigory tomorrow, and even though I'm furious with him—or maybe because of it—I need to do this. Play this for him. "Please don't," I say, casting Markus a pleading look when he turns in the doorway.

"Why not?"

"I need to play this piece for him. I've been working on it for nearly a week."

"No shit? Like I hadn't noticed. You're lucky I haven't gone crazy from your incessant banging away at the same notes."

"Please," is all I can say, even though I should apologize. This piece has become my own little rebellion that I need to finish. If I don't get to play it for Grigory, all the hard work is wasted.

"I don't like this, Clara. I don't get a chance to talk to him before Friday, and with the way things are, I'm afraid another lesson will only make matters worse."

"It won't," I say. "I can handle a lesson. I really need this."

Markus considers for a moment. "Okay then."

* * *

When Grigory opens the door to the practice room the next day, I trudge straight up to the piano, setting up the first pages of the Rachmaninoff piece instead of waiting for his instructions.

Grigory lifts a bushy brow, and when he joins me by the piano and sees the sheet music, his expression turns decidedly skeptical.

I fume. Rage burns like hot coals in my belly. But instead of backing out, I let it fuel my determination.

"Start with a scale." He leans back in the chair beside me, crossed arms and the baton dangling from his fingers.

I'm determined not to let him intimidate me. "Which scale?" I ask with a flippant edge.

Lowering his chin, he spears me with dark eyes, and his tone becomes dangerously low. "D-minor. Four octaves. Slowly."

I must have lost all sense of self-preservation because I start in a half-fast tempo, defiance burning in my fingers.

Grigory tries to stop me with a hand gesture, *the arrogant bastard,* but I stubbornly keep going until he grabs my wrist.

"Slowly." Irritation oozes from him, and I can't help but gloat inwardly. I did this—knocked this arrogant control freak off balance and instigated some kind of emotion in his impassive demeanor.

Driven by reckless anger, I try to snatch my hand away. But his grip is like steel, and the impossible strength weakens my determination.

"Clara." The firm warning breathes life to my instinctive submission, which had drowned in my agitation. So I obey and let him control the warm-up, torn between my own emotions.

When we're done with the warm-up, Grigory makes an annoyed gesture to the sheet music in front of me. "Let's hear it."

My rage simmers back up, and I spread my fingers above the keys, determined to show him I can do this. But it's not without a good splash of anxiety in the mix. Because I get why he's skeptical. Rachmaninoff had an enormous hand, and his music reflects it. Furthermore, this is a big turn from the melancholic and calm pieces I've played with him this far.

But I can't accept that he's right. Not after working so hard. So I push my angry hands into the keys, and I'm surprised by the force the music rings out with. I keep up the pulsating energy, and somehow my fingers keep pounding all the right keys, rolling on in furious motions of their own accord.

I play through the climax, even though I had decided this part was too risky, and when I lift my hands, I'm high on the rush.

I did it. I fucking did it!

My hands quiver on top of my thighs, and I want to lift one to wipe at my damp forehead, but I force them to remain in place. It's about the only thing I can control though. My heaving chest and pounding pulse won't settle, and my nerves are rattling as I wait for Grigory's response.

He doesn't say anything. I don't even think he moves. But he must surely be impressed. Right?

After a minute without any response, I chance a glance up at him. His face is like stone. No surprise or amazement. Not even a slight pull of his lips to show he's impressed. He's just blank.

"Play the left hand from the top," he says, stomping down my last sliver of triumph like the dying embers of a fire.

I gnash my molars together and stare at the keys. *What the hell is his problem?* We shared something deeply intimate together, and he keeps acting like nothing happened, and now he can't even acknowledge my accomplishment. I may not be one of the virtuoso pianists he's used to, but this is huge for me, and he knows it. He just doesn't care to show it, and it enrages me.

Yet, I obey and play the left hand.

Of course, I obey him.

Grigory pushes me hard throughout the rest of the lesson. The baton keeps swishing through the air, striking my right arm, which still hasn't recovered from the last two lessons. I want to yell and throw curses at him, but instead, I whimper pathetically, grinding my teeth together and squeezing my eyes shut to hold everything down.

Halfway through, my arm is so sore Grigory can barely touch it without me wheezing and pulling away.

Adamant about keeping up the rain of blows, he lifts his chair over me. Then he goes at it on my left arm.

He stops touching me altogether. His guiding breaths are the only help I get, and it's far from enough. It's terribly lonely sitting here under his control, receiving nothing but punishment and cold distance. My anger morphs into a heavy sadness that settles deep in my chest, and I'm constantly on the verge of falling apart. But I bite it down, refusing to allow the humiliation of him seeing my tears.

When Markus comes to get me, I'm sore and worn down from the inside out.

Grigory steps into the middle of the room, leaving my side at the first chance he gets, and I clench my jaw as anger and hurt squeezes around my chest.

Markus comes up behind me and lays his hands on my shoulders. "Looks like someone's been naughty," he says, probably seeing the horror show on my arms.

I fold them together against my stomach, covering the ugly splashes of red, blue, and yellow on my right one. The left one is mostly just red and pink with angry welts, but I hate it just as much. Today the marks are nothing but a symbol of Grigory's cold distance and it hurts to even look at them. Even when I avert my gaze, my arms won't let me forget, screeching about what transpired with a constant burn.

Markus tilts my head back to study me, and the humor in his eyes disappears immediately.

"Come here," he says softly, urging me to turn around, folding his arms around me.

I curl up on the bench, pressing myself into the safety of his body, away from Grigory and his cruel distance.

Markus strokes my hair a few times, then turns his attention to Grigory. I can feel his demeanor shifting even before he speaks. His hand stills in a firm grip on the back of my head, and his posture becomes rigid.

"You and me, we need to talk," Markus says with a sternness that could rival Grigory's any day.

"I've got time Monday afternoon," Grigory says in a tight tone.

"That won't work. Lunch tomorrow or we do it right here and now. But I'm not leaving Clara like this, so she'll be here too if we do it now."

Grigory makes a disgruntled sound, clearly not happy about the idea of me being present for their conversation. Frankly, I don't want to be there either since I have a feeling it won't exactly be a comfortable chat.

"Lunch tomorrow, then," he says.

Markus grabs my things and helps me up from the bench.

"I'll see you tomorrow," he says in a curt tone and leads me toward the door. He doesn't instruct me to thank Grigory for the lesson like he usually does, but wraps a protective arm around my waist and takes me home.

"What are you going to talk to him about?" I ask once we're in the car.

"Him taking better care of you." Markus is looking straight out at the road with his features set in a serious expression.

I take a ragged breath, feeling emotionally wrought. "Why is he acting like this?" I haven't told Markus about the lesson, but I sense he already knows the gist of it.

Markus is silent for a while then sighs. "Grigory hasn't had a sub in a while. His last two relationships didn't work out well, and he's been quite closed off for a while. I think he needs a reminder how things work when you have a woman under your control."

I stare out at the bustling city for a while. Grigory has the domination part down to a tee, but the taking care of me part not so much—at least not after the punishment—so I see what Markus means.

After a while, Markus turns to me with a remorseful expression. "I'm sorry you had to go through this." Returning his eyes to the road, he mutters, almost to himself, "I really didn't think it would be this bad. He used to be good at taking care of his subs."

"What happened?"

Markus is deep in thought for a moment before he speaks. "When I met Grigory, he didn't do relationships. I guess he didn't have the time or just wasn't interested. But then he started to seem like he was ready for something serious. He saw this French girl for a year, and although they weren't exclusive, he wouldn't see others, and it was clear she meant a lot to him. But then one of his good friends went and snatched her up before Grigory got a chance to figure out that he wanted more."

"What a bastard," I mutter.

Markus shrugs. "Technically she was fair game, and the guy didn't mean to do it. It just happened. Chemistry and attraction and all, you know. I think Grigory blamed himself more than anyone else. So when he met Magdalena a year later, he dived headfirst in." Markus's jaw tightens like the sheer thought of this Magdalena makes him angry, then adds, "Too fast."

"How so?" I ask when he doesn't elaborate.

"Well, let's just say she did quite the number on him. He hasn't had anything but the occasional one-night stand since they broke up two years ago."

"What happened?" It's more than clear it was something bad.

"Sorry, Clara, but this is not my story to tell."

That's it. I don't get more information out of him.

* * *

Friday, I wake up early after a long, restless night. My eyes are heavy, refusing to stay open for more than seconds at a time, my body limp and unmoving. It feels like someone has given me a shot of horse tranquilizer that numbs my body but refuses to work on my brain.

I hear Markus moving around the apartment, getting ready

to leave, and finally I force myself out of bed to go find him. I trudge into the hallway, wearing checkered shorts and a spaghetti top, hugging myself to ease the chill on my skin as I blink against the light.

Markus pulls me straight into a warm hug, letting me slump against him.

"Can I take a break from the piano today?" I ask in a raspy voice. After all, I have learned something from the punishment.

He pulls me out at arms-length to study me. "Sure. I'll tell Grigory I've allowed it."

"Thanks," I mutter.

"Spend the day taking care of yourself. Take a warm bath; eat some ice cream."

My tight expression eases a bit as I try to bring a smile to my lips. Markus always takes such good care of me, always knowing what I need.

It doesn't end just because he leaves. During the day, he calls several times to hear how I'm feeling. It helps for short periods, but ultimately, my dispirited mood is unshakeable. I spend the whole day on the couch, trying to sleep or keep my attention on the TV—both with little luck.

When Markus comes home late in the afternoon, I greet him in the hallway in the same outfit as this morning. I follow him into the kitchen and watch with round eyes as he unpacks chocolate, ice cream, and popcorn.

"Time for an *Ice Age* marathon." He gives me a radiant Markus smile, and for the first time all day, my mouth curls up into a genuine smile. The unease that has gnawed at me throughout the day slips into the background as I curl up at Markus's side on the couch and watch *Ice Age,* but it never fully leaves.

— CHAPTER 14 —

"Can I have the day off again today?" I ask Markus the next morning, picking at my breakfast without eating much.

"You have to spend at least thirty minutes warming up. The rest is up to Grigory. He comes here at two."

I give him a long, blank stare. "Why is he coming here?" *And on a Saturday.*

Markus pours more coffee into his mug and adds a splash of milk. "Because I've asked him to." Leaning back in his chair, he takes a swig, watching me casually like there's nothing odd about Grigory coming here.

"Was that what you talked to him about yesterday?"

"Part of it," he says, being as vague as when he told me about Grigory's ex the other day. Apparently, Grigory's privacy is important to him.

"But isn't this your day off?" Markus is away a lot during the week, so when I don't shut myself in with the piano like last week, we usually spend the weekends together.

"I'm going for a cup of coffee with some friends I haven't seen for a while. It will probably be a few hours, so the two of you will have some time on your own. You need to settle things after last week."

"It's not necessary." I'd rather not see Grigory at all. "I'm fine."

He gives me an *are you kidding me* look. "Sure, and fish can fly." With a tsk-sound, he gets up and starts clearing the table.

"Markus, I really don't want to see him." I imbue the words with all the urgency I can muster.

Finishing his coffee, Markus sets the mug beside the sink with a clunk. "I really don't care what you want at this point. The two of you need to work things out." He turns to face me and leans back against the counter, hands pressed to the surface. "Grigory has been cranky all week, and you keep retreating to your little hidey-hole and poking at your food without saying a word. I'm frankly fed up with it. Both of you."

"I'm sorry, Markus." I feel terrible I've treated him this way. "I'll start talking to you. I promise. Just please don't make me see him. It's not necessary."

Markus scoffs and levels me with an irritated glare. "Right? You'll just magically grow wings and fly up from that pit of yours, all happy and unflappable?"

I hate when he's being sarcastic, but I can't blame him. I know I've been a shitty submissive the past week, and God knows I won't magically get better. But the idea of seeing Grigory has my stomach tied up in all kinds of twisted knots, and I can't see how we're supposed to work things through.

By talking?

Grigory having a sensitive talk seems as likely as me growing wings.

Markus moves to leave and turns in the doorway. "And one more thing, I told Grigory he may hit you somewhere else if your arms can't handle it." His mouth twists. "That is, if he makes sure to pick you up afterward."

"Are you kidding me?"

Markus walks away, and I rush up from the chair to follow.

"Why would you do that? Are you trying to make everything worse?" *Fuck.*

Markus continues to the bedroom where he takes a fresh shirt from the closet and drops it onto the bed. "Maybe it will give the two of you the kick you need to realize what a mess you've ended up in."

"So you're going to make everything worse?"

Markus shrugs and pulls off his sweater. "If that's what it takes to make it better."

"That's so fucked up."

"Yeah, well, it already was."

I gawk at him, horrified and confused. "Are you saying I have fucked this up too?" My throat tightens, tears welling up in my eyes. I feel so helpless in all of this, yet Markus makes it sound like I'm to blame as much as Grigory.

"Gosh, no. I'm sorry, sweetie." Markus rakes a hand through his hair and pulls me into a hug. "I'm a bit on edge too. Both of you have shut me out and put on irritable attitudes. But this really is Grigory's mess, and I can't blame you for acting out. I know it's been hard for you."

"Then why do I have to pay for it?"

"Because whether you want it or not, you're involved. The

alternative is to end this altogether, and to be quite frank, I don't think any of us wants that." He pulls me out by my shoulders. "Do you want that?"

I lift a hand to dry the corners of my eyes as I consider not seeing Grigory again. The thought alone wrenches at my heart, and my answer is without doubt. "No."

"Yeah, me neither. I quite liked seeing how much you thrived with the lessons, and it's good for Grigory too. He hasn't played with a submissive in a while, and I like sharing you with him. He just needs to get his head out of his ass and remember that a sub comes with a responsibility."

I press my cheek against his bare chest and wrap my arms around his waist. "Will you be here when he comes?"

"Sorry, sweetie. I need to leave half an hour before. But he's promised to take good care of you."

I flex my hands nervously against his back. "I don't like this."

"I know." Markus tightens his arms around me. "But you just have to do as Grigory says. He'll take charge."

"Of course he will," I mutter with a wry note.

Markus chuckles and leans back, brushing my hair behind my ear. "Yeah, he will. And you like it."

I roll my eyes, unable to deny it.

He slips his hands under my T-shirt and pushes it up my stomach. "Take a warm bath with me, sweetie. It will calm your nerves."

"Thank you," I say sincerely, lifting my arms to let him undress me. Markus always has a cure for my trembling nerves and I really love him for it.

* * *

My anxiety ramps up when Markus leaves, and I pace back and forth for half an hour.

When the doorbell rings, I glance around like I could find something to help me out of this situation. But the only thing that would save me is not opening the door, and that idea has ice-cold shudders running down my back. I don't even want to consider the consequences.

So I scurry to the hallway, and with a quivering hand I pull open the door.

Grigory's eyes are the first thing I notice. Dilated pupils and taut face muscles make him look wild and dangerous. Like he's about to jump me. I take a step back and he follows me in, so close I scramble to keep distance, almost stumbling over my own feet.

He swings the door shut, and the echoing slam is the only sound as he glares at me. I feel like a cornered rabbit facing a hungry lion. He scans my body, from my feet, over my tight pants, the crimson spaghetti top, and to the small braid at the side of my head. Then back to my right arm. I don't miss the feral twitch of his mouth as he studies the vivid colors of red and blue begging to be noticed, confirming I'm the prey here.

But the marks are not the worst. When Grigory's eyes trail back up and linger a moment too long on my chest, I glance down to see the small peaks of my nipples jut out behind the fabric.

Fuck, fuck, fuck. How did I forget to put on a bra? I usually go without one when I'm home with Markus—but not today!

I all but bolt to the music room, unheeding polite manners. Frantically, I scan the room for something to cover myself with, but my cardigan is in the living room, and there's not even a blanket in here.

Grigory follows a minute later. "Sit down," he orders gruffly, pointing to the piano bench with his evil metal stick.

Curling my arms over my chest, I hasten to obey. It's not a conscious choice. It's pure instinct that kicks in at the sound of his command.

With even strides, Grigory closes the distance between us to stand beside me. I feel trapped. It doesn't matter there's enough space to run around him or squeeze around the other side of the piano. Just knowing I'm alone with him is enough to stir a feeling of utter defenselessness.

At the opera, the professional surroundings protect me. I know there are other people close by, and being at a workplace demands a certain degree of professionalism. At least, that's the illusion.

Here, I'm completely at his mercy, alone with him in a private home behind thick walls and locked doors.

He takes my right arm and drags his fingers over the bruises, applying some pressure here and there. I can't hide my discomfort. My battered arm hurts, as does his detached way of examining it.

Lowering my head, I turn away to hide my taut expression.

But I know he sees it anyway. I can feel his scrutinizing eyes on me, and that man's ability to catch the smallest, most discreet details is scary.

"Give me your left arm." There's no trace of sympathy in his voice, and he inspects my other arm in the same rough manner. The bruising isn't as bad here, but when he presses the pad of his thumb into a particularly sore spot, I let out an involuntary whimper.

"Hmm," he grumbles, giving me back my arm.

I fold both arms around myself again, needing the illusion of protection. But even the psychological comfort is useless as I feel him looming over me, taking in my every nervous twitch, every ragged breath.

"Take off your pants," he orders, waving his baton impatiently at my legs.

I gape up at him, about to sputter my outraged protest. But when I see the impossibly low eyebrows and the grave line between them, all my protest goes *swoosh.*

My fingers go to the button and zipper, fumbling to get them up. I feel utterly defenseless as I slowly push down my pants, revealing my bare thighs and the skimpy red thong.

He must see my discomfort since he says, "Don't worry. I've already seen it all down there, haven't I?"

It's the first time he even refers to the punishment, and it's cold and detached.

Tears prickle behind my eyes. I have no idea why he's acting like this. Ever since the punishment, he's shut me out. I don't get it. Shouldn't you grow closer after such an intimate night?

Now he's just cruel.

I should get up and walk out of here. Pull my pants back up, at least. Anything. But I remain frozen, trapped under his command, growing weaker with each second.

Grigory doesn't give me the courtesy of looking away. And why would he? He's seen it all, like he says. He watches blatantly as I push the fabric farther down, over my knees and down my ankles, stripping away the protection.

As soon as I have them off, Grigory snatches them from my hand and tosses them to the sofa.

This is almost as humiliating as the last time we were in here together. If not more. That night, Markus was here to lend me some support, and despite Grigory's stern authority, he also showed me compassion. That night, I was a human being with feelings; now I'm just a body.

My muscles wind into tight coils when Grigory sits beside me, and when I put my fingers on the keys, they are stiff and shaky, and nothing sounds like it's supposed to.

Grigory pushes me without giving me pause to process the violence he inflicts upon me. As a result, I play even worse and thus receive more strikes. It's a cruel circle, and when he abruptly breaks off the lesson after barely half an hour, loneliness is squeezing my chest, threatening to burst free in streams of tears.

I start gathering my sheet music in my folder. It's not that I have any reason to since I'm not going anywhere with them, but I need something to do to avoid facing Grigory. The knot in my throat grows bigger by the second, my breathing coming in staggered heaves, and I'm sure I'll break down the moment the front door closes. Maybe sooner if it takes too long for him to leave.

He opens the door to the hallway, and I chance a glance his

way, a bit stunned he's leaving without a goodbye. But most of all, relieved.

My relief quickly withers though, as he turns in the doorway and catches my gaze. "Come to the living room when you are done here." Then he disappears before I get a chance to say anything.

My head pounds as I stare stiffly at the empty doorway. I had completely forgotten what Markus said about Grigory and me needing to work things out. Is that what Grigory wants now? To talk? How is it even possible when he's taken this cold distance?

Is he going to force me to spill all my most private feelings and not say a word himself?

I wipe a stray tear from my cheek and force down the oncoming flood. I need to get him out of here. But how the hell am I supposed to do so when I can't even utter a word without risking breaking into tears?

Glancing around the room, I decide a good start would be to put on my pants—get my physical shield into place.

But I can't find them.

I go to the sofa where he put them and look under and beside it. But they're gone. With panic prickling in my nerves, I search the room even though I know I won't find them.

Has he taken them?

I can't face him like this, half-naked and vulnerable, with red stripes painted all over my arms and thighs.

Maybe I should stay in here and refuse to come talk to him. Or better, run to the bathroom across the hall and lock the door until Markus comes home—or Grigory breaks it in.

Would he do that?

Any other day I would say no. But today I don't dare to think he wouldn't. There's this dangerous energy lurking behind his eyes, and it scares me to be honest.

Markus trusts him, I remind myself. They've been good friends for many years. Grigory is not some kind of lunatic.

I berate myself mentally. I should stop making up all these childish worries, grow a pair, and tell him straight out to leave. What difference does it make if I break out crying anyway? Like he said, he's already seen it all—including my tears—and it might even help underline my point.

With newfound resolve, I push my shoulders back and go to the living room, prepared for a stand-off with a stern Grigory and an unyielding set of eyes.

But what I find catches me off guard.

Grigory is sitting at the far end of the large sofa, by the chaise lounge, arms resting on his thighs and remote in his hand, scrolling through Netflix. His gaze is distant, jaw tight.

Without looking up, he pats the sofa cushion beside him.

Gulping past the constriction in my throat, I gather my nerve. "You need to leave," I say. Crossing my arms over my chest, I try to force a little confidence, but it becomes more of a hugging myself kind of gesture when Grigory lifts his gaze to me. "Please, leave," I quickly add before my resolve fades.

In one fluid motion, Grigory gets up, and I grow smaller with each approaching step he takes.

"Please, just go," I beg in a shaky voice when he stops in front of me.

"Come sit with me on the couch." Grigory puts a hand on my arm, but I step back, hugging myself harder.

"Just go." Tears are brimming in my eyes now, and any moment they'll spill over.

"Clara," he says, using a dominant tone, "we need to spend some time together away from the piano."

I can't believe this man. He thinks he can get his way by using an authoritative tone. Normally he could, but a surge of anger strengthens my resolve. "Markus said you'd take care of me." Pointing back to the music room, I say, "That wasn't taking care of me."

"I know." Grigory drags a hand through his hair, and I'm taken aback by the genuine regret flickering in his eyes. With the way he spoke a moment ago, I expected him to go even more dominant and put on a reproachful tone. Instead, he listens. "I haven't taken care of you the last two weeks, but I'd like to correct my mistake now."

I flicker my gaze back and forth between his eyes and try to gauge if there's a catch. But I can't find any.

"Will you please let me hold you?" he says, holding out his hand for me but not touching me.

There's a strange urgency in his eyes like he truly needs this, and I remember what Markus said about Grigory and aftercare. It doesn't add up with anything he's done since the punishment, but he seems so genuine, and I get the feeling there's some underlying reason for his distant behavior that has more to do with him than it has with me. For the life of me, I don't know what it might be, but I can't refuse his sincere request. My arms fall to my sides and Grigory understands the meaning and tentatively reaches for me.

I let him pull me to him, and I feel his shoulders drop with a relieved sigh as he presses me to his chest. I feel it too, the relief. I've longed for this for more than a week, and the startling tenderness in his arms knocks the resistance straight out of me. Suddenly, I'm weeping into his chest, unable to hold back anymore.

"I've got you," he reassures, and there's that strange urgency again. "I've got you, *devochka*, I'm here now."

His soothing words only spur on my tears, and I sink into him as my legs shake under the force of the sob rising in me.

Lifting me into his arms, he carries me to the sofa and lets me curl up in his lap as he rocks me like a child. "Don't worry. I'm here now."

I want to ask him why he wasn't before, but all I can do is soak his white shirt in tears as I keep crying with no seeming end.

I have no idea how long it goes on, but Grigory never tires of comforting me. He keeps holding me through the storm, and his firm grip makes me think he might actually need this as much as I do.

"Sweet Clara," he murmurs, pressing small kisses to the top of my head. "I've got you now," he keeps reassuring as he caresses my back with circular movements.

His soothing words break down my defenses, and I press myself to him with a lack of restraint that shouldn't be possible with someone I barely know. But even though I'm somewhat disturbed by the way I let myself go, this feels right. And when the tears finally let up, I feel calm—more than I have at any other point since the night in the music room.

Grigory lets me sit curled up in his lap a while longer with my hand splayed on his chest and my head tugged into the crook of his shoulder. It's so peaceful I think I could sleep here, feeling his steady heartbeat and listening to his even breaths.

But the bubble breaks when Grigory lifts me onto the couch to sit beside him—at least for me it does. With the desperate need to be held having faded, it's no longer as easy to be so carefree about the close intimacy. Grigory, though, seems quite comfortable as he wraps his arm around my shoulders and holds me to his side.

"Relax, Clara. I'm still here," he assures and wraps a blanket over my legs with his free hand. Then he starts a movie, and as we watch in silence, I gradually sink back into the comfortable intimacy.

Feeling Grigory's carefreeness helps. Somehow, he seems even more laidback than when we're at the opera, and I wonder if it's the casual setting or the much-needed aftercare. He even laughs at the movie once in a while. It's a lovely sound—deep and rumbling.

It makes me comfortable enough to ask one of the many questions that have been swirling in my head lately.

"Why did you shut me out after the punishment?" I tense the moment I hear myself speak the words. It's too personal. And when Grigory's arm tenses around me, I mutter a quiet, "I'm sorry," and try to pull away.

But Grigory won't let me. Holding me firmly in place, he presses his other hand to my cheek to turn my head up to face him. His features are set in a hard expression when our eyes meet. "You've messed with my ability to see straight, *devochka*."

How? Why? I want to ask, but all words seem to have been sucked away in this charged moment, full of something unsaid yet very important.

When I finally do speak, the words don't make any sense. "I didn't mean to." I look away. Gosh, this is embarrassing. He thinks I'm the one who messes with his head. It's the other way around.

When I chance a glance back up, Grigory is smiling. It's the same wide grin he wore when I staggered into the hallway at the opera, thinking I could find C3 myself. "Are you sure?"

This time, I don't see the mockery I thought I saw that day. Actually, his smile is quite warm, and I find my own lips tipping up in a smile even as my cheeks go positively red. "I'm sure."

"Good. Because otherwise I'd have to punish you."

This man... I fall forward, burying my head against him since I can't hold his gaze any longer. He wraps me up in a warm hug, and there's that deep, rumbling chuckle again, which makes me all mushy inside.

"Thank you," I whisper into his chest.

"For what?"

"This."

"God, Clara. This is what I mean," he says, holding me so close it almost hurts as he places a long tender kiss on top of my head.

I'm not sure exactly what he means, but it's clear this means much more to him than I had ever dared to hope.

— CHAPTER 15 —

The sound of the front door startles me. Reality hones back in and infiltrates the peace with murky water as I realize I've forgotten all about Markus.

I dart up so fast I would have tripped in the blanket if it wasn't for Grigory grabbing my arm.

"*Devochka*," he says, demanding my attention. "What's the rush?"

Turning to him, I all but stutter, "I need to greet Markus." *I don't want him to find me curled up in another man's arms like this.*

"No running," he admonishes. "I don't want you to fall."

At my nod, he releases me, and I go as quickly as I can without running. It's only when I'm halfway through the room I realize I'm still not wearing any pants. I have no problem with Markus seeing me like this, of course, but I don't want to flaunt the fact that I've gone pantless with another man. So I hurry back to grab the blanket and wrap it around me as I scurry toward the hallway.

"No running." Grigory's stern voice makes me stop dead in my tracks.

Squeezing my eyes shut, I haul in a loud breath, then continue at a less hazardous pace.

Grigory's command is branded into my system when I reach the hallway. It confuses the hell out of me when I sink into Markus's embrace. I know it's irrational, but I can't chase away the feeling of having done something wrong—like cheating.

Taking a step back, Markus peruses me. His narrowing eyes reveal that he sees the conflict in my face. It's truly uncanny how easily he reads me sometimes.

"Grigory and I are gonna have a talk. Do you want to be in the music room or bedroom meanwhile?" he asks.

I choose the bedroom since I won't be able to focus on the piano right now.

With hurried steps, I make my way back through the living room. I feel Grigory's eyes on me all the way like a stern reminder not to run. I don't return the look; It would only stir up more confusion.

In the bedroom, I flop onto the king-size bed and grab my Kindle. But the whirlwind in my head takes up all the space in my mind, and I can't concentrate on the words. So instead, I try to figure out where my sudden unease comes from.

Markus wanted Grigory and me to spend time together like we did—repair the damage from the lack of aftercare. So technically, I haven't done anything wrong.

At least not on the outside.

On the inside, though, my emotions are like an elastic band pulled taut between the two men. Before today, it was difficult to control how I felt about Grigory; now it's impossible.

What happened today was much more than some long overdue aftercare. It was intimate on a very personal level. It broke open my defenses and pulled forth all the things I've been trying to hide.

I can no longer deny that I have feelings for Grigory. My every instinct tells me I can't have feelings for two men. But I do.

I love Markus. He's my dominant, my protector, and best friend—the man who sparks a vibrant need deep within my belly.

Yet, I crave Grigory with an urge bordering on obsession. I crave his touch, his stern eyes, and his all-consuming power that renders me speechless—snuffs out my last ounce of will and leaves nothing but pure submission.

But I'm not sure the two can coexist. I'm scared the pull toward Grigory will draw me away from Markus, or I'll pull away from both men because it's more than I can handle.

Forty excruciating minutes pass in the company of these thoughts.

When Markus finally comes in, I'm sitting on the bed, fumbling with the sheets.

"Why so tense, sweetie? Grigory says everything went well after you got the piano lesson over with. Didn't it help to spend some time with him?" Markus closes the door and takes a seat on the bed.

"It did." I push up to sit on the mattress. "A lot," I say, but my words come out with a disheartened tone.

"Then, what's wrong?"

I'm not sure where to begin, so I start by telling him the first thing that popped into my head when he came home. "I'd forgotten you when I was with Grigory."

"No!" he exclaims, mouth agape with feigned shock. "Are you saying you don't think about me every moment, every waking hour?"

I can't help the laugh that bubbles up, and I swat at him. "You know what I mean."

"Of course, I do. You think you've done something wrong because you haven't thought about me while being with Grigory."

"Yeah," I admit tentatively.

"You know, it's okay to like Grigory."

"I'm not sure I just *like* him," I say with a worried grimace.

"I figured." Lifting his hand, he trails his fingers over my forehead and cheeks like he's trying to soothe away the worry lines.

I stare down at the sheets and start fumbling again.

"Feelings are to be expected when you play with this sort of dynamic," Markus continues. "And I'm not afraid your feelings for me will diminish because things evolve between you and Grigory."

"You're not?" My eyes snap back up to him, relief making my heart beat a little more freely.

"Of course not." He curves his palm around my cheek, and I lean into it. "I love you, Clara. You're mine, and you'll stay mine—no matter what happens between the two of you."

I nod eagerly. Gripped by an urge to manifest his words, I fall forward and bury my head in his lap. "I'm yours," I whisper and pull in a loud breath to steady the strong current of emotion.

"And I love you too."

"All mine," he confirms, curling his hand around my nape.

We sit like this for a while, both consumed by the power exchange permeating the very air between us.

"I want to give this a try," Markus finally says. "You, me, and Grigory."

I slowly push back up. "What do you mean?"

"I want to take it further than the piano lessons. Spend some time together, the three of us. See what happens. I like dominating you with Grigory—see how you blush beneath two men." He gently pinches my cheek and smiles. "You are damn cute when your cheeks redden and you get all flustered."

I lower my eyes, feeling warmth flow to my cheeks. "You can accomplish that all by yourself."

"Yeah, but it's fun having someone to share it with. Plus, it's good to see Grigory with you. He really enjoys your submission, and it's been too long since he had a sub."

I remember him mentioning this earlier, but he never fully explained. "Was it because of that woman he was with?" Magdalena, I remember him calling her, and even though I don't know anything about this woman, my reaction to the thought of her is as strained as Markus's.

His lips pull into a grim line. "Yeah. Things ended quite badly between them."

"I'm sorry," I say, at a loss for better words.

"Don't worry about it, sweetie. That's not for you to deal with. But I do want to know what you think about upping the dynamic between the two of you?"

I curl my lips between my teeth, trying to hide the smile that wants to break free at the idea.

Markus smiles, and as his face lights up, I can't help my own from following suit.

"There's no use in demanding an answer, huh?" he says with warm amusement. "It's all written right here." Taking my chin in his hand, he gives my head a small shake, and I all but beam at him.

Markus wraps both my hands in his. "We'll continue slowly. No sex or kissing. Just dominance and the occasional beating. At least for now." He winks at me, making a myriad of butterflies flap in my belly.

But it's not just Markus's flirty wink. It's also the idea of something sexual with Grigory. The thought of his large fingers slipping down my pants and between my folds has blood rushing to my cheeks and my sex, making me all hot and bothered.

"You really aren't good at hiding your thoughts, sweetie." Markus lifts an amused brow and gets up, dwarfing me with his tall size. "Take a few minutes to process the new information, then come to the kitchen. There's pizza."

* * *

I put on my checkered shorts and a thin cardigan and saunter through the living room to the kitchen.

I'm not sure why I expected Grigory to have left. After all, he hasn't said goodbye. But I'm not sure I'd expect him to, and Markus hadn't mentioned him joining us for dinner. So when I see him sitting by the dining table, I halt in my tracks.

He looks up from the bottle of wine he's opening, and the air lodges in my throat, my eyes immediately darting to the floor. I wasn't prepared to see him again this soon.

Keeping my head lowered, I go to take a seat beside Markus, and I can feel Grigory following me with his gaze. It makes me want to crumble to the floor. There's never any firmness in my legs when that man watches me.

My belly growls when I see the pizza box from my favorite Italian place. But the hunger clashes with the nerves twisting in my stomach. The last dinner the three of us had together was less than comfortable for me, and today has marked a huge change, bringing the three of us into unchartered territory.

Not only has Markus announced he wants to take things further, but I have also put my feelings out in the open—to both men. I all but told Markus directly, and the way I was with Grigory said it all and then some.

I pull out the chair beside Markus, but a stern "uh-uh," makes me pause.

Looking at Markus, I see him pointing to his other side. My heart skips a beat when I see the burgundy pillow on the floor by the end of the table. Right between the two men.

How did I not notice it before?

My feet are like lead, and with each hesitant step I take, they grow heavier. My breath is coming in ragged drags when I finally stop in front of the pillow.

I can't do this. I can't submit to both men at the same time. Not after everything that's happened today. But even more so, I can't do it of my own free will. Too many emotions are stirring within me, and I need a firm hand to settle the mess. I've already given so much today, and giving this—kneeling of my own accord—is too vulnerable.

"Sit down," Markus says, but it's more of a suggestion than the firm order I need.

So I just stand here, growing more anxious by the second as the two men start taking pizza onto their plates.

Grigory takes a sip of his wine, then leans back in his chair, arms crossed over his chest as he watches me. But he doesn't just watch. No, his eyes bore straight through my private sphere, shoving away all will and strength until my legs are about to give in.

I lower my eyes, but it doesn't help. I can still feel the weight of his gaze, and I want to combust under it—sink to my knees and become small. Give up my free will and submit.

So I finally do. Slowly, I sink to my knees, defeat and relief warring to win the upper hand.

Defeat wins when I glance up and find Grigory's attention back on the food in front of him.

I slump and stare into the velvet pillow, which Markus has bought specially for me. It's usually calm and peaceful being here, but right now the uncertainty of this whole situation is deafening. The words barely even register when the two men start a conversation, and loneliness creeps up on me. I feel excluded down here. I don't even get a piece of pizza. Am I supposed to wait until both men have eaten?

I was so excited when Markus told me he'd ramp up the dynamics, but this wasn't what I expected.

"Eat, sweetie." Markus pulls me from my nervous thoughts, holding a fork with a piece of pizza down to me.

Looking up, I meet his warm gaze, and it eases some of the pressure on my chest. It's terribly embarrassing being fed like this, but I'm already on the floor at both men's feet, and I figure I can't sink much lower. So I accept the pizza and stare at Grigory's socks as I chew.

Large squares in black, burgundy, and gray create a simple pattern with thin red lines running across. Per se, they are quite mellow—especially compared to those modern socks in all the neon colors of the rainbow—but on Grigory, they are vibrant. He always wears a white shirt and black slacks. It looks good on him, but it also seems somewhat restrained, and if I had to guess at the color of his socks, I would think they followed the same strict regime. But here, where no one sees, his clothes get to have a little more life and color.

Another piece of pizza comes down in front of me. This time, it comes from the other side, in a large palm.

Hesitantly, I reach for it, but Grigory pulls his hand back. Gazing up at him with confusion, I'm met with an intense expression that seems to hold both power, lust, and care. It's a heady combination that knocks me off balance yet locks me in place.

He reaches his hand back out to me—right in front of my mouth, leaving no doubt as to what he means.

I swallow, glancing at the piece of pizza in his hand and then up at him. He raises his brows in silent command, and with a deep inhale, I bow my head and eat the pizza from his hand.

"Good girl." The deep rumble of his voice hits straight into my submissive core, and when he moves his hand over my hair in languid strokes, a surge of humble gratefulness rushes through me. It fills every cell and fiber of my being until there's nothing else—just my gratitude and a profound calmness that makes my breath flow in a deep, even rhythm.

There's nothing lonely or excluding about sitting down here. On the contrary. I feel treasured and protected. And when Grigory holds another piece of pizza down for me, I bow my head in deference and whisper, "Thank you."

— CHAPTER 16 —

I start Sunday by cooking Markus breakfast while he, for once, sleeps in.

I'm in a bright mood for the first time in days, feeling a rush of excitement every time I think about how Grigory said goodbye to me last night.

My legs could barely support my weight when he helped me up, and my head was buzzing like I'd had three colorful cocktails. If Grigory hadn't held onto me, I think I'd have collapsed right there on the pillow.

Two weeks ago, I would have felt foolish for losing my balance, but when Grigory looped an arm around my waist and held me against him, I only felt cherished and cared for.

"Such a pretty little girl," he said, brushing my hair behind my ear. "You like sitting on the floor and eating from my hand, huh?"

My cheeks went fiery. But instead of letting embarrassment swamp me, I went along with the current, leaning into him and soaking up the safety he offered.

"You don't have to practice more today." He hugged me closer with both arms and held me for a long minute. Then he pressed a kiss to the top of my head and helped me back onto the pillow.

I wanted to protest at the loss of his arms, and I still feel a pang of yearning whenever I think of the large hand stroking my hair one last time before leaving.

I miss him.

A few days ago, fury and hurt would have filled me at the thought of Grigory, and now I'm pining for him. I can't quite wrap my head around how it came to be. Our time together yesterday wasn't enough to erase all that happened after the punishment.

But I guess that's just Grigory. He has an uncanny ability to haul me from one end of a spectrum to the opposite. There's no in-between with that man.

Although yesterday didn't erase everything, it has given me hope. Hope for more. It's dangerous, but I can't help it.

It seems like this thing between Grigory and me means something to him too. What he said and did yesterday has made me realize that him shutting me out must stem from some internal conflict that has nothing to do with me—at least not directly. He needed the aftercare as much as I did, but for some reason he couldn't give it to me before. I'm not sure if it's because he's conflicted about getting involved with his best friend's sub, some old hurt that lingers, or something entirely different.

But right now it doesn't matter. I'm confident I'll soon get to submit to him again, and today I'm with Markus and shouldn't think about it. So I flip the last batch of pancakes onto a plate and bring them into the bedroom alongside my newfound confidence and serve breakfast in bed.

After breakfast, Markus moves in on the couch with the comforter, pillows, and all, while I go to clean up in the kitchen. When I come back, he pulls me under the covers with a sudden yank, making me squeal. My eyes light up with excitement when I see he's prepared to watch *Paddington* on the large screen. I love all things cute and playful, and I love it even more that I can share them with Markus.

He makes some laugh-inducing imitations of Paddington as we watch. "My uncle always kept a marmalade sandwich in his hat in case of emergency," he says with an impeccable British accent.

I erupt in some heart-fluttering bursts of laughter, and I feel all but floaty after having been tense for so long.

After the movie, we go for a walk in a nearby park to enjoy the sunny weather, and I ask about Grigory and the unusual piano lessons.

Markus tells me it began when he told Grigory I wasn't playing much piano, and he wanted me to get back into a good practice routine.

"She just needs a motivational beating." Markus imitates Grigory with a terse expression and Russian accent, then continues in his normal voice. "But I'm not as sadistic as Grigory, so I told him it's more up his alley." He shifts back to the Russian accent. "You just send her here, and I'll do it if you can't manage yourself."

Imagining Grigory's flat expression, I sputter a laugh. This man isn't as humorless as he appears at first glance.

"We had some fun with the idea of combining it with a piano lesson," Markus goes on. "And it ended up sounding like a rather good idea. The lessons could help with your motivation, and I thought the discipline would work well on you. And well... it would be a lot of fun. There's that too." He gives me a mischievous smile, then adds, "And of course, Grigory couldn't decline the offer of hitting a sweet, submissive girl."

I gaze up at Markus as I fold my arm into the crook of his elbow. "When am I going to see him again? I mean, outside the piano lessons."

"Today." Markus grins, probably having predicted my gawking surprise. "He comes over in an hour."

"That's so soon." I did not see that coming.

"I know. But I didn't want to give the two of you time to drift apart after you've just found each other again."

"It shouldn't be your job, should it?" My boyfriend playing matchmaker for another man and me seems wholly wrong.

"Well, this is an unusual dynamic, so should and shouldn't doesn't necessarily count." Markus considers for a moment. "But no. This is Grigory's responsibility, but he's been in a bit of a weird place lately and I want to help him not fuck this up."

"Don't you get jealous?"

"No. Not really."

"I don't get it," I say. "I'd be sick with jealousy if you dominated another woman."

"I must say I'm a bit surprised how easy this is too. But I really like seeing Grigory with you. I think you've awoken something in him that he's shut down for a long time. I like helping him find it again even though it means sharing you."

"You wouldn't rather find someone else for him." I hurry to add, "I mean, not that I want you to. But I still don't get why you would help another man to be with your sub."

Markus stops and his features are serious as he turns to face me. "Clara, you're very submissive, and seeing these last couple of months how profound it is, I'm no longer sure I'll be able to fulfil your needs myself. Especially not when we go back to our normal lives in the fall. I guess I could use some help."

I draw in my chin, taken aback. "As in letting me be with other men on a regular basis?"

"I don't know. I haven't fully thought it through. Right now I just want to see where this goes."

Markus takes my hand and starts walking again. My throat suddenly feels tight with emotion, but as Markus breaks the silence with another Paddington imitation, the tension quickly breaks, and we fall back into the easygoing Sunday mood.

* * *

When we get back home, I scurry around the apartment for half an hour, nervous energy coursing through my veins, then jump astride Markus on the couch and ruffle his hair.

"Tell me something," I say. "Anything to calm this nervous mess you've made."

Markus lifts a brow. "I've made?"

"Yeah, you're the one who didn't give me time to prepare for Grigory coming."

"Believe me, no matter when I told you, you would have

found your own way into this jittery mess. Unless I waited until the last minute. Or better yet, just didn't tell you."

The doorbell rings, and I jump off Markus when he moves to get up.

"I really don't like that kind of surprises," I say, grabbing the nearest pillow into my arms.

Markus gives me a cocky grin and rakes his hand through the mess I've made on his head. "No? You seemed to like it a lot when I surprised you with the first piano lesson."

"Not the surprise part," I call after him.

I try to remain calm as I hear Grigory's deep rumble mix with Markus's more lyric voice in the hall. I can't make out their words, but the tone is light and humorous, and it settles some of my nerves.

Markus returns a few minutes later. "Be a good girl and crawl out to Grigory and greet him."

I get up and start walking toward the hall.

"I said *crawl,*" he admonishes.

I halt, glancing up at him with round eyes. There's no reprieve in his strict expression, so I end up sinking to the floor.

"Sorry, Markus," I mutter, crawling through the living room with a mix of timid restraint and eager anticipation.

"Much better," he says.

In the hallway, I crawl toward the polished leather shoes without lifting my gaze. A few feet away, I stop, kneeling with my head bowed.

My breathing comes in heavy drags of air, my heart beating like a restless drum.

The shiny shoes move closer, stopping an inch from my knees. I hold in a breath. The intoxicating shift in power is already messing with my head.

Even if the room was pitch black and Markus hadn't told me it was Grigory, I would know. His sheer air of authority is unmistakable.

A familiar hand settles on my head, heavy and calm. Only the thumb moves in small motions back and forth.

I close my eyes, feeling the weight, the warmth. Listening to his even breaths. I try to imitate the rhythm and almost succeed, but when he sinks onto his haunches in front of me, my breath picks up pace again.

I glue my eyes to the narrow patch of floor between us, too overwhelmed by the proximity to meet his gaze.

Luckily, eye contact is not what he wants. Cupping the back of my neck, he pulls my forehead to his chest, draping the other arm around my back.

I suck in a loud breath, but this time it's a settling one. He couldn't have received me in a better way. So I surrender myself, safely cocooned in his powerful presence.

Time drags out into a blur, and the only remaining beat, which lets me know it hasn't stopped altogether, is the steady thumps of Grigory's heart. We sit like this for a couple of minutes, just feeling each other.

When Grigory finally loosens his hold, he takes my chin and guides my head up to meet his eyes.

His face softens in the same tender expression as when he met me in the lobby the first time after the punishment. For a second, it frightens me. *Will he push me away again like he did back then?*

I hold onto his eyes, searching for something to warn me about the shift. But it doesn't come. He just strokes my cheek, keeping me fixed in a trance with his unwavering eyes.

"Stay down here," he says, rising to his feet.

He takes off his shoes and places them beside my sandals. My shoes look tiny next to his. *I'm* small next to him. My eyes glide up, taking him in—black slacks, white shirt with the top buttons open, broad shoulders, and stern features. He's so intimidating with his raw masculinity and sophistication all wrapped up in one heady package.

"Come." He brushes my hair tenderly as he passes me, moving toward the living room.

I'm about to get up when he stops me.

"Stay on the floor."

He doesn't even need to glance my way to know what I'm doing. The realization makes my blood surge a little faster as I follow him on all fours, grateful for his order to stay down here. Being on the floor stabilizes me in the uneven power dynamic.

Grigory takes a seat at one end of the long sofa, and even though I would love to follow and kneel before him, I don't dare to without an invitation. So I take a kneeling position in the middle of the room, displaying my submission without aiming it directly at him.

My eyes flicker up to Markus on the chaise lounge, and I consider if I should sit with him on the sofa instead. It feels strange kneeling here with no one having told me to, but there's not enough room for me up on the couch. Physically, three grown men could easily fit between Markus and Grigory, but I'd feel like a lamb between two hungry wolves. It's safer down here.

So I lower my gaze and stay put. If they want me somewhere else, I'm sure they'll let me know.

"Such an obedient girl you have." Grigory's voice is full of approval.

"Isn't she?" Markus responds.

There's a brief pause, and my fingers twitch on my thighs as I grow acutely self-conscious, sensing all attention in the room aimed at me.

"How about a cup of coffee?" Markus asks. "It's too early for scotch, right?"

"Coffee sounds good."

Raising his voice slightly, Markus addresses me. "Go make two cups of coffee. Black for Grigory and a splash of milk for me."

I crawl to the kitchen and start brewing coffee, relieved to get a reprieve from the dominant energy sucking out all the air of the living room. While I wait for the water to run through the machine, I lean against the counter and listen in on the conversation in the adjoining room.

"She's very submissive," Grigory states, and my insides go all mushy like it's a high compliment. It sounds like one with the way he says it. "When did you find out?"

"As soon as I saw her." Markus chuckles. "She gave off this sweet submissive vibe right from the start. I tried to go easy since I didn't want to scare her off, but I couldn't help myself and all but ordered her to meet me after the concert. And boy, was I relieved when I found her waiting for me. An hour later, I knew for sure."

"It's deeply rooted in her. There's no doubt," Grigory agrees. "Are you the first one she's submitted to, or had she explored it before?"

"I think I knew before she even suspected. You should have seen her the first time I spanked her. Those big eyes went round like saucers when she found out I wasn't joking around. Then she realized how wet she was, and she went completely rigid." He adds with a smug tone, "Well, that's until I made her come."

My face goes beet red. Why, by God, must he tell Grigory that?

"I could imagine," Grigory says, amusement lacing his voice. "The masochist in her goes hand in hand with her submission. Pain can bring her into a submissive space, but I also think submission allows her to handle large amounts of pain."

"You might be right. But I'm far from the incarnate sadist you are. I don't think I've ever come close to reaching her pain limit. Only when I punish her, and you know how it is then. Her pain tolerance is hampered by all the emotions—guilt and regret. So you don't get the full picture. I've got a feeling she can take much more than I'm comfortable giving."

Their voices become hushed, and I hold my breath, trying to make out the words. But the coffee machine is too loud, and I don't think I could hear them anyway, so when the machine beeps, I find mugs, pour coffee, and add a splash of milk to one.

I bring the mugs to the living room and serve them one at a

time with my head bowed and both hands folded around the ceramic. Then I return to my kneeling position in the middle of the room.

Someone takes a sip, and there's the clink of a mug being placed on a table.

"Where does your schedule bring you after *Tosca?*" Markus asks.

"I'm conducting a couple of concerts in London with Andrei Kovalev and the London Philharmonics," Grigory says.

I flutter my eyes up, a bit starstruck. Andrei Kovalev is one of the most renowned pianists in the world, and along with the London Philharmonics—and Grigory, of course—it doesn't get any bigger.

"That sounds great." Markus sounds almost as impressed as I feel.

"Yeah, well, I would have liked another pianist. But the concert planners insisted on Kovalev, and my manager insisted I took the job." Grigory huffs.

"What's wrong with Kovalev? He's a great pianist."

"If flashy notes and rapid cadenzas are all you want, sure. But we're playing Rachmaninoff's first piano concerto; you need some emotional depth for that."

"You can do with a challenge. I know you like it. And who knows? Maybe Kovalev just needs the right conductor to show him the way."

"I've got challenge enough here," Grigory says with a wry tone. "I don't think I've seen an opera house in such a mess before. The entire organization is coming apart at the seams. No one has heard about communication, and people barely know what their responsibilities are. I'm considering rehiring the entire staff and starting from scratch, just to save the trouble."

"I knew they had more than a few challenges, but I thought it was mostly some internal conflicts." Markus sounds taken aback.

"Well, you'd better not fall ill at the premiere because we have no stand-in for you." Grigory's frustration is palpable. "At least none I would ever allow on such a big stage."

The two men keep talking for a while, and I keep my eyes cast down, zoning out to the soothing sound of their voices.

At some point, the room goes quiet, and self-awareness creeps up my spine as I feel the weight of their attention shifting to me. I don't dare look up.

It's only when Grigory clears his throat that I lift my gaze.

Large brows accentuate dark eyes, and harsh features evoke thoughts of something wild and untamed. He sits on the edge of the sofa with his arms resting on his thighs, swamping me with his undivided attention.

Crooking his index finger, he beckons me to him and pulls the burgundy pillow across the floor and between his legs.

My heart beats a little faster at the sight of my kneeling pillow between Grigory's feet. Tentatively, I peer at Markus and get a go-ahead nod.

With all the grace I can muster, I crawl across the floor and kneel on the edge of the pillow, too overwhelmed to move closer.

But it isn't enough. Grigory repeats the finger motion, and I inch farther in.

"More," he says in a low voice.

A gentle tremble takes residence in my limbs as I move closer, settling right before him—so close I inhale his masculine scent.

With a slow hand, he pulls my head into his lap. The proximity spikes my heartbeat, and my fingers clutch the edges of the pillow. It's too intimate.

We have exchanged so few words, and yet I have a feeling he knows me intimately—the way you know someone after many late nights of laughing and crying. We haven't spent a single night together, yet he has seen those extremes. He's seen my beaming smile when he compliments my piano playing, and he's seen me coming apart in his arms after he's punished me. But I practically know nothing about him. Not more than you can read on Wikipedia. And now I sit here, trapped by his hand, enclosed by his legs.

My breathing turns shallow, my pulse thrumming with rapid beats. This is happening too fast. I need distance. Time to adjust—get to know him before I let him take another part of me.

"Give me your hands," he says gently.

Reluctantly, I release the velvety fabric and reach my hands up. Grigory's large hands close around mine, swallowing them up completely. It's no better than iron manacles snapping shut.

I shift on the pillow, my breaths coming still more ragged.

"Shh," Grigory soothes, lifting our gathered hands to rest on the back of my neck, stroking his thumbs along my skin in reassuring caresses. "Deep breaths, *devochka*. We are just going to sit here for a while."

I feel utterly trapped, my hands locked into his, the weight of them pinning my head into his lap. The air has a hard time reaching into my lungs in this crouched position, and it takes a couple of staggered tries before I can manage a deep one.

"Good girl. Keep going. Just like that."

Slowly, I get my breathing under control and realize there's no threat in Grigory's hands. Rather, they are familiar and secure. I've felt them so many times, and they've never failed to soothe me. It's only the lack of them that has truly hurt me.

So I give in to the lull of being trapped, not needing to talk or think, just being here where he's put me.

Grigory and Markus pick up their conversation in hushed voices, and I listen to the deep rumble of Grigory's accented voice right above me. However, I don't hear the words. The sound glides over me as a calming soundtrack, the meaning inconsequential.

At some point, he releases my hands back into my lap and starts caressing my back. Long, languid strokes travel up and down along my spine, pulling me deeper into the trance.

I don't notice the room has gone silent before I feel a shift in Grigory. Moving a hand up under my hair, he curves it around my nape, holding me in place as he presses the other flat against my back.

Something is about to happen. I can feel it in the air.

"Take a deep breath, *devochka*."

I inhale loudly. Right as I push the air back out, Grigory lifts his free hand and lets his palm fall onto my back with a thud, large and heavy, pushing the rest of my breath out in one hard gush.

Pain blossoms in my back and all the way through my chest. I heave for new air, but shock has narrowed my windpipe.

"Slow breaths." The sound of Grigory's urgent inhale penetrates the fog of panic before it can settle, and I drag in a long breath. Only half the air goes into my lungs, but it's better than before.

"That's it," he croons, picking up the soothing motions on my back again.

I fall into the gentle rhythm of his touch, but the shock hasn't quite waned when Grigory lifts his hand again and slams it onto my back by the sheer force of gravity.

I let out a choked wail as the air rips from my lungs and pain crashes deep into my back.

Tears prickle the corners of my eyes, panic slithering around my lungs. "Stop, I can't do this," I croak, pushing at Grigory's legs. It's too much, too fast. I can't let him rip me apart like this again.

"Breathe through it, *devochka*," he urges. But I can't. His words barely register. All I can feel is the pounding need to get away. I shove at him, my safeword hanging on the tip of my tongue.

Something moves hurriedly in the room, feet thumping across the floor, but I can't process the information through the wail of sirens and flashes of red in my brain.

Two hands grab my waist from behind, and I yelp, my muscles stiffening with fear.

"Clara, it's me," a familiar voice whispers in my ear.

Markus.

"I'm here, sweetie."

A small gust of air moves past the restriction in my throat, and another familiar voice speaks, deep and accented. "That's it. Breathe."

I can't think, I can't move. I can only follow the order I've obeyed so many times before. So I breathe. It's all I can do.

Markus leans over my back to whisper beside my ear. "Who do you belong to, Clara?"

"You," I croak between staggered breaths.

"That's right. You're mine." He strokes my sides, up and down, letting me know he's got me.

Grigory's hands are still heavy weights on my back and head, but they no longer feel threatening. Like Markus's, they are a source of protection.

"If I say Grigory may hit your back, what do you do?" Markus asks in that husky tone of his that leaves no doubts about who's in charge.

I choke out the words. "I let him do it."

Grigory's satisfied rumble is the first response I hear, and it goes straight to my core, mending my shattered determination and lighting fire to my submission.

"Good girl," Markus says, but all my attention has shifted to the hand on my head, the thumb stroking gentle patterns on my hair.

"I think she's good to go again." Markus's voice has become a distant sound, and I barely notice when his hands disappear and he moves away.

Grigory starts stroking my back again. "Such beautiful

submission," he murmurs with startling reverence, like my submission is something sacred to be cherished and protected.

A rush of something deep and calm fills me to the brim. It's so strong I can hardly contain it, yet I'm floating in a peaceful state where everything is in place, overwhelmed and calm at the same time.

Grigory rests his hand beside my spine and presses my head into his lap. I know what's coming, yet I remain calm.

The hand lifts and crashes onto my back, shoving the air from my lungs. Pain bursts deep inside my body, filling me with an urgency unlike anything I've ever experienced. But it's brief, morphing into a weighty feeling—like a heavy blanket covered in a sheen of lead.

"Good girl," Grigory croons, stroking the entire expanse of my back, covering it in soothing warmth.

Another blow lands with a hard thud. Then the stroking starts anew. He keeps going like this, and I cling to his legs every time his palm slams down. But at some point, I even give up this small resistance, and my hands fall limply onto my thighs. Then I just sit here with my head buried in his lap, accepting everything he gives me.

My eyelids fall shut, refusing to allow in any disruptions, and my ears feel like they are filled with cotton, only letting the rumble of Grigory's voice in. A floaty darkness wraps around me—but not a threatening kind. It's the kind of darkness that holds out all thought and concern, leaving me in a peaceful emptiness. Only Grigory, the pain, and the comfort exist.

"Is it okay if I remove her blouse," Grigory asks, and I

vaguely notice Markus say something.

Markus must have agreed because fingers lift the hem of my blouse, slowly traveling upward, skimming my sensitive skin as they go.

I try to lift my arms in compliance, but they don't seem to work. Nothing seems to work. Not my brain, my arms, or words.

A small mewl is all I manage as Grigory lifts my arms, one at a time, to free them from the sleeves. Then he carefully lifts my head and pulls the fabric over before putting it back on his lap. I barely even react when the clasp of my bra pops open and fingers slip the straps off my shoulders.

I gasp when he presses his palms to my back. I've felt those hands on my shoulders and arms many times, but never both of them pressed against my naked back. The heat is immense and I feel more vulnerable than I ever have with him.

Slipping one hand up to rest on my nape, he moves the other in circles all over my back like it's new land that needs to be explored. The intimacy is overwhelming, and tears spring to my eyes even as tiny moans slip past my lips.

"Take a deep breath," he says, his hand stopping on one side of my spine.

Grigory lifts his hand as I drag in a large gulp of air, and when I release it, his hand falls onto my back, heavy and hard, making me cry out. The pain is much sharper without the barrier of fabric, and it steers me straight for panic.

"Stay with me, *devochka*," Grigory urges and starts stroking again. "I've got you."

His words call upon my every instinct to please him, and

when he hits me again, the pain quickly changes. The sharp burn morphs into a thrumming energy that swamps my mind and drives me deeper into the thoughtless world where only Grigory and his all-consuming power exist.

One moment I'm swamped by painful brutality and the next it's warm tenderness. The contrasts crash against each other, rendering me so utterly powerless I weep. Not from desperation. It's calm and cathartic tears of surrender.

Grigory reaches a finger down to feel my wet cheek. It doesn't make him stop. He just starts murmuring continuous endearments in between strikes. "That's it, *devochka*," he croons as I draw in a deep breath. Smack! Pain erupts on my back. "You're doing so well." He tenderly rubs my skin, then another blow hits with a violent gush. "Such a good girl."

I can't take it anymore. I start shaking, my mind a blurry mess. Yet somehow, I receive each blow with a burning desire to give him whatever he wants—be worthy of his appraisal.

Three rapid blows rip a raw screech from my throat. Then a sob breaks from my chest. And another. I grapple at his slacks, desperate to find purchase in the torrent of pain and emotion.

But it only lasts a moment. When Grigory leans down over me and rains tiny kisses over my back, his hands stroking and holding me everywhere, the storm settles. I'm surrounded by him in all possible ways. There's no room for anything else. Not thoughts, overwhelming feelings, or pain. I go limp again—every bone and muscle useless, tears falling in a quiet stream.

Grigory lifts me into his lap and rocks me while whispering words of comfort. I cry like a child into his shoulder, shaking through the shock still rattling my body. My foundation is like a hundred tiny tectonic plates quaking against each other. But Grigory keeps it all together, and I welcome the vulnerability of falling apart in his arms.

Vaguely, I register that Markus comes to sit beside us. Grigory passes me to him, and Markus gathers me in his lap. Burying my head against his shoulder, I inhale the familiar fresh scent of his aftershave. It's safety and comfort, like the feeling of his arms encircling me.

"Are you okay, sweetie?" he asks, stroking my hair.

I nod into his shoulder and sniffle through the receding tears. I feel torn apart and shaken up, yet I'm more than okay. It doesn't add up, but a lot of things that have happened recently don't seem to.

"You liked Grigory hitting your back, huh?" Markus leans back to watch me with a warm smile.

I dry my moist cheeks and smile back at him. "Yeah." *I really did.*

"I enjoyed watching." Markus gently strokes my cheek. "You are so beautiful when you give up control like that."

"You don't mind that it isn't you I surrender to?" I say in a low voice as to hide it from Grigory even though he's sitting right beside us.

"If it was anyone else, I would. But I trust Grigory."

I'm not sure trust is the only matter making it okay for Markus, but it's the most tangible one. There seems to be a certain chemistry between the two men that allows them to share effortlessly—a strong friendship and a lack of jealousy that makes this dynamic seem natural.

"Are you okay with going back to Grigory?" Markus asks. "I think he would like to hold you some more."

I glance at the man beside us. He's as grave and unreadable as ever, showing no signs of wanting me back. But when I agree and Markus passes me back to him, Grigory's arms say everything. He pulls me against him in a tight hold, cupping my head in his large hand as he rocks me like it's second nature.

Markus disappears to the chaise lounge and turns on the TV at a low volume. I barely notice the sound, and I don't think Grigory does either. We're both caught up in the intense energy between us—the stark intimacy that comes from letting someone rip you apart then put you back together piece by piece. Grigory seems to take as much joy in the mending as the tearing, and I slowly drift off as the pieces fall back in place, leaving me calm and safe in his arms.

— CHAPTER 17 —

There's a steady flow of people in the lobby at the opera the next day—tourists coming to snap pictures, employees coming and going.

I'm early as usual and grateful for the bustling life. The windowless space can be quite eerie with nothing but my nervous breaths and restless pacing to fill the silence.

No pacing today though. Today I'm calm enough to sit on a bench and take out a book about the romantic piano virtuoso Franz Liszt. He is one of my great idols, and I've been wanting to find out more about him for some time now.

I become so engrossed with the pages I don't notice Grigory coming until he's suddenly here, towering above me.

He takes the book from my hands, and I tentatively glance up at him, almost expecting him to scold me for my inattention.

But he just looks the cover over and says, "Great book. One of the best I've read about Liszt." Then he takes my bookmark and closes the book around it before offering me his hand.

"Good to see you," he says once I'm on my feet, so close I have to lift my chin to meet his eyes.

A huge smile wants to break free over my face, but I contain it to a shy, fluttery one as I say, "You too."

Grigory puts my book in my bag and hangs it on my shoulder, then takes my flowery folder in one hand and presses the other to the small of my back to guide me along.

A tourist comes rushing up and asks if he can have a picture, and more follow at his heel when they notice it's Grigory Volkov. I've never been with a famous person before, and to be quite frank, all the attention makes me uneasy—and that's on top of the jittery nerves Grigory causes.

As with everything else, Grigory handles the situation with authority and proficiency. "Sorry, busy day," he says, barely throwing a glance in the tourist's direction as he keeps on walking. Somehow, he manages not to come off as rude despite the brusque rejection, and the tourists quickly disperse.

I can't help but marvel at him—this famous man who has plenty of confidence and command to match his status. Peering up at him with admiration as he opens the door for me, I wonder if anything can ever throw him off balance. Well, besides the lack of aftercare, apparently.

Small crinkles form at the corners of his eyes when he catches me looking—a hint of a warm smile.

I scoot past him and wait beside the door for him to pass and lead the way. But instead of walking ahead of me like he usually does, he puts his hand on my back again, keeping me at his side as he leads me through the halls.

It's a small change, yet it feels big, and for once I feel comfortable enough to start a conversation.

I ask which Liszt pieces he has played, and I can't help

gaping as he rattles off the long but no way nearly preemptive list of deeply virtuosic music that I can only hope to play myself one day.

"Have you played any Liszt yet?" he asks.

"I've been wanting to for a while, but I'm afraid I won't be able to handle it with my small hands." Liszt was notorious for having had a large hand.

Grigory chuckles and lifts a brow. "You know, Rachmaninoff had an even bigger hand than Liszt. You had no trouble playing his music, so I think you'll do just fine. But of course, you may not want to start with his *Transcendental Etudes.*"

He opens the door to the usual rehearsal room, and I walk past him with a huge smile plastered to my face. So he *was* impressed with the Rachmaninoff piece, after all.

The lesson proceeds as usual. Grigory has great demands and doesn't hold back with the baton. But to balance out the discipline, he lets me feel his hand whenever I'm overwhelmed or just to give me a break.

I'm in good spirits when Grigory wraps up the lesson and tells me to pack up my things.

"Thanks for the lesson," I say when I step up beside the piano, ready to leave. Markus isn't coming to get me today since his vocal coach needed to push their appointment. Besides, I've told Markus he doesn't need to pick me up every time. I've been here enough to know my way in and out by now.

Grigory puts his hands on my shoulders and studies me with a gentle look that makes my knees go soft. "How are you feeling?" he asks.

"Fine," I say with a shy nod.

His eyes narrow like he's searching for confirmation on my face. "It was hard on you yesterday." It's not a question or something I have to consider. It's simply a statement.

And he's right. I've never tried anything like it. Markus doesn't hit me more than what is pleasurable, and I only cry when he punishes me. But what Grigory did really hurt. Yet, it was never more than I could take.

"Let my driver take you home," he says.

"I'm fine with the metro," I say, not wanting to be an inconvenience, but he already has me by the arm, leading me out of the room.

"Nonsense. That's what I have him for. Besides, I'm going home myself, so I might as well take a small detour."

We walk in silence for a while before my nerves at this new situation settle enough for me to ask a question. "Where do you live?"

"Well, my address is in Vienna." He gives me a humorous smile. "But my temporary residence is at the Grand Hyatt near Tiergarten. Just until I find something permanent here."

Tiergarten, that's the opposite direction of Markus's place, making it a huge detour. But I don't mention it. He seems determined to take me home, and to be quite frank, I'm grateful for avoiding the metro and all the people. Plus, this is nice, just talking to him.

"What kind of place are you looking for?" I ask.

Grigory tells me about his house-hunt as we walk to the car, and I listen attentively. Despite all the intimate times we've shared, Grigory is still a mystery to me, and I'm more than eager to know more about the man behind the stern face and powerful authority.

"Herr Volkov, Fräulein," Grigory's chauffeur greets us when we arrive at the underground parking garage.

Grigory gestures for me to go ahead when the chauffeur opens the back door, and he rounds the car to get in on the other side himself.

I'm about to buckle my seatbelt when Grigory leans over and hauls me across the leather seat. Large arms close around me, and I lean back into him, releasing a long breath.

God, it's so easy to forget everything when he holds me like this, and the twenty-minute car ride is all too short.

When the car pulls up in front of the modern apartment building where Markus lives, I reluctantly try to straighten and move to get out. But Grigory keeps his arms closed around me.

"There's no hurry, *devochka*," he says softly, his breath ruffling the hair behind my ear, tickling the sensitive skin.

I sink back into him, easily accepting his decision to hold onto me a while longer.

"Give us ten minutes," Grigory tells the chauffeur. The middle-aged man steps out of the car, leaving us in a silence charged with sizzling energy.

Our breaths are the only sound, and they meld together in a heavy rhythm that intensifies as Grigory slides his hand under my jacket and grips my waist. Leaning in, he skims his lips across my neck in a hint of a kiss. I shiver, from head to toe, my skin coming alive with prickling sensations.

His breath is hot against my neck, and I think I moan as I unconsciously buck my hips, heat pooling between my legs.

His other hand comes up to my neck, fingers moving in feather-light strokes above my windpipe, tracing my collarbone. I can't help leaning my head back. There's a dormant threat somewhere in his touch, and God, I want it. I want to know how it feels when his massive hand wraps around my slender throat, rendering me utterly helpless, completely at his mercy.

"You have no idea what you do to me, *devochka*," he rasps, and for a moment I can hardly breathe. It's only when he takes a loud inhale beside my ear that I remember to part my lips and suck in air. "Wednesday, at two p.m. I'll come get you in the lobby."

Slowly, he drags his hand across my stomach, freeing me from his capture. It's the worst freedom imaginable. *I don't want it,* is all I can think when I slide across the seat to get out. But I can't not have it.

I open the car door and cast a final glance back at him. His eyes are full of hunger—the same primal hunger I saw when he came to Markus's apartment to teach me a few days ago. Actually, it's the same look that has flickered in his eyes so many times since the first time I met him.

At this moment, it strikes me. He's wanted me right from the start, and *fuck,* I want him more than I've wanted anything for as long as I can remember.

— CHAPTER 18 —

Wednesday, Grigory receives me in the same way in the lobby. I'm not sure why he doesn't ask me to meet him in the rehearsal room. He must know I've come here enough to find my own way. Though I won't ask about it because I don't mind. In fact, I like it a lot. Especially now that he guides me along with a hand on my back and we talk as we walk down the hallways.

Grigory tells me he's brought a piece by Liszt for me—a romance in e-minor—which he thinks will be a good introduction to his music.

"It has the same expressive melancholy as many of the other pieces you've played," he says, giving me a warm smile when I beam with excited anticipation. "I think you'll like it."

Grigory couldn't be more right. The piece is breathtaking—so much so that I find myself welling up as he plays it for me. He plays with such inherent emotion it's impossible not to be touched. And maybe it's also that I'm touched he has found such a beautiful piece for me. It may be a small gesture, but to me it feels like so much more.

We spend most of the time going over the technical details, and when Grigory ends the lesson, I can hardly wait to get home and start on it.

"I have concerts both tomorrow and Friday," Grigory says, standing in the middle of the room with his arms crossed over his chest, watching me as I gather my things. "Next time will be Saturday. I'll meet you in the lobby at four p.m."

Saturday marks the start of tech week—the last week before the premiere, full of all kinds of different final rehearsals. It's the busiest week in the process of setting up an opera, and I wonder why Grigory doesn't cancel. He must be swamped as is.

Remembering the car ride home two days ago, I blink up at him from under lowered lashes, and a hopeful spark takes residence in my chest. Maybe he wants me here as much as I want to be here?

The little kernel of hope grows throughout the next few days. I spend all my time by the piano, driven by an uncontrollable urge to impress him.

Markus comes in a couple of times with a worry-line marring his forehead, asking if I'm okay. I can't blame him. The last time I spent so much time in here, I was angry and hurt, trying to push down a ton of emotions I could barely grasp.

This time, though, it's pure joy that drives me. So every time I flash him a wide smile and tell him how far I've gotten, the line in his forehead fades and he gives me a kiss, leaving me to it with a warm expression in his eyes.

* * *

Early Saturday afternoon, I receive a text from Markus.

Change of plans. Grigory doesn't want you here until eight tonight. Make sure dinner is ready when I get home, so we can eat together before you leave.

I frown. I've never been at the opera so late, and something about this change makes me uneasy. Though, I'm not sure why.

Immersing myself in piano practice the rest of the day, I try not to think about it. But when I step into the large lobby ten minutes to eight, I wish Grigory would have told me to come another day.

A week from today, the new season has kicked off and the building will be buzzing with life in the evenings. But right now, it's dead in here. Only a slight buzz from the city outside reassures me there's life close by. The large space is shrouded in an ominous atmosphere now with the chandeliers off, the only light coming from a few lamps on the walls.

The place feels abandoned, like some creepy old building that incites ghost stories.

A few years ago, being here would have scared the shit out of me. Empty places and being alone in the dark would have such an effect. I'm embarrassed to admit it wasn't just childhood fears. Even the first year after I got my own apartment, I would sleep with the lights on, jumping at every little sound. I tell myself I've gotten over those fears, but now and then I find myself in a situation like this that will stir them up.

Trying to squash them with rationality, I remind myself there are people here. Grigory, at least, must be somewhere, and probably other people too. But they can be anywhere in the enormous building, so the thought does little to soothe me.

My footfalls create a hollow echo as I cross the stone floor to sit on a bench. I take out my book and try to preoccupy myself, but I can't stop glancing around the lobby with an ominous feeling stirring in my stomach.

The minutes tick by at a snail's pace, and when the digits on my phone show it's eight minutes past eight, there's still no sign of Grigory.

I wonder if there has been a misunderstanding? Grigory is always on time.

I put the book away and start pacing. My anxiety is getting hard to ignore, and when it's sixteen minutes past eight, my heart is thumping in my chest. I'm on the verge of bolting out of here, but I decide it's better to call Markus first.

I press his name in my call log and bring the phone to my ear. But right as I hear the first ring, a door opens across the lobby, and I spin around to see Grigory standing at the staff entrance.

He's holding the door open, looking impatient, so I scurry across the room.

I don't get as much as a nod or a hi. He grabs my upper arm and drags me along with hastened steps. But I don't care. I'm just happy he's here and I don't have to walk the empty hallways alone. They are even more creepy than the lobby, darkness swallowing up the silence until you trigger the light sensors.

After irrational fears wreaking havoc on my nerves for almost half an hour, I'm in no mood for talking. Plus, Grigory seems more brusque than usual, so I'm not sure I'd try talking to him even if I hadn't been so wrought up.

When we get to the rehearsal room and start the lesson, I get to feel the brunt of Grigory's mood.

He goes into strict conductor mode, pacing the room with sleeves rolled up as he makes large hand movements.

"Crescendo," he exclaims, singing along to the rising melody.

I try to follow him as well as I can, but his demands are too great. He wants a more lyric melody, larger dynamic contrasts, and more intensity in the mid-section—things you usually save for a more advanced state of learning a piece. Three days is by no means enough to reach such fluency, not even if you bust your ass by the piano as I've done.

Halfway through the lesson, I ask what kind of technique I should use in the mid-section, trying to spur a change of direction. But he writes me off.

"It's fine the way it is," he says and continues down the path he's set out on.

His demands only grow throughout the lesson, and he doesn't even try to hide his dissatisfaction. "No, no, no," he exclaims. "Don't drag the tempo. Play the right hand alone."

It's like he's forgotten he only gave me the piece a few days ago. Or maybe the mighty conductor has suddenly grown tired of working with an amateur like me. Like Liszt himself. He supposedly said he didn't want to work on technique with his students. They could attend the conservatory to learn such basics.

A feeling of inferiority stabs through me. A man like Grigory should spend his time teaching professional pianists who can live up to his demands.

The feeling lingers throughout the rest of the lesson, and when Grigory finally lets me leave a little past nine, exhaustion is a heavy burden on my mind and body.

I try to shake off his cold behavior by telling myself he has probably just had a bad day. But it's not much help. A bad day doesn't justify such behavior, and he affects me too deeply for me to write it off so easily.

The way he acted was hurtful, really, and I feel so beat I don't want to return on Monday like he has asked me to—or rather, ordered.

When I get home, I ask Markus if Grigory is okay, saying he seemed restless.

"It's been one of those days where everything goes wrong," Markus explains. "Costumes that aren't done on time, people who have received wrong information, a sick obo-player and no replacement. He's probably just stressed."

"Doesn't he have people to fix those things?"

"He does. But I think some of the positions at the opera need rehiring. Unfortunately, communication problems are the order of things in this house. The last conductor didn't bother with much else but the music. I think it's one of the reasons they wanted Grigory so badly—he's known to get involved with every part of the process and won't settle for less than perfect."

I remember them talking about this last Sunday when Grigory came here, so it makes sense. But it's hard being around him when he's so closed off.

"Maybe we should take a break with the piano lessons until the premiere is over?" I suggest, although a bit reluctantly.

"It might be a good idea. I'll talk to him tomorrow."

But when Markus comes home the next day, he tells me I am

to show up as planned Monday evening.

"Did he work out the coordination problems?" I ask.

"Unfortunately not yet," Markus says, then adds with a smile, "but I think your piano lessons give him a break from all the stress."

Or rather a stress outlet, I want to say.

I must have frowned because Markus grabs me by the shoulders and studies me closely. "Is everything okay? Did something happen?"

I consider telling him about the lesson, but as I watch closely, I notice Markus looks tired. Maybe the problems affect him too. So I shake my head and smile. "It's fine." And it really is. I can handle Grigory having a bad day.

* * *

But it's not just one bad day. Grigory is brusque and closed off again Monday night. He drags me down the hallways with a bruising grip on my arm, and after having released me by the piano, he doesn't touch me again for a long while. Not even with his baton.

He walks around the room while I play, swinging his arms like he's conducting a vigorous piece of music, hurling verbal reprimands my way.

"It says *piu agitato,* not *piu lethargico,*" he exclaims when I play the mid-section of the Liszt piece.

I get a sense he's using the lesson as an outlet for frustrations that have built up during the last couple of days. I don't think it's personal, but the thought is as good as a Band-Aid on an open wound. Being used like this hurts, and his verbal outbursts cut into my submissive soul like a searing knife.

A few good lessons were all I got before he put his walls back up.

I do my best at the piano—and I'm convinced I'm doing a pretty great job, considering I've barely had the piece for a week. But like with the Rachmaninoff piece, there's no recognition for my hard work. He demands a degree of detail that is entirely unrealistic at this point, and his frustration grows with every slip I make.

My hands start trembling and slipping on the keys. It gets so bad that he stops me and flips through the sheet music in my folder with an angry frown on his brow. Then he slams another set of pages up on the music stand and steps back into the middle of the room, rolling up his sleeves.

"Play," he orders.

The piece in front of me is one I know well, and when we worked on it a few weeks ago, he seemed satisfied. But there's no satisfying him today; he keeps pushing me to bring out more expression.

I grow more and more discouraged, playing worse and worse, and as a result Grigory becomes still more frustrated.

He comes up behind me, tugs my hair behind my shoulders, and snakes his broad hand around the front of my neck. He doesn't press, but the threat is there, right against my windpipe, and I can feel my pulse throbbing against the collar of his hand.

"I want to hear the yearning and frustration. Like it's the last time you get to stroke the keys." His words are a dangerous threat, like the hand around my neck.

I remember sitting here and wishing I could lean back against him and feel more than his hands. But not like this. Not with this rage radiating off him. Not with his hand wrapped around my throat.

His voice becomes a sneer against my ear as he leans in. "I want to hear you play like it's the last thing you do before I take your breath."

What the fuck? My hands fly up to pull at his wrist, but he only tightens his grip. The heel of his hand presses into my windpipe, his fingers squeezing the sides of my neck, and it gets harder to breathe as the pressure builds in my head.

I scratch at his hand, trying to grab onto it and relieve the pressure, but he's too strong. And when he growls a low, "Don't," right into my ear, I stop.

My hands fall into my lap, the fight seeping from my limbs. My instincts know no logic or self-preservation with this man. They only know obedience.

He pulls in a sharp breath, mocking me with the fact that I can't do the same. Or maybe he gets off on this?

Fear pulses in my veins, but I'm not sure that's all. I'm not sure the pounding of my heart isn't as much fucked up arousal as rising panic.

I let out a tiny whimper—the sound of helplessness. Grigory responds with a low rumble as he tightens his grip, cutting off my air.

Panic builds, angry red colors and sharp fear overriding everything else. I heave for air but only manage a small wheeze. I heave again. Still nothing. So I claw at his hand, nails digging into skin. Still no air.

I'm about to burst into full-on fight mode when the hand disappears. Air expands my chest painfully as I heave in an all too large gulp.

"Play!" Grigory's hard command jolts me from my panic like an electric shock.

It doesn't matter that he plays mind games on me, cuts off my air, and humiliates me. There's no way I can disobey him.

So I lift my hands to the keys and play—with everything I have.

Grigory remains behind me, his forceful energy burning into my flesh. I want him gone, and I want him closer. But I can't have either, so I let all the anger and yearning seep through my fingers and transform into the most deep-felt music I've ever played.

When I lift my fingers from the keys, I feel raw and exposed. Somehow, opening myself up to him through the music is more vulnerable than letting him rip me apart until I sob and cling to him.

"That's it," Grigory's massive hand slams into the piano. "Not even Andrei Kovalev can manage such depth of emotion."

It should be a complement of grand proportions, comparing me to one of the world's best pianists, but it feels like an admonishment.

He fists my hair and pulls my face back, so I stare straight up into his dilated pupils. "Same time tomorrow. I want to hear you play like this again."

Then he releases my hair and leaves the room.

Is that it? Are we done? Or will he come back?

I stare blankly at the open door, listening for the click of his square heels. But they never return. There's nothing but jarring silence—and my heart that beats like the frantic wings of a caged bird.

I have no idea how much time passes before I finally rise from the bench, gather my things, and walk into the hallway. My feet are heavy, my body numb, and the only thought swirling through my tattered mind is that I won't be able to meet his demands tomorrow. I simply don't have it in me—he's torn it all out.

When I get home, Markus also seems to have had another rough day, so I try to plaster on a smile, not wanting to worry him. But it's far from genuine, and he sees right through it like he always does.

He comes into the kitchen while I'm cutting carrot sticks by the kitchen island. Propping his hip against the counter beside me, he asks, "What's eating at you, sweetie? Has something happened in the lesson?"

I bite my lips together. Grigory might have grabbed my throat, but he usually hits me, so it doesn't seem like a big deal. But it's not just that he grabbed my throat—it's the way he did it. It's the lack of touch and comfort. It's his cold distance. But how can I tell him without sounding needy? I don't want to make a big fuss about it, so I keep my eyes trained on the task before me and shake my head. "Everything's good."

The moment the words leave me, I want to hit myself over the head. I always tell Markus what's going on, but I'm so confused I don't know how to cope with these feelings even though the answer is right here in front of me.

"Are you sure?" he says.

He seems concerned, but I still can't make myself tell him what's happened. The memory is too humiliating to let it out in the open. So I nod and say, "I'm just tired. You know, he has high demands and it takes a lot of focus to keep up."

"Yeah, tell me about it. The rehearsal today wasn't exactly a walk in the park. But everything came together so much better in the end."

For a moment, the memory of Grigory's cold distance fades as I remember how I played at the end of the lesson. I put the knife on the cutting board and turn to face Markus. "He really knows how to get the best out of people." At least when it comes to music.

"He does, but it's only because the potential is already there." He strokes his knuckles over my cheek with a look of tender pride, and it's clear it's me he's talking about. "You know, it's not just because he gets to discipline you that he likes your lessons."

I remember how Grigory compared me to Andrei Kovalev today, and the bad things surrounding the compliment fades for a moment.

My eyes flutter down, and I smile shyly as Grigory's words play through my mind. Looking back up, I say, "Grigory compared me to Andrei Kovalev today."

Markus's lips spread out in a bright smile. "Did he now?"

"He said he couldn't even play like I did." I can barely believe I'm remembering correct as I hear myself say the words, but the memory is clear as day, and despite Grigory's reproachful façade, he must have meant it. Grigory never throws around idle compliments.

Markus leans down to kiss me and holds my chin when he pulls back to say, "I'm so proud of you, sweetie."

I feel it too, the pride radiating from his eyes, and I allow myself to bask in this moment and enjoy the high compliment I couldn't enjoy earlier today.

Why couldn't Grigory make me feel like this?

"How about some yellow crazies?" Markus asks, wagging his brows enthusiastically. "I think we could both use some TV time tonight."

I nod my head eagerly. "Definitely."

The feeling of being rejected doesn't go away, but it wanes as I bring dinner to the living room ten minutes later and settle on the couch beside Markus to watch some crazy minions until we both are about to fall asleep against each other.

* * *

Grigory is relentless the following night. He keeps pushing me, demanding more emotion—or maybe demanding any emotion at all?

I feel numb, unable to feel my fingers or the music, and with every hard reprimand I get, I retreat further into myself.

Grigory growls with frustration. "This isn't working," he exclaims as I'm playing.

With a startled jump, I rip my hands from the keys. For a second, I think he's going to end the lesson as he just watches me, and I feel a gush of relief.

But the next moment he's at my side, pulling me up with a bruising grip on my arm. A hard yank turns me around, making me lose my footing. Then he shoves me over the bench, and before I know it, my head hangs toward the floor, my ass sticking in the air.

Frantically, I try to push up, but his hand is already a vise against my back. I achieve no more than flailing my arms and whipping my head back. Another large hand shoves up under my skirt, pulling my panties and stockings down in one tug.

Panic wraps around my lungs, spiking hard when I reach back for my panties and end up with my hands pinned to my back.

"Please," I beg. "Wha..."

My words die when three hard smacks collide with my right cheek, followed by three more on the other. Fire bursts through my nether region, shock screeching through my system.

Grigory steps back, leaving me hanging over the bench, alone and exposed.

I scramble to get up and cover myself, drying away a few stray tears rolling down my cheeks.

"Sit," Grigory orders before I barely have my clothes adjusted.

My ass burns when I sink onto the padded bench, and I'm quivering all over.

"Stop thinking and play!" Grigory commands.

I don't know what happens. His degrading brutality is a fist around my neck, but at the same time, those six blows have forced all thoughts from my head, and his demanding tone snaps my focus into place. Like yesterday, my body obeys him, leaving me shocked as my fingers dance over the black and white keys.

I play like it's the only thing left in the world. My breath synchronizes with the rising and falling melodies, and all my feelings seep through my fingers, breathing life into the notes. I feel removed from myself, yet more present than I've ever been. Like I'm reduced to the movement of my fingers and the music they make.

Grigory makes me play the piece over and over until he's finally satisfied.

"That's it for today," he says with an impassive tone.

Hurriedly, I gather my sheet music in a pile on my folder, stacking my cardigan and bag on top of it.

Thoughts seep back into my head in one big muddy cocktail of confusion, anger, and sadness. A small sliver of pride. But most of all, longing. I long for Grigory to pull me into his strong arms and hold me, whisper reassuring words and tell me everything's okay.

Glancing up at him, I nearly drop my things to run into his arms. But my head kicks into gear again before I go through with it and risk a harsh rejection, which would make everything worse.

Grigory is facing the window, rolling down his sleeves and combing back his hair, and he doesn't send a single glance my way. So I hurry out of the room, devastated by his cold distance.

With hasty steps, I make my way down the empty hallway, and when I see the bathroom sign, I set into a run. I lock myself up in a booth and fall back against the door, squeezing my eyes shut to keep the tears from spilling. There I stay until I have enough control over myself to not feel like I'll combust any second.

I manage to keep myself together on my way home, but as soon as I step into Markus's apartment, I break down.

I scurry through the living room and into the bedroom with tears streaming down my cheeks, hoping Markus won't catch me in this state. Luckily, I make it to the bed without seeing him. But I know it's only a matter of minutes before he'll come to seek me out. I haven't greeted him like I'm supposed to, and it would take a miracle to get a grip on myself before he comes.

As I expected, only a few minutes pass before I hear footsteps outside the door. I'm curled up on the bed, sobbing uncontrollably. There's nothing I can do to stop it when I hear Markus approach and feel the mattress dipping.

"What's the matter, sweetie?" Concern hangs heavy in his words as he pulls me up into his arms. "Did something happen with Grigory? You were sad last night too."

I confirm with a nod, unable to get any words past the sobs racking my body.

Only when the crying at long last slows can I tell him what happened in the last two lessons—the choking, the spanking, the verbal strikes, and not least, the lack of comfort.

When I've finished, he remains silent. It's not like him, so I look up to find his features taut.

"That's not okay at all," he says gravely. "He should have taken care of you."

A month ago, I would be astounded he doesn't react to Grigory's harsh way of treating me—only the lack of comfort—but with all that's happened since I met Grigory, it kind of makes sense.

Markus pulls me to him again and holds me close. "It's not okay," he repeats, and I can feel the anger in his tight arms. "I'll make sure he fixes this."

It helps to be held like this, but it's not enough to shake Grigory's cold demeanor, and I feel unwanted and alone even though I'm clearly anything but here in Markus's arms.

— CHAPTER 19 —

I wake up feeling despondent, and Markus has to use a strict tone to get me out of bed before leaving. But as soon as he's gone, I'm back beneath the covers with the blinds drawn.

The darkness weaves around me, making the world small and manageable.

A few times I venture into the living room and try to watch some TV, but the sunlight pervading the room is sharp on my eyes and reminds me there's an entire world outside. So I retreat back into the safety of the dark bedroom.

Markus calls a couple of hours after he's left, and his concern for me is palpable through the phone. "Have you had anything to eat?"

I shake my head, and he has to repeat the question to get a monosyllabic answer out of me.

"Go grab something as soon as we hang up and then go take a warm shower." It's his firm tone that leaves nothing up for discussion, so when we hang up, I go to the kitchen with bare feet and a thin cardigan wrapped around my half-naked body.

I stare into the fridge for several minutes despite the cold air making me quiver. There's nothing I want to eat here, so I end up closing the door and grab an orange and a handful of almonds.

Once in the shower, the warm spray is soothing on my tense body. I stare into the white tile as the water runs through my hair, making it stick to my shoulders, then over my naked skin before reaching the drain where it swirls a couple of times before disappearing. It keeps going and going, making the same journey again and again.

At some point my legs tire of holding me up and I lean back against the chilly tile and glide to the floor.

Without warning, tears start seeping from my eyes. I'm not sure where they come from or why they fall. But they won't go away again. Like the water, they keep falling and falling.

If someone saw me, they probably wouldn't notice I'm crying. There's no sobbing or sniffling, only tears merging with the water from above. But my state of mind would be easy to read from the way I hug my legs and rock myself.

The water hammers against the tile, filling the otherwise deafening silence. Only a single sniffle breaks the constant sound once in a while, reminding me the world hasn't stopped moving. It's only me.

I have no sense of time, no idea how long I remain like this. It feels like an eternity, but when I leave the steam-ridden bathroom and sink back under the covers, it's barely eleven.

Time moves on broken legs as I lie here staring into the darkness, cursing the yellow edges of light around the blinds. I should do something. Anything. Play the piano, read a book, listen to some music—somehow break free from this paralysis that has seized me. But I can't make myself move.

When Markus calls in the afternoon, trying to get me out of bed, all he achieves is me crying on the other end of the line. *That* I do quite ardently, however, sobbing loudly, apologizing on pitiful whimpers. When he gently tries to nudge me by suggesting I watch TV or go for a walk, it only gets worse.

He ends up backing down with a sigh. "At least try to get some sleep," he says before he has to go.

But I can't sleep either, and instead, I alternate between crying and staring into the dark room.

He didn't ask me why I'm so devastated, only told me it was okay and he was there for me. I'm relieved he didn't, because even if I tried, I couldn't give him an explanation. There are no thoughts in my head—no anger or sadness directed anywhere. Just a painfully dark void.

* * *

When I hear the front door open early in the evening, I'm still lying in bed, crying for the hundredth time. More than anything, I want to be alone. I can't handle the inevitable inquisition about my mood, which I've been waiting for all day.

Footfalls sound outside the bedroom, and I pull the covers over my head when the door opens, light encroaching upon the darkness. Keeping dead still, I tighten every muscle to keep my crying in check. Hopefully, he'll leave if he thinks I'm sleeping.

Hard heels click over the hardwood floor, and I hold my breath as the bed sinks behind me. Carefully, he pulls the covers from my face, and gentle knuckles stroke my wet cheek.

I pull in a sharp breath. It's not Markus.

I'd recognize this hand anytime, no matter how light the touch.

It's Grigory.

His hand is much larger than Markus's, but the size is not what gives him away. It's the devastating tenderness of his touch that I've never felt the likes of before.

Caresses are often fleeting. Impatient. But when Grigory touches me, it feels like he has all the time in the world. It's like he could keep comforting me for hours without tiring.

It's heartbreaking. Because I know it's a hoax. I know the fleeting reality of his touch. Soon it will be gone, his cold distance the only thing that lingers.

I quiver with the effort of holding back the tears. It was hard when I thought Markus was here, but Grigory's presence is fuel to the flame—a turbulent wind that drags up all my carefully restrained emotions.

"Shh, *devochka*," he whispers, and what's meant as a reassurance hits me as mockery. It's not enough. I need more, yet I need less—for him to go. I hate that he's only here when it all snaps, and I hate that he sees me like this. I'm not crying and sniveling, but my wet cheek and shaking body say it all—not to mention the fact that I'm lying here in the dark this early in the evening.

Removing his hand, he rises from the bed, and that's when I crumble.

A desolate sob rips from my throat, opening the floodgate to an endless stream of tears.

He just came, and now he's leaving?

My chest tightens painfully, and my muscles lock into a cramp-like state as I curl around myself, hugging my legs to my chest and crying into my knees.

He'll probably get Markus now because he doesn't want to handle this sobbing mess I am. It's so humiliating.

I wait for the devastating sound of footsteps leaving.

But it never comes.

Instead, I hear the rustle of fabric—a jacket being removed? Then the faint clicks of shoes being placed on the floor. The mattress sinks again and Grigory lifts the covers to crawl in behind me. Without hesitation, he pulls me to him like it's his right.

Fury and longing crash together in one big storm. The memory of his sharp words and closed-off distance cut through my mind—being left alone and desperately needing his calming touch.

I need it now too, but I'm too hurt and angry to accept his comfort. So I pull away.

Emptiness shoots through me the moment I lose the connection, and my sobs become ugly sounds that have me heaving for air.

He pulls me back to him and locks me into the vise of his arms and legs, rendering my struggles useless. There's no give, and my need to feel him soon drowns out my stubbornness, and the fight slowly dwindles.

"It's okay. I'm here now," he whispers, kissing my temple.

His gentle care makes me so weak. My defenses crumble and I meld in his embrace in utter surrender. There's no way for me to resist.

Grigory neither seems surprised nor spooked by my condition. He just holds me as I cry out all my pent-up frustration, anger, and longing that have accumulated over the last few days—or maybe longer. Perhaps it all started with the punishment in Markus's music room? Or even the first time I met him? I don't know. He makes me so confused.

One thing is for sure though. This means a whole lot more than I could have ever predicted.

Sobs shake my body and rip ugly sounds up through my throat, but I no longer feel like I'm being torn apart. Not when Grigory holds me. He holds it all together so I can fall apart without breaking.

I lie here, shaking and crying in his arms as he whispers soothing words and every so often strokes the hair from my face.

But the fierce grip of his arms is at odds with his gentleness. It's not a normal, relaxed embrace. He's actively holding onto me like he's trying to subdue me. But I've stopped fighting long ago and am now only clinging to him. It's something else. Like he knows I need his strength so I won't feel like I'm slipping away into nothingness. Like he knows how safe it makes me, knowing he's strong enough to protect me.

Or maybe it's because he needs this as much as I do?

It's a surreal thought which I normally wouldn't dare to dwell on. But I need it to calm myself, so I let the hope fill me as I squeeze closer to him, feeling the broadness of his chest and the welcoming warmth of his body.

It takes a long while before my crying stops, but at no point do I feel like Grigory is trying to hurry it along. He gives me the time I need.

When I'm out of tears, I'm empty. But no longer alone and abandoned. It's a freedom to let go, and I lie limp and lifeless, yet peaceful, in his arms.

Grigory slides his hand under my camisole, splaying it on my stomach, and it's only now I realize how little clothes I'm wearing. Panties and a top. That's it.

Momentarily I tense up, startled by the intimacy—afraid he'll take advantage of the moment.

But the hand just rests there. He's not trying to feel me up or make this into something sexual. Of course, he isn't. This is Grigory. He might tear me apart emotionally and wield his dominance like a cruel power over me, but he hasn't once tried to use it for sexual purposes.

I trust him in that way—to not cross the lines Markus has set.

The realization makes me sink into him. I want his warm hand on my stomach more than anything. It sucks out the tension twisting in my belly and soothes the nervous prickle in my skin.

I wonder how it would feel if he removed our clothes and pressed his bare chest against my back.

The thought makes my back arch, my hips sway back. Just an inch. It's a discreet motion, but enough for my ass to press against him—and realize he's erect.

I startle in surprise, and his hand presses against my lower stomach like he doesn't want me to pull away.

I stop breathing for a moment. Feeling him like this is torture of the sweetest kind. It sets up a simmering heat deep within my core and makes my nerve endings prickle to life. I want him—so badly it hurts. But I can't.

Grigory's breathing has become heavy like mine, ruffling the hair on my shoulder.

"God, Clara. You don't make it easy," he says, holding his hand firmly to my stomach to keep my butt connected to his erection.

"What?" Something about the way he says it makes me think he's not just talking about this sexual tension between us.

He nuzzles his nose against my neck with surprising affection and whispers, "Staying away."

My breath stutters, and I'm not sure if it's the tickling sensation on my neck or hearing that he tries to stay away from me.

Why is it so important to stay away?

The darkness shuts us inside our own little secret world, allowing us to say the things that are too intimate or vulnerable to say in the light of day.

"Is it because I'm with Markus?" I ask. "Because you don't want to share?" I feel almost hopeful as I ask the last part, but then I remember I don't want him to be averse to sharing because then we can't keep seeing each other.

Grigory's voice becomes dangerously low. "If I have to share to get you at my feet, I'll share."

A moan slips past my lips and I arch back into him. He's clearly not happy about sharing, but he'll do it anyway because he wants my submission—badly maybe even. It almost seems too good to be true, but I allow myself to believe it here in the darkness.

"Relax your hips, *devochka*, or I'll have to leave."

I stiffen as I realize I'm all but grinding against the hard length straining behind his pants. "I'm sorry," I say.

Grigory lets out a hushed chuckle. "Me too."

Relaxing my hips, I ease the pressure on his cock. God, I want this man in so many more ways than I could have ever imagined, and it's painful to lie here and feel the need reciprocated and not being able to do anything about it.

Trying to distract myself, I return to the unfinished conversation. "If it's not Markus, then why do you need to stay away?"

Grigory sighs like he's about to admit something personal. "I didn't want another sub."

"Why?" I ask, for once comfortable enough to prod.

"It's a long story," he says with a note of defeat that sounds so foreign in his voice.

I consider asking if it has something to do with his ex—or maybe exes—but when Grigory starts stroking his hand in slow circles on my stomach, I realize how depleted I am. Suddenly the mere action of forming a few words seems like a huge task.

"Try to get some sleep," he whispers.

It's not a difficult order to obey. My limbs go heavy, my mind blurry, and within minutes I'm drifting off into peaceful sleep in the safe cocoon of Grigory's arms.

* * *

I wake up in an empty bed in a pitch-black room. Even the yellow lines around the blinds have faded, and suddenly I miss the reminder that there's life and light outside. The darkness no longer feels safe. It's lonely and stifling.

I sit up on the bed, feeling foggy and sluggish.

Grigory was here. He lay behind me and held me while I cried. Then he caressed my stomach until I fell asleep.

Didn't he?

I can clearly recall the feeling of his body pressed against mine, but I'm not sure it was more than a vivid dream.

He was here, wasn't he?

I can hardly believe it, but the echo of his touch is too real. It couldn't have been a dream.

Disoriented, I stagger through the dark room with a rapidly growing lump in my throat. I'm not sure what's worse, finding out he was never here or he was here and left me again.

I tremble, partly due to the chilly air and partly due to the exhaustion lingering in my body.

The muffled sound of the TV seeps in through the door, but I don't hear any voices so I prepare for disappointment as I grab the handle and push the door open.

Light assaults my senses, and I blink toward the sofa where I see two figures.

Rubbing my puffy eyes, I look again.

There he is. Lounging on the sofa, feet on the coffee table, watching TV. Calm and confident as always. Markus is at the other end of the couch, but I don't see him. I only see Grigory.

Barely able to believe my own eyes, I stare at Grigory, afraid he'll disappear if I look away.

I have to bite my lip to hide its quivering, and I'm about to break into new tears from pure relief.

Lazily dragging his eyes from the screen, he watches me with his characteristic set of stern features which are impossible to read. Has he retreated again? Is he still caring? Or impassive? Time stops as I wait to find out.

With fluid motions, he gets up and walks to me, one stride at a time until he's finally here, right before me.

I can't hide anything. All my emotions are painted in vivid colors across my face as I stare up at him with wide, teary eyes.

He can have it all if he wants, or he can throw it away and break me in the blink of an eye. There's no in-between, and I can do nothing to help or hinder. It's all up to him.

He watches me with an intent gaze that has become no easier to decode after more than a month of knowing him. I want to yell at him. *Do something! Make a decision!* But I can't. I remain breathless like a defendant awaiting a verdict.

Finally, it comes. He reaches out his arm and pulls me to him. I sag against his chest, releasing a heavy sigh as I cling to him. It's all or nothing. I can't hold back.

I shake in his embrace, my arms squeezed together between our bodies like I'm afraid the monsters will take them if I release them into the open. I feel like a child being comforted after a nightmare.

But there was no nightmare, no dream. He's actually here—very real as his breath stirs my hair, his lips pressing kisses to the top of my head. His white shirt is just as real with its smooth fabric which I've felt many times before and come to associate with him, and the steady beating of his heart is calm and vivid against my ear.

Slipping a slow hand around my waist, he guides me to the couch and places me where he sat. Then he goes to the other end and takes the blanket Markus hands him. I follow him with my eyes the whole way, afraid he'll disappear if I don't.

Grigory folds the blanket around my shoulders, then takes a seat beside me and tugs me into his side.

I have barely glanced at Markus since I blinked against the light, and right now I'm too desperate for Grigory's touch to feel bad about it. Grigory has given me a small opening, and I rush straight in and take all I can get. I'm running on pure survival instinct, and Grigory is the only one who can keep my lungs from collapsing under the heavy weight in my chest.

So I lean my head against him, curling my hand around the white fabric.

Normally, I would take it slower, test the waters. But not today. And what is *normal* with this man anyway? The first time I was alone with him, he hit me and forced his dominance upon me, and since then it's been a never-ending series of pushing and breaking my boundaries. So what if it's me who, for once, acts in total disregard of norms and polite restraint?

I make myself sound braver than I am, because really, I'm only so carefree because Grigory doesn't seem to frown upon my clinginess. He barely even seems surprised at how I hold onto him. He simply looks down at me and places a kiss on my head, then returns his attention to the crime series on the TV, seemingly wholly unbothered by my extreme behavior.

Despite his immediate focus being elsewhere, he clearly hasn't forgotten me. I feel it in the way his arm tightens around me every so often, the small, reflexive kisses on my head, and the sporadic caresses. It seems unconscious, like his need to take care of me is almost as instinctive as my need to feel him. *Could it be?*

It's been a long time since I felt such a sense of belonging as I do in his arms, and if someone tried to take me away, I would kick and scream like a crazy person. I need him. The mere thought of losing him again makes my chest hurt. The thought festers, reminding me how lonely it felt when he left me alone in the rehearsal room—left me alone on the piano bench after hitting me. The memories are like a python slithering around me, slowly constricting my lungs.

I let out a gasp when I realize how tight my chest suddenly is.

"Breathe, *devochka*," Grigory murmurs into my hair as he tightens his arms around me.

It becomes both easier and harder to breathe. But I don't mind the latter when it's Grigory's arms restricting my breath. I bury my head in his shoulder, inhaling his masculine scent, once again overcome by the relief of feeling him.

We sit here watching TV for a long time. No one speaks, and I get a feeling it's what we all need. We've all had a long week in our own way. I've struggled fruitlessly to please Grigory and am emotionally drained. The two men have worked hard on the show, which premieres in two days, and there has clearly been a lot of pressure this week.

Now, they both finally seem to relax. Markus sits, half lies, on the chaise lounge, his head resting on the back of the sofa as he watches the TV with heavy eyelids. Grigory has made himself comfortable with his feet on the coffee table, his body angled to me as he holds me close. He seems less closed-off than usual—calm in a way I rarely see him. It's like he has eased up on the inhuman self-control, which is as much a barrier as an impressive force field.

My eyes fall to his socks. Today they are midnight blue with vertical lines of white and light blue dots. They still aren't exuberant, but compared to the rest of his attire, they are lively. As I sit here with my head leaned against his chest, studying his socks, I have a feeling I get to see a bit more of him than everybody else.

It seems illogical since I often feel like I don't know him at all and he keeps pulling away from me.

But then there are moments like this when I feel the closeness on some level that doesn't require words or tons of information—maybe even closer than words can bring me. It's like I know him in a way more intimate than knowing his favorite color or how he grew up. Like I get more direct access to the deeper layers when he tightens his arms around me and gently kisses my hair—showing me a kind of affection that is entirely at odds with the strict exterior he meets the rest of the world with.

Or maybe he meets other people with a similar kind of care? After all, I haven't seen him interact with enough people to know. It's hard to imagine though.

Markus breaks me out of my thoughts. "Are you guys

hungry?" he asks, lazily turning his head toward us.

I shake my head, for the first time meeting his eyes.

"How much have you eaten today, Clara?"

When I feel Grigory watch me too, I shrink, the weight of all the attention too much to bear.

"An orange and a handful of almonds," I mutter, catching the concerned pinch of Markus's brows before burying my face against Grigory's chest.

Grigory doesn't comment on my worrisome lack of appetite, but responds by stroking my hair and squeezing me to him.

"Burger and fries?" Markus's question is not directed at me, but the worry for me lingers in his tone.

I feel Grigory's nod, and then I hear Markus's voice as he calls up a takeaway place.

When the food arrives, Markus unpacks the brown paper bag on the coffee table and tries to entice a burger into my hand. But I refuse to loosen my grip on Grigory to take it.

"You have to eat something," he says with a sigh.

I shake my head. *I'm not hungry.*

Markus looks to Grigory with a question in his eyes, then returns to the chaise lounge with his food. It hurts to disappoint him like this, and suddenly I feel wrong and sad again.

I want to change my mind and ask for a burger, but I can't feel my stomach and I can't bear to let go of Grigory—not even to eat. So I remain frozen while gradually slipping further down the dismal slope.

Grigory shifts into a position that allows him to eat while still holding me. It doesn't take long before he too attempts to feed me, holding a French fry up to my mouth. But I'm stuck in my refusal and shake my head even as the knot in my belly grows.

A minute later, another French fry comes to my mouth, this time along with a firm command. "Eat."

I can't bear to disobey him, so I hesitantly open my mouth and take the fry.

It tastes bland at first, but as I keep chewing, I realize how hungry I am. It's like my stomach is waking from several days of hibernation, and the next time Grigory holds a fry to my mouth, I eagerly take it. I'm almost embarrassed about my eagerness after having rejected several times, and I'm grateful no one comments on my sudden shift.

A few French fries later, Grigory holds his burger up for me to take a bite. Luckily, he doesn't try to hand me my own—my hunger still can't compete with my need to hold onto him. So I gratefully eat when he keeps alternating between feeding me and eating himself. Before long, we have consumed two burgers and two portions of fries like this.

At some point, I look at Markus and see him watching me with an amused smile as if saying *gotcha.* I lower my eyes, feeling blood gather in my cheeks. But I can't help looking up again, and this time with a smile.

It's strange sitting here, curled up against Grigory while Markus lounges at the other end of the sofa. On some level, I feel bad about being so obvious about my need for another man. But the small exchange with Markus reassures me enough to let my guilt slide and remain snuggled against Grigory.

— CHAPTER 20 —

The day before the premiere is dark Thursday. Everyone rests before the big day, and it's both needed and deserved.

Grigory told me to take the day off too, so Markus and I continue in the same vein as last night, watching TV and ordering in—the only exception being I'm now curled up against Markus since Grigory isn't here.

Unlike Markus, I haven't been working hard, but I still need this break. I'm exhausted after all the emotional turmoil, and even though it helped to see Grigory last night, I still haven't fully recovered from everything. On top of it, I'm shocked by my broken state yesterday. It seemed wholly excessive.

I know it must have been a reaction to Grigory's cold distance, but a few terrible lessons shouldn't be enough to break me? I might be prone to intense emotions—good and bad—but I don't think I've ever reacted so out of proportion to anything before.

On the other hand, Grigory has an uncanny tendency to push me to the edge. The last month has been a rollercoaster of highs and lows, so maybe I shouldn't be so surprised.

Markus seems to find my breakdown quite natural. He

concurs the harsh piano lessons are the cause, and when I voice my concern for how extreme it was, he says, "Remember, we *are* playing with some extreme dynamics."

Grigory also didn't seem taken aback. I was sure my meltdown would be more than he'd like to take on. After all, I'm not his, so it would only have been natural if he'd let Markus take over, or at least included him. It would have hurt terribly, but I would have understood.

Instead, Grigory remained perfectly calm when I broke into ugly sobs. He even crawled into bed with me and let me bawl my eyes out in his arms. Not even my fight deterred him. Then he stayed the rest of the night, letting me cling to him like my life depended on it until I fell asleep in his arms.

I don't get him. Whenever something intimate happens, he pulls away, suggesting he can't handle intimacy or doesn't care about me. At other times, everything points in the opposite direction and he makes me feel cherished and cared for. He can be more gentle than anyone I've ever met and this kind of intimacy can't be forced.

My head hurts trying to figure him out. It's not what I need right now, so I shove away the confusing contemplation to focus on being here with Markus.

Though soon, Markus directs my thoughts back to Grigory. "It seems to have helped to see Grigory last night?" he asks as the squirrel in *Ice Age* chases its acorn.

I nod, wishing Grigory was here today. But of course, I don't say it.

"Good. I'm glad to hear," he says genuinely, then turns back to the TV.

It still takes me aback how much Markus takes care of me. He must have been the one to arrange for Grigory to come over last night, and I wouldn't be surprised if he had confronted Grigory head-on, telling him to fix things. Markus might be one of the most easygoing and diplomatic people I know, but he won't hesitate to call someone out if need be.

It's hard to imagine Grigory receiving such critique without shooting his adversary down with an arrogant rejection. But it seems like there's a mutual respect between the two men, and I think Grigory actually listens to Markus.

I find it strange that Markus has to intervene to make Grigory mend his own mistakes. Grigory has plenty of willpower on his own. Yet, this is the second time Markus made Grigory come over after several days of cold distance.

It would be easy to think Grigory only wants the dominance and violence of it all and only comes over out of some sense of duty to Markus. But then I think about the way he held me last night and the things he said, and the idea dissipates.

Nothing makes sense about that man.

When Markus and I are lounging on the couch after our second movie, I try to gain some information to help put together the puzzle. "How long have you known Grigory?" I start. I know they've been friends quite a few years but haven't heard the full story.

Markus considers for a moment. "Seven, maybe eight years. The first time I met him, I was singing one of the minor roles in *La Bohème* in München. Grigory thought I should have been the lead, and you know Grigory. He makes things happen. So when the production was revived a couple of years later, I was singing Rodolfo." He says the last part with a wide smirk, clearly proud about the role, which must have been one of his first big ones.

"Was that how you became friends?"

"Well, we hit it off from the start and met up whenever we were in the same city. When I sang Rodolfo, we were already good friends. We have a lot to talk about, even besides music. Like our shared interest in hitting women."

His suggestive look makes me smile shyly.

"We've helped each other through some rough times," he goes on. "Grigory has supported me through the ups and downs of my career, helped me land big roles and gain contacts. Plus, he's always been good at putting things into perspective, even with relationships." He goes quiet for a moment, his eyes distant. "And he was there for me when I lost my dad."

Markus was close to his dad, who died from aggressive lung cancer some years before we met. It happened very suddenly. The man had gone to the doctor with a small cough, and three months later he was dead.

Markus often becomes distant like this whenever he talks about it. I wish I had known him back then so I too could have been there for him. But I'm glad he at least had a good friend.

I take his hand and we sit in silence for a few minutes before Markus heaves a sigh and continues.

"A year later, I returned the favor when Grigory went through a bad breakup. I think I was the one who stopped him from withdrawing from his impressive career and let it all crumble around him."

"Grigory? Dropping everything?" I think I'm half gaping. *Are we even talking about the same man?*

"Yeah, it was pretty bad. He has this secluded house in a Russian forest, which he went to. I thought he just needed a couple of weeks away from everything, but then I heard he was about to walk out on his contract with the opera in Vienna." Markus makes a wry expression. "I could barely get to him because of all the damned snow in that forest."

This must be because of the woman Markus told me about a few weeks ago after Grigory had shut off the first time. What was her name…? Magdalena, I think. He's only mentioned her once, but the name stuck since something bad clearly happened between her and Grigory.

I badly want to ask about it, but like a few weeks ago, Markus is clearly not going to divulge more information. Just talking about this has darkened his entire demeanor. So instead of pressing on and risking him getting irritated, I change the subject.

"Have you ever shared a submissive with him before?" I remember Markus once telling me he and Grigory had been dominating together at BDSM clubs, but I don't know if it has ever been for more than one night.

"A couple of random women we've met at BDSM clubs and a sub he was seeing a while back."

"So, not any of your former submissives?"

"Clara, I've only had two long-term submissives before you, and I'm not sure either of them truly classified as submissive. At least not outside the bedroom." He lifts a hand to stroke my cheek. "You're the first woman I've seen Grigory show any kind of interest in since his break-up two years ago."

"Really?"

"Yeah, he's grown quite lackluster in that department. A few one-night stands here and there. I'm not sure he even goes for submissives anymore." Markus shakes his head and flattens his lips. Then a new thought seems to appear as the corners tip up in a small smile. "It's been good seeing him with you. You've awoken a spark in him that's been dead for a long time."

My own smile grows wide at his words.

But then I come to think about the women he might have been fucking while I've been seeing him, and a sick jealousy slithers into my belly. I want to be the only woman he sees—in every way. But I can't be. I belong to someone else, and Grigory needs to sate his sexual needs somewhere.

I want to ask if Grigory has been with someone recently, but I don't want to reveal my jealousy—and I'm not sure I want to hear the answer.

The unjustified feeling keeps rearing its ugly head throughout the evening, and with it comes a whole slew of new fears.

Suddenly, the idea of Grigory being with another woman is no longer the worst thought as I realize the end is closing in. After the premiere, there are no more rehearsals; will it mean no more piano lessons? Grigory might be leaving town to work on a project elsewhere and only come back for the remaining shows. Even if he doesn't, this will end anyway when I go home in ten days. Will I ever get to see him again then?

Tomorrow might be our last day together—that is, if I get to see him at all. Just because I'm going to the backstage party doesn't mean I'll get more than a quick greeting. He'll be busy talking to all the other people battling for his attention—all more accomplished and talented than me. I wouldn't stand a chance in such a crowd.

Then he'll move on and forget about our summer fling—or whatever this is.

But I won't. Grigory's dominance is branded into me, and I know my need to submit to him won't soon die down.

I try to tell myself it'll get better when I go home and stop seeing him—like a detox. But I've already tried suppressing my reactions so many times I want to laugh at the idea.

But maybe, just maybe, it won't all end here. Maybe I'll see him again when I visit Markus in the fall or at New Year's. The optimism is short-lived. That's in several months and Grigory might not even be in Berlin during those few days I'm here. Plus, with his current track record of pulling away whenever things get intimate, the chances this will go on seem less than minuscule.

So I try to shut down my hopes to avoid getting hurt. But I know it's already well past too late.

— CHAPTER 21 —

Markus is already getting ready to leave early in the afternoon on Friday. The show doesn't start until seven p.m., but he has to warm up, get make-up done, change clothes, and all those kinds of pre-show stuff. Plus, on premiere nights he likes to be more than early.

My mood has been shifting back and forth all afternoon. One moment I've acted like a flustered teenager who's just had her first kiss; next, I've felt dreary, wanting to stay in bed the rest of the day.

I sit on the sofa, deep in my own thoughts, when Markus comes in. He's wearing a deep blue suit and a white shirt, his hands working on the matching tie. He looks incredibly sexy in that outfit. The color brings out the blue in his eyes, which sparkle with life and anticipation today.

My thighs clench together, and I bite my lower lip. Judging by his cocky grin, he knows all too well how he affects me.

His newly polished leather shoes squeak as he moves across the floor with determined strides. Placing a hand on the armrest, he leans in and pushes the other hand between my legs, cupping my sex. "No masturbating today," he says in a husky tone. "You have to wait until tonight."

I let out a frustrated groan when he pulls his hand away. I already feel hot and needy, and waiting until after the show seems like torture. At least I know there's a good chance it won't drag on from there. It wouldn't be the first time if he hauls me to his dressing room and fucks me right then and there. It's a good way to release the pent-up energy that has built up during tech week, he often says.

"Grigory will meet you when you get backstage tonight," Markus says, absently stroking the side of my neck with his fingertips. "I have an interview."

The sound of Grigory's name sparks something in me. A restless yearning and a titillating energy. But most of all, dread. The realization this might be the last time I see him has hit me like a hammer, and just thinking about him has tears pressing behind my eyes. It will only get worse when I see him, I'm sure. Without Markus at my side, I won't be able to handle it.

I stare unblinking at Markus. "Can't I just go to your dressing room and wait for you there? It will probably take some time before I can get backstage anyway, and I know my way around."

"No," is all I get in reply. No explanation.

"Why?" My question comes out high-pitched as dread shoots through me. W*hat if he pulls away again?* And even worse, *what if he wants someone to help release his pent-up energy too?* Then I'll run along at his heel, tears pressing behind my eyes, while he flirts with other women. I can't take that.

"This is not up for discussion." Markus's stern expression silences me. "I want you to do exactly as he says." He pauses to make sure I get it. "Do you remember I told you he would never do anything I'm not okay with?"

I nod.

"Good. Keep that tucked inside your pretty head." He brushes a lock of hair behind my ear and strokes his thumb over my cheek. "I don't want you to forget it. Do you understand?"

"I won't."

"Can I leave you alone with him then, knowing you'll be a good girl," he presses his index finger to my forehead, "and that your worry system won't go off with blaring alarms and red lights?"

I smile at that. "Sure," I agree, rolling my eyes. "I'll do my best."

He leans in and presses a long kiss to my lips. "I'll see you tonight," he says with a wink, and then he's on his way.

I've got a hunch he'll take me to his dressing room right away. I hope so. Heat is already pooling between my legs, and I will be in dire need of a distraction after seeing Grigory. Markus's cock buried deep inside me will do the trick.

* * *

Not long after Markus has left, I begin preparing for the big night. I start by retrieving the evening gown hanging in the closet.

I spend a minute admiring the beautiful burgundy dress, remembering when Markus surprised me by taking me dress shopping for this occasion back in June. I fell in love with it the moment I saw it on the rack, and it was a great disappointment when my tiny bosom couldn't fill it out.

Markus insisted I got the right dress no matter the cost and paid extra to have it fitted. I think he wanted me to wear it as much as I did.

It's perfect for me. The color goes great with my brown hair and light skin, and the upper part hugs my body in all the right places, the elegant V-neck enhancing my small breasts, the tight fit showing off my narrow waist. But what I love the most is the deep back and the long skirt that flows in lively waves from the waist. It's the perfect combination of sexy and elegant, and I can't wait to wear it.

But first things first. I take a bath, put on make-up—a little more than usual, though still keeping it natural—and do my hair. My brown locks fall in pretty waves when it's newly washed, so I make a small braid at the side and let the rest hang loose. Then I hurry to get some food into my stomach before finally slipping into the dress and finishing with a pair of black heels.

Standing before the mirror, I feel beautiful, sweet, and sexy all at once. Markus will love stripping the shiny fabric off my body. Or maybe he'll push it up around my hips so he can admire it while fucking me.

Maybe Grigory will like it too.

I shake my head. It doesn't matter what he thinks. If I have too high expectations, it'll only hurt when he takes one look at me, then turns back to whatever he was doing when I came. So I force myself to move away from the idea.

It's too late though. The thought keeps popping back up like an annoying fly you try to swat away. And who am I kidding? It doesn't matter how low I keep my expectations. It will be a cut to my heart every time he looks at one of the many other beautiful women who, unlike me, are available.

I leave the apartment with the thought of him watching other women hanging like a dark cloud over my head. Most of all, I want to go back inside and crawl into my checkered shorts and drop onto the couch with a good animation movie. I'm in no mood for fancy opera houses, cultured people, and famous conductors.

When I walk into the opera half an hour later, it's a whole different place than I've seen it during the summer. Throughout the last week, I've come to expect a hollow emptiness when I enter the lobby, but tonight the place is buzzing with life and excitement.

Opera is no longer as ceremonial as it used to be. You can easily show up in a pair of jeans and a nice blouse without anyone looking twice at you. But on a premiere night, everyone is dressed up—long gowns and fancy suits. I've always loved the festive atmosphere of it. Tonight is no exception, and I slowly feel my gloom lifting as the energy rubs off on me.

I leave my jacket in the coatroom and find my seat in the auditorium. These kinds of places never fail to amaze me. The space is huge and mesmerizing. Red upholstered seats, golden balconies, and ornamented walls bathe the old auditorium in glory and splendor.

Markus has gotten me one of the best seats, right in the middle of the front row on the first balcony, where both sound and view are perfect.

The air hums with anticipation. Idle chatting ripples through the space, mixing with the warm sounds of a few musicians fiddling on their instruments in the orchestra pit.

I flip through the program, and when I land on the part with a large picture of Grigory, I linger a bit too long before turning the page with an angry motion that rips the paper.

Annoyance spikes in me. *Why does that man need to be everywhere?* I manage to get him out of my head for one minute, then he pops up somewhere else.

The mention of Markus behind me is a welcome distraction, and I listen in on two ladies' conversation for a minute. One says she has seen him at another show and holds him in high regard; the other chimes in, saying she has heard only good things about him and can't wait to see him in this production.

A smile forms on my lips. Markus's career is really taking off. I have a feeling he'll soon get the call from The Metropolitan Opera that he's always dreamed about.

The lights go down and the audience starts clapping, all eyes turned toward the left side of the pit. I follow the direction and my heart flips when I see what has caught everyone's attention.

Grigory walks in through the orchestra with long, firm strides, taking his place on the podium and making a couple of quick bows toward the audience. His usual slacks and dress shirt have been upgraded to a three-piece suit with a white waistcoat, white butterfly, and a black jacket. His hair is combed back, and he radiates authority and confidence as he towers over the orchestra. Everyone can see he's in his element.

My mood takes a sudden turn as I gaze down at the familiar figure. I hate that we are separated by all these people and that he's leading the orchestra and not me.

Up here, I feel small and insignificant. I'm one tiny person among a thousand people. Even when I go backstage and the number reduces to a tenth, I still won't stand a chance.

He's surrounded by beautiful, competent people who have all excelled at their craft. How can I compete with them? I'm just a plain, young woman—a poor student with no special talent.

Fuck. I shouldn't think like this, but it's difficult not to in these surroundings.

Grigory turns to the orchestra and lifts his hands, baton held in the right one. With an energetic gesture, he starts the show, and the first three chords boom out into the auditorium. The music grabs me, stirring up chaotic feelings. Not even the beautiful scenery will ease my building tension when the curtain rises.

It's only when Markus comes on ten minutes later that my focus begins to hone in on the stage. Before long, an ethereal flute melody introduces his first big aria, "Recondita Armonia." It's one of my all-time favorites, and I inhale a deep breath at the beautiful sound. The melody affects me the same way as "Der Lindenbaum" from *Winterreise,* and when Markus starts singing, I finally sink back in my seat. His voice effortlessly fills the large auditorium, floating above the beautiful harmonies, enthralling everyone who hears.

Markus gets a long round of applause before the opera goes on, and I'm clapping so hard my hands hurt. I'm so proud it's my man down there making an entire audience cheer.

When the music continues, I let it consume me. For long

stretches of time, I almost forget about the man directing it all from the podium in front of the stage.

Sometimes, my eyes fall down there, watching his energetic movements, but the story unfolding on stage quickly pulls me back. It's only when the curtain closes that my attention rests fully on him.

His hair is a wild mess—it seems to be the only thing in the world that doesn't want to submit to his will. He shoves it away from his forehead as he bows to the audience. Then he steps off his podium and walks through the orchestra, disappearing beneath the stage. It takes me back to Monday when he left the rehearsal room without a word. I know how irrational it is, but it feels like it's me he's walking away from—me he's leaving again.

The lights come on, and people file out between the rows only to return half an hour later. All the while, I sit here, staring at the empty pit with a heavy feeling in my chest.

How am I supposed to move on and forget him when I go home? I'm not ready for this to end. I'm not ready to never see him again.

I want to kneel before him and show him my deep devotion. Give in to his every demand and let him push me to the limit—and beyond—then let him put me back together, piece by piece. I want to feel his large hand, which is the most dangerous and reassuring thing in the world.

But I can't have any of it, and seeing him after the show will be a stark reminder.

Before I know it, the lights dim, and the audience receives Grigory with another round of applause.

And so, the show continues.

It's breathtaking all the way through. The singers are amazing, making their characters seem as evil, tragic, and in love as they are supposed to be. The production is riveting and aesthetic with splendid costumes and scenery. In short, the show is every bit as formidable as the opera house made it out to be.

But it's an emotional roller coaster ride of tall highs and deep lows for me. When the curtain falls for the last time after three hours and the audience finally tires of the never-ending clapping, I'm exhausted and longing for Markus's bed.

But I know me being here and taking part in this big night means a lot to Markus. So I suck it up and follow the throng of people to the lobby to get my coat and find a staff member who can let me backstage.

It takes twenty minutes before I finally have my jacket and get a hold of someone with a guest list. I end up in a large backstage lounging area full of dressed-up people, who are laughing and drinking champagne. I don't fit in with my disheartened mood, and the din of voices is an assault on my weary mind.

Not wanting to be in the middle of it all, I step to the side and scan the crowd for Grigory. But all the faces make me dizzy and I can't find him.

"Champagne?" a waiter asks, holding a tray with champagne flutes up in front of me. I glance at him, slightly confused, and give a shake of my head. The opera has really made a spectacle of this. On the other premiere nights I've attended, you may help yourself to a flute of bubbles—if there even is champagne.

I take another look around. And there he is. In all his masculine glory, his hair in an untamable mess, posture tall and proud, radiating authority.

It takes a second for me to notice the woman he's talking to. Silky black hair reaches all the way down her back, and her long red gown hugs sensual curves I can't compete with. Her full lips are colored the same alluring shade of red as the dress, making her ooze sex and femininity.

A heavy rock falls into the pit of my stomach. Maybe this is the type of woman Grigory prefers?

I gulp against the constriction in my throat and have to avert my eyes to dampen the unreasonable envy digging into my chest. But it's no help. My head is already mocking me with images of Grigory taking the gorgeous woman hard and fast as she moans her pleasure.

Tears press behind my eyes, dangerously close to breaking free.

I have to get out of here.

But I can't think or act. I remain rigidly in place as my eyes flicker back and forth over the room.

I don't know where to go. To Markus's dressing room? Or even better, home?

No, I can't do that to Markus.

Maybe I should start by getting out of this room—find the toilets to get some peace to think?

It seems like a good idea.

I will my legs to move, but the signal reaches them too late. Just as I'm about to take a step, a pressing sensation prickles my skin, making me look up—right into Grigory's hard gaze. His eyes bore past my defenses, ripping them to shreds like flimsy paper.

I freeze—a deer in headlights.

Without releasing my eyes, he shuts down the conversation with the beautiful woman and walks toward me with long, measured strides that make people move to the side. He doesn't even seem to notice the crowd. All his attention is honed in on me.

It reminds me of a majestic lion in a zoo that once stalked toward me, baring its teeth and growling. Only this time, there's no fence to keep me safe from the predator.

My heart hammers like it's about to leap from my chest, and everything around me melts away. I take a step back. And another one. But he's already here.

He grabs me without stopping and drags me from the room, his hand like an iron cuff around my wrist.

"What... where..." I'm too stupefied to get more out.

I struggle to keep up with his long strides as he hauls me through the crowded corridor. There's no room for embarrassment. My brain has kicked into some state of emergency, only allowing me to focus on the man dragging me away.

The din of people dies out as we get deeper into the maze of halls. We go down through a stairwell, and I almost trip, but somehow Grigory steadies me, despite all his hurry.

A new hall meets us with a menacing silence. The clicks of square soles and thin heels are the only sounds ringing between the narrow walls.

We round a corner and Grigory unlocks a door and shoves me into a small room. It's only slightly bigger than the usual rehearsal room—an upright piano, a small sofa, and a table. It looks unused. Desolate. And when the door swings shut behind me, I spin around to meet a set of wild eyes and flaring nostrils.

The hairs on the back of my neck stand on end as I realize how vulnerable I am. We are far away from everyone else. No one would hear me down here if I were to scream.

Does Markus even know where I am?

Markus. His words from this afternoon pop into my head. *He would never do anything I'm not okay with.*

My heart picks up speed. The last time he said those words, he was sending me off to be dominated and disciplined by a man I didn't know.

Now said man is watching me like I'm his next meal.

I frantically look around the room for somewhere to hide—somewhere to run.

But Grigory's blocking the door, there's no window, and I can't move, anyway.

There's only one thing to do. I lower my gaze to appease the predator, staring at my shaking hands as the silence creeps in, announcing the storm.

A minute passes like this, but it feels like ten. Finally, I can't stand it anymore, and my eyes flicker back up. It's only a fleeting glance through lowered lashes, but it's enough.

I shouldn't have done it.

In the blink of an eye, he's over me, yanking me to him with such ferocity that I slam against his chest, the air shooting from my lungs with a loud gasp.

His massive hands roam my body, up and down the naked skin on my back, over my butt, and into my hair, gripping it close to the roots. I struggle to remain on my feet. If it weren't for his arms pressing me to him, I would drop to the floor.

It's too much. I start squirming, but he only tightens his grip and digs into my neck, scratching with his teeth and nibbling my skin.

A grunt is my only warning. Suddenly, he bites down. Hard.

Pain shoots into my shoulder and panic rises in my chest. I shove at him, but there's no room to gain leverage. So I dig my fingers into his chest. But Grigory just wraps his arms around my slender figure—so far that his fingers come back around to dig into my stomach. It effectively traps my arms between us so I can barely move. I'm a defenseless animal caught in the claws of the mighty predator. He's strong and solid; I'm small and frail.

The helplessness creeps to my head, blurring my thoughts until I feel like I've downed three flutes of sparkling champagne.

A squeak, maybe a moan, comes up through my throat, and my lips fall apart to let it out. In this moment, something inside me snaps—a switch flips, shutting off my head. I can't think straight. I can't think at all.

I collapse in his arms, sagging against him while whimpering like the defenseless animal I am.

He feels it, the moment when I give in. A guttural groan rises in his throat and something in him changes. His violent hands relax, molding around the curves of my waist, almost gently. But his bite remains, hard and unrelenting.

Pain, tenderness, overwhelming helplessness. It all mixes together, working like a heavy drug on my mind.

My head falls back, and Grigory shoots a hand up to catch it, cupping it in his warm palm.

Without thinking, I press my pelvis up against the hard bulge in his pants. My moan spurs his teeth deeper. And deeper.

My skin is going to break. The notion stabs into the fog, threatening to burst the thin veneer keeping me safe from the pain.

I hover on the edge between hypnotic submission and jarring insanity, swaying dangerously.

And then, I fall, crashing into the pain that splits my neck.

I whine desperately and start struggling. But even as I use all my strength, I only manage pathetic squirms.

It's like he doesn't even notice and I'm getting truly scared. Something primal has taken hold of him, and he seems to have lost all control.

Panic screeches at the corners of my mind, threatening to take over. My breath is jammed in my throat, and tears prickle behind my eye.

Suddenly, he releases me—both his teeth and arms disappear.

Swaying where I stand, I wonder how I don't collapse. Is he still holding me?

I don't realize what's going on before the zipper on my back is pulled down and a strap falls off my shoulder. I try to pull away again, but Grigory holds me in place while slipping the dress off with frightening ease.

The smooth fabric slides down my body, and I stare at it as it pools around my feet. Then I'm spinning around, tripping out of the heap of fabric as Grigory pushes me forward. Before I know it, I'm pressed down over the table with a steely hand flat against my back.

I want to tell him to stop—ask for a break. Ask what he's doing. But no words come out. Only small whimpers. Everything else is caught in the impenetrable fog filling my head.

Instead, I start kicking. My legs fly up and down behind me, but Grigory has strategically stepped between them, so I'm hitting nothing but thin air. So I try with my hands, flailing blindly behind me, trying to catch… something.

I manage to get hold of Grigory's arm, squeezing and trying to shake it. It gets me nowhere, so I dig my nails in, but he seems oblivious to my struggle. I don't even think he feels my nails sinking into his skin, and when he reaches down to grab my pantyhose, I lose my grip anyway.

The fabric burns across my skin as he rips it down, the sound of tearing nylon mixing with his hard breaths.

I grab onto the edges of the table, desperate for anything to stabilize me. Because Grigory won't do it. He's so caught up in his lust I don't think he's capable of taking care of me at all.

Please stop, I want to say, but I can't get the words out. My breath heaves in my lungs, my throat wheezing as I try not to hyperventilate.

Then everything stops.

As if he senses my growing panic, Grigory leans in and closes warm hands in a gentle grip around my arms. Words finally come to me. It's not a *no* or a *stop.* It's a plea for him to protect me. "Grigory, I'm scared," I whimper.

"I know," he soothes. "It's okay. I've got you, *devochka*." The tender words confuse the hell out of me. It doesn't add up with anything else he's doing. Yet, the thick fear lifts from my mind, and when he gathers my arms in one big hand on my back, I drift into a cloudy haze.

He holds me for a while, and when he lifts my hands up to lie at each side of my head, I'm limp and pliant.

I don't move a muscle. Not even at the sound of a belt buckle followed by the scratch of a zipper.

"Good girl," he says, his hand traveling along my spine, firm yet gentle.

But when he reaches my panties, his energy shifts again. Slowly, he wraps his fist around the lace, and I feel the dormant violence in his grip, bracing for it with my hands curled around the table edge.

With one hard tug, he yanks them down. The brutality makes me jolt, and I whimper as nails scratch over my ass. I try to keep myself calm, but my breathing is already labored again, and when two fingers slip into the wetness between my folds, panic builds anew.

The foreign touch is invasive, and when Grigory breaches my opening, I whimper and squirm. It's almost a violation. I've never agreed to this, not verbally or physically. There has been no preamble or build-up, just Grigory hauling me away and stripping me bare.

I whimper a little louder, but it sounds like a moan, and to my horror, I realize my legs are spreading, welcoming the intrusion.

Fuck. What's happening to me? I'm not sure I want this. Not this way. It's too sudden—too violent. Yet my body seems to be of another opinion.

Grigory pulls his fingers out, leaving me relieved for a split-second before the sound of breaking foil crashes into my senses with a startling realization. *This is really happening. He's going to fuck me.*

And then what?

I'm already fighting a hopeless battle to keep myself on steady ground through all of this. If Grigory fucks me, I'll fall for good, crashing in the gravel at his feet with no way back up. Then I'll lie there, staring up at him, unable to move or act, fully at his volatile mercy.

The prodding of his cock at my entrance hauls a keening sound from my throat. It's fear, desperation, and want all wrapped up in one messed-up cocktail that makes me push up my hips even as I bang my fists against the table.

I shake my head from side to side as tears drip down my cheeks, but I can't say any of the words swirling in my overloaded mind. *No. Stop. Shrek.* Any number of words could make this stop, but I can't get them out. *I'm not sure I want to.*

Grigory pushes the crown inside, and fear bands around my chest, making me wheeze.

If he leaves me after using me, I will break. There'll be nothing but a hollow shell left, rattling alone in the dust, staring after Grigory even long after he's out of sight.

His cock presses farther, stretching my inner walls. There's nothing I can do, and silent tears spill from my eyes as he takes the last thing I have to give.

Pinning me by the waist, Grigory slides all the way inside. I'm so wet there's no resistance. Then he pulls back and hammers into me with one hard thrust that rips through my entire being, shocking and painful. A shrill scream fills the small space, bouncing back and forth between the walls. I swing my head back, my body bowing and bucking in a hopeless effort to contain the pain.

Then everything goes blank.

Everything disappears.

Except for the man who has taken it all.

His cock throbs inside me as he holds still, filling me to the breaking point, blotting out every thought I ever had. I can't speak, think, or move. The only thing I can do is accept his total power.

So I do just that. I go limp with a small mewl, collapsing over the table, my hands dangling over the side. There's no use in fighting anymore. He's got the last piece of me now.

"That's it, *devochka*," he croons, the praise soothing the last sliver of doubt from my mind. "Good girl."

He starts moving inside me. First, it's slow and careful, but within seconds he's pounding into me with primal ferocity. Every thrust shakes my body—shakes me to the core. It's painful yet freeing.

A raspy growl erupts from his throat and he clenches his hands around my waist. Fingers dig into my skin as his pleasure builds.

The feeling of his oncoming climax evokes an ardent gratitude in me. I'm grateful he wants to sate his need in me—that I'm the one to receive his dominance.

He comes with a few hard jerks, and the need to belong to him burns so hot it scorches me from within. I moan and buck with something beyond pleasure—something as raw and instinctive as his dominance. Clutching my hands around the edges of the table, I seek purchase in the onslaught of emotion.

When he pulls out, it's like losing a vital part of myself, and in its wake a desperate need arises, making my hips buck in a shameless plea for more.

He doesn't let me tumble in my misery for long before he thrusts two fingers inside me, no less merciful than when he took his own pleasure. He jabs them in and out, making a slick sound that reveals how impossibly wet I am.

Pushing a third finger in, he picks up speed, and I moan at the painful stretch. His other hand starts playing with my clit, and my eyes roll back. I can't take it. It's too much. Too much pleasure, too much pain.

The two seem to coexist quite perfectly, and I release a long moan that stretches into a scream as the orgasm rips through me. It shakes my entire being, jerking and yanking at my body, tearing at my mind.

Grigory keeps pumping his fingers, dragging my orgasm out. When he finally withdraws, I crash hard. I slump over the table, every bone and muscle limp and useless. Only my erratic breathing bears witness that there's still life.

Grigory caresses me with long strokes. Fingers slide up under my hair, curling around my nape with a startling gentleness, then back down along my back, reverently stroking my waist, and on to caress my butt.

Soon, the shaking sets in. Erratic shivers rip through my body like they are trying to shove me out of it.

Ever so gently, Grigory lifts me into his arms and carries me to the small sofa, where he settles with me in his lap. I clutch the lapels of his shirt, needing something to grab onto as I feel like I'm being ripped apart from the inside.

But I'm not. Grigory covers me with his jacket and bands his arms around me, holding me together through the violent trembles. I shed a few silent tears, but they don't feel threatening when I'm here, enclosed in his arms.

I don't know when or how long it takes, but at some point, my body settles. Grigory keeps rocking and caressing me, and slowly I drift into a peaceful place where it's empty and quiet. Calm and safe.

There's no place in the world I'd rather be than here in Grigory's arms.

— CHAPTER 22 —

I blink my sleepy eyes when Grigory carefully rustles with his jacket. He reclines against the corner of the sofa, legs stretched out on the cushions. I'm still in his lap, my head on his chest, legs entangled with his. I don't know how long I've been out, if I've been sleeping or my mind has just been on standby.

Lifting my head to see what he's doing, I catch a glimpse of his phone before he puts my head back on his chest and gives me a reassuring squeeze. Only half a minute passes before both his arms are wrapped around me again, soothing me into the calm darkness where nothing can reach me.

I'm almost dozing off when the door opens. I snap back with a jerk, scrambling to sit up and see who it is.

"Shh, it's just Markus." Grigory holds me in place, the hand on my head keeping me nestled safely against his chest.

With confusion muddying my mind, I angle my head under his hand to see Markus approach us with determined strides. He stops at the end of the sofa and leans in to grab my legs. He pulls me to him, flips me to my back, and hauls my hips over the armrest. I fumble for Grigory who's been my anchor since he ripped solid ground away from under me. I'm not ready to lose the security of his arms.

Grigory doesn't let me drift for long. He just shifts to accommodate my new position, grabs my arms and pins them beside my head so I stare straight up into his burning eyes.

Without preamble, Markus pushes inside me. I hadn't even heard him open his pants, and I gasp, staring up at him with wide eyes. He's pure lust and possession as he fucks me, taking his pleasure without consideration.

Usually, I love when he takes me like this, but we're not alone. There are two sets of sharp eyes on me, and the realization slams into me. I still can't speak or think, and when I try to reach for Markus, urge him to stop, I remember another man has my arms pinned to the couch—another man who's watching me being used.

I squirm on the couch but get nowhere. Grigory's grasp only allows useless flailing with my lower arms, and Markus has my hips pinned to the couch as he keeps pounding into me.

Helplessness settles heavily in my stomach as I realize I once again have no say. This time, though, there's nothing intoxicating about it. I just feel dirty and exposed.

I know it's no use, but I can't help putting all my feeble energy into my struggle. My pulse throbs in my ears, and I thrash my head from side to side as I heave for air.

When Grigory releases my one arm, I'm about to start flailing, but then he grabs my chin and forces my gaze to his.

I stare straight up into the dark depths of two eyes that hold power, care, and possession, all in one heady mix. Everything stills—my heartbeat, my erratic breathing, and my struggling body. I realize Markus has paused, holding still inside me.

"Breathe, *devochka*," Grigory urges, his voice calm and soothing, his thumb running along my jawline as his palm cups my chin.

I pull in a shuddering breath as relief floods me. It's not dangerous being here. There's no degradation or taunting power in those eyes. He takes care of me, this powerful man. And so does Markus. I might be helpless, but I'm also safe here between the two men.

Grigory lifts his eyes and gives Markus a nod before returning his attention to me. Markus starts again, and all the while he slams into me, Grigory's eyes hold mine captive—physically as well as mentally. They make sure I don't slip into the confusing blur that is my mind, and the sheer power in his gaze renders me unable to move. When he's got me, everything is calm.

Grigory releases my chin when Markus slows his pace to abrupt jerks revealing his oncoming orgasm. I shift my gaze in time to see him when he comes inside me. *Mine,* his intense eyes say as they lock onto me, and I let out a small moan of surrender.

A satisfied smile forms on Markus's lips as he pulls out. He leans down and lifts my head to meet his in a heady kiss that sucks whatever little energy I had regained straight out of me.

I sink into the couch when he pulls back, heavy as a rock.

Large hands grab me under my arms and pull me onto a lap—Grigory's lap.

For the second time tonight, I melt against him—a listless heap of limbs. There's no energy left. Not the tiniest sliver. If someone told me to get up, I might start crying from the sheer enormity of the task, and if someone asked me a question, I don't think they'd get any response at all.

Wrapping the soft material of his jacket around me again, Grigory presses my head into his shoulder and wraps an arm around my waist. Sleep is already pulling at me, and if no one stops me, I'll quickly drift off.

The sofa creaks as Markus sits beside us. "People are asking about their conductor," he says, slightly out of breath. "If you want to join the party, I'll make sure to get her home in bed."

Grigory can't leave me!

I clutch his shirt in my fists, clinging to him with all my might. At least, that's how it feels. In reality, my hands are probably only holding loosely onto the fabric.

I feel the shake of Grigory's head. "I'm more needed here." He tightens his arm around me in silent reassurance. "That is, unless you want her."

Markus responds with a warm chuckle, "No, it's okay. I have her tonight. And someone needs to celebrate the premiere, so if the two of you won't do it, I guess I'll have to." He gives me a squeeze on the ankle. "Are you okay to stay here with Grigory for a while?"

I give him the only answer I can muster. Snuggling closer into Grigory's embrace.

Grigory's laugh is a soothing rumble against my ear.

"I think that says it all." Markus's voice is laced with amusement. He squeezes my ankle again. "I'll come get you later. Grigory will text me if you need me."

A moment later, I hear the creaking of the door and the click as it closes. I hold onto Grigory a few minutes longer until I'm sure no one will come and take me away from him. Then I let go of everything and slip back into the peaceful place where the whole world is right.

— CHAPTER 23 —

I wake up a couple of hours before noon, feeling woozy and confused as the evening before slowly comes back to me.

Markus is fast asleep beside me, arms draped over the pillow and the covers bunched around his waist. I reach up to slide a hand through the curls of his dark hair. It's more black than brown, several shades darker than Grigory's deep, warm brown with a couple of white streaks at the temples. I wonder if Grigory's hair would feel as soft as Markus's if I were to run a hand through it.

How would he react? Swat my hand away to avoid the unruly mess becoming even more unruly? Maybe if I kept trying, he would give in and close his eyes to enjoy the feeling?

I smile at the idea. I'd love to play with Grigory's hair, but I haven't dared to touch it yet. Maybe soon though.

Markus barely stirs as I keep messing with his hair. I think he might have been drunk when he came back to get me last night, but I was too drowsy to really notice—too focused on Grigory.

I was not happy when Markus tried to take me. I remember wrapping my arms around Grigory's waist and refusing to let go, and I think I even whimpered.

The sound of Grigory's deep chuckle was just as soothing as his arms when he hoisted me up and carried me all the way through the winding corridors and out to the cab.

I was no easier to get rid of when he set me on the backseat beside Markus. He had to grab my hands to get me to release his neck.

"Don't worry, *devochka*," he said, still holding my wrists. "You'll see me again soon."

"Will I?" I asked, doubt straining my voice.

"Yes." The firmness in his answer relayed his sincerity. It was enough to keep me from grabbing him again, even though my fingers jittered with the need.

He brushed his knuckles over my cheek one last time before stepping back and closing the door. Tears welled in my eyes, but I was too tired for such strong emotions, and when Markus pulled me to him, I quickly drifted off.

I barely remember getting home and into bed. I've slept like a child. Even so, an antsy feeling lingers—like I'm missing something.

As I gradually wake up, more images flicker before my inner eye, making a mess of my mind. If I thought I was confused before, I'm not sure what to call it now. What happened last night was crazy. I've never tried anything like it. I was genuinely scared, my struggles not just a means to feel an erotic kind of helplessness. Yet, everything was okay. At least it ended up being so. From the outside, it would have appeared like rape, but I don't think Grigory could ever truly rape me, no matter what he did. My need to please and obey him is too strong.

The feeling of being so utterly at his mercy still lingers—scary yet intoxicating. In some sense, I'm still at his mercy. I can't control my feelings when it comes to him. It's like a bottomless pit, and he alone holds the power to push me deeper or pull me up.

When I finally decide to get out of bed to find some breakfast, I feel sluggish and on edge. And sore. Inside and out.

My inner walls feel raw, and when I lift my camisole to inspect my hips, I find bruises and burns which evoke a wealth of conflicting emotions in my groggy mind.

Markus joins me in the kitchen half an hour later, wearing nothing but briefs, blinking the sleep from his eyes.

I walk straight up to him and slide an arm around his waist, beckoning him for a hug. He openly accepts me, kissing the top of my head and stroking my arms.

"Are you okay?" he asks against my head.

I nod and mold myself closer to him. "I think so."

He holds me for a few minutes before I take a step back to gaze up at him, my hands still flat on his stomach, seeking the comfort of his skin. "How was the party?"

The atmosphere lightens as Markus tells me about the after-party. He's in a great mood despite clearly being hungover. He adamantly denies the latter whenever I ask about it. But it's clear from his sluggish demeanor and lack of appetite he's had more to drink than he lets on.

He might be the one who's the master mind-reader, but I know him too, and I keep teasing when he keeps denying.

"I think you're getting a bit too frisky for your own good," he says. "You'd better go take a long bath to cool down."

I give him a sly smile as I clear off my plate and start scouring the kitchen cabinets and fridge in search of potato chips and cola.

Batting my eyes innocently, I place the typical hangover cure in front of him.

"You're really pushing it, aren't you?" He scowls, scarily good at covering up his amusement. "If I were you, I'd hurry on to take that bath."

When I linger, he adds in a firm tone, "Now," barely containing his smile.

"Okay," I say with a bratty edge and scurry out of the kitchen. On my way through the living room, I hear the rustle of a chips bag and the pop of a soda can, and I can't help smiling widely. Lucky for my ass, Markus doesn't see it.

The hot water is soothing on my ravaged body. I study all the sore places with a strange fascination. A huge, throbbing bite mark on my left shoulder makes me feel like prey; a couple of burns remind me how brutally Grigory ripped the clothes from my body; bruises on my waist and hips are already turning blue, bearing witness to the ruthlessness Grigory gripped me with. On top of that, my inner walls feel raw, and there's a dull pressure in my lower stomach that I ascribe to his deep thrusts.

I can't stop pressing down on the bruises even though they're sore. They are all marks of territory, and I feel a strange sense of pride at seeing them on my body—seeing Grigory's marks on me.

But when I step out of the shower and take it all in through the mirror, the feeling shifts. The bruises become lies. Betrayals. Something that essentially holds no meaning.

I'm not his.

I belong to someone else.

His possession is only an illusion.

I stare at them with a heavy sadness squeezing my chest, and I have to spend several minutes getting a grip on myself before I can go back to Markus.

The rest of the day passes at a slow tempo. I snuggle up against Markus on the couch, watching TV and reading—whenever my preoccupied mind allows it. Every so often, Markus asks if I'm okay and wants to know how I felt about what happened last night. I don't want to go into details about the mess in my head, so I just say I feel a bit off—and fragile—and that it's nice to have him here, holding me and taking care of me.

I don't tell him I wish someone else was here too.

Whenever the thought appears, I unconsciously press down on a sore mark, needing to feel connected to Grigory. Once I realize what I'm doing, guilt stabs into me. The feeling could easily consume me, but with Markus's easy-going disposition close by, I manage to keep it at bay most of the time throughout the day.

We read the first reviews of *Tosca* together, which have high words for the new production. They all mention Grigory, saying how huge a force it is for The Berlin State Opera to have him at the wheel. The singers also get a lot of praise, and particularly one reviewer highlights the wonderful surprise of the rising star Markus Richter who has a bright career in front of him.

For the next hour, both Markus and I are high on the praise he has received.

In the afternoon, Markus gets a call from Grigory. He sits beside me on the couch while chatting about the great reception of the show. Hearing Grigory's deep rumble through the phone sparks all kinds of different feelings in me, and my skin hums with nervous expectation that has me shifting on the couch.

Halfway through the conversation, Markus disappears into the bedroom, and I sit here hoping for something, not knowing what. That they're talking about me? That Markus will come back and tell me Grigory enjoyed seeing me last night? A simple promise to say hi from him?

I watch Markus hopefully when he returns, but he only smiles and reclaims his seat on the couch to watch the TV show running on the screen.

* * *

We spend Sunday in the same calm tempo. I enjoy being with Markus, but memories of the premiere night keep popping into my head and stirring up confusing feelings.

Whenever I go to the bathroom, I pull at the neck of my blouse to reveal the bruise on my left shoulder. I watch it with eye-widening fascination, followed by a jumble of messy feelings.

On the weekends, I typically wear my checkered shorts and a camisole, but I don't want to flash the marks in front of Markus if I can avoid it—they are a symbol of something private between Grigory and me. Sharing them with Markus feels like an invasion—or maybe it's guilt that makes me hide them. So I've put on jeans and a blouse that covers the bite mark on my shoulder—at least most of it. The deep redness and a few streaks of blue still bleed up over the neckline. I think I would need a turtleneck to cover it up entirely.

In the afternoon, I ask Markus what he would like for dinner.

"You don't have to worry about dinner today," he says, leaning in to kiss me, his hand lingering on my thigh as he hovers in front of me.

"Thanks," I say with a smile. "What are we having?" He has probably planned to take me out to celebrate the premiere or found some delicious takeout place he wants to try.

"You'll see." He repeats the kiss and his hand slips up to tangle in my hair, holding me in place as he demands entrance to my mouth. I melt beneath him, and when he pulls away, I'm hot and panting, having forgotten all about dinner and secret plans.

When the credits of the second movie of the day roll early in the evening, Markus says, "Time to get ready. Go take a shower and find something nice to wear."

"Where are we going?" I ask, jumping to my feet.

"Ask Grigory."

My jaw drops, my legs suddenly quivering. "Grigory?"

"Yes, Grigory. The man who fucked you raw a couple of nights ago." Markus grins. "He's picking you up at six and taking you to dinner."

"Aren't you coming?" I fall back onto the sofa, my hands grabbing onto his.

"No. It's just the two of you."

I want to ask why, but another type of panic grips me when I glance at the clock. "Why haven't you told me earlier? I barely have an hour."

"I know how nervous you get, sweetie." He rubs my thigh in a reassuring gesture. "I didn't want it to affect our day together."

Outrage flickers inside me—along with panic and antsy surprise—but I know he has a point, and I can't blame him.

The next hour passes in a flurry. Markus might have spared me the anxiety throughout the day, but now it comes crashing with a vengeance. I dart around in hazed confusion as I scramble to get everything done—shower, apply make-up, and find the right clothes—the latter being an impossible task. All the clothes I have here are either too sexy or too casual, giving off the wrong signals in some way.

Markus ends up coming to my aid and chooses a cute, red swing dress with a V-neck at the front and back.

"Won't I be too dressed up?" I ask, my voice a pitch too high.

He grabs me by the shoulders. "Relax, Clara. Take a deep breath. Grigory always wears formal attire, and he's not gonna take you to the next best pizza place."

He's right. So I quickly slip into the dress.

When I watch the result in the mirror, I notice, to my great horror, that the bruise on my left shoulder is too far up for the wide strap to cover it. I could have hoped the bright red color would camouflage it somewhat, but the bruise stopped being red long ago, goddammit. It screams for attention with its stark bluish-purple color.

"Fuck!" I dart back to the bedroom, flipping through my few clean cardigans and blouses in the closet. Luckily, the one covering up the mark the most is black and suits the dress, but it only barely does the job. If it slides down even half an inch, the bright colors will pop out for the whole world to see.

Ten minutes to six, I stand by the curb, panting and hot despite my light clothing and the chilly evening air. I keep shifting my weight from foot to foot, fumbling with the folds of the skirt. My eagerness to see Grigory has driven me down here early, but now I regret it. I could have spent the last ten minutes calming my nerves in Markus's arms, but instead I chose to stand here where the anxiety keeps building and building.

When a black Mercedes pulls up to the curb five minutes later, my stomach is in knots.

The chauffeur gets out and circles the car. *"Fräulein."* He greets me with a polite nod and the German *Miss* as he opens the door for me.

I feel Grigory's eyes on me before I see him. All my defenses hit the ground like a crashing pile of bricks, and I freeze, unable to act or think. I don't get to dawdle long before Grigory leans over to pull me into the car and across the seat until my legs are pressed against his.

The door slams shut, and my tension builds as the air thins out in the small space. There's not enough room to be here with this all-consuming power field.

Like he knows exactly what he's searching for, Grigory turns my back to him, a strong arm locking around my waist as he pushes the cardigan off my left shoulder.

I suck in a gulp of air, feeling his eyes on the large blue mark he's made. I can't see his reaction, but I can hear it in his deepening breath.

He taps the mark gently, then presses slightly. It's not hard, but enough to make me bite my lip to contain the discomfort. The pressure becomes harder until he's digging his fingers into the muscle. I whimper, and in return he makes a deep rumbling sound. Then he pulls my cardigan back up like he got what he wanted.

Looping both arms around me, he places a kiss on my head, so gentle my eyes glide shut of their own volition. I sink into him, suddenly filled with an intense rush of being where I belong. The world hones in on this very car. Everything else—the traffic lights, cars, people out there in the street—blurs into nothingness.

"You looked beautiful in your burgundy gown Friday night." Grigory brushes my hair from my shoulder and presses his lips to my neck. "You still do," he whispers, his warm breath prickling my suddenly over-sensitive skin.

"Thank you," I say on a long exhale, heat spreading from the inside at his compliment.

He lifts his hand to trace a finger down my neck. A shudder erupts down my arm, and an involuntary moan falls over my parted lips. He curves his palm around my shoulder and starts a slow journey down my arm, easing the prickling chills while his breath lingers on the crook of my neck.

I angle my head to the side, giving him access to the vulnerable spot, and my back arches as my entire body hums with need.

"Not tonight, I'm afraid," he says in a low murmur, gripping my arm tightly while nuzzling his nose against my neck.

I want to let out a plaintive whimper, but instead I turn around and curl up against him, and he angles toward me to press me closer to his chest.

The next twenty minutes pass in silence, the sounds of the city a low murmur outside the car. It's so peaceful I wish we could skip dinner and keep driving around.

All too soon, the car stops, and the chauffeur steps out to open the door for us.

Grigory takes my hand and leads me down a crowded street. Feeling eyes on us, I grow uncomfortable with all the attention. When walking hand-in-hand with Markus, the lingering glances don't bother me, but we're only eleven years apart. Grigory is more than twenty years older than me, and on top of that, the power shift is much more potent between us.

I try to let go of his hand and walk behind him to make room for people going in the opposite direction, but he keeps me firmly in place at his side, and his confident strides make people veer to the side for us.

We end up in an intimate Spanish restaurant with a rustic interior and a lot of small tables standing a bit too close for my taste. There are many people here, and I'm not happy about the idea of sitting at one of those small tables.

"Guten abend, Herr Volkov," a waiter greets Grigory in German. *"Ihr üblichen tisch ist bereit."*

I think he says something about the usual table, so Grigory must be a regular here.

The waiter guides us to a table in the back, and I breathe a sigh of relief when I see it. A room divider and a couple of tall plants separate it from the rest of the restaurant, giving us our own secluded corner where none of the other guests can see us, and we can't see them.

Grigory gestures to the inner corner, and I give him a slight smile as I slip onto the wooden chair.

Instead of taking a seat across from me, Grigory moves the other chair to the end of the table, making me feel trapped in the small nook. But it doesn't bother me much. I like being close to him.

The waiter returns with menus, and when he's about to give me one, Grigory holds up a hand to stop him. My heart flutters. When I peek up at the waiter, I expect to see the same condescension I remember from the snooty waiter at the French restaurant a few weeks ago. But if there is any, this man doesn't let on.

Grigory orders drinks in fluent German, and I understand enough to know he asks about the wine selection and chooses a glass of red for himself while ordering a cola for me.

When the waiter leaves and Grigory peruses the menu, my self-consciousness starts rearing its head. I'm not sure what to do with myself as I have no menu to study, and my eyes flit around, my hands fumbling in my lap.

When Grigory casts a glance at me, I'm quick to lower my gaze. Peering up again, I find him studying the menu with a small smile tugging at the corners of his lips. Seeing him like this, relaxed and approachable, rubs off on me, and I stop fumbling, finding some calmness in just sitting here.

The waiter brings us our drinks and appetizers—small bowls

of olives, aioli, and bread. Grigory orders by pointing to the menu, and I get the feeling he keeps the interaction silent on purpose to keep me out of the decision-making.

I gather enough to know we must be having tapas—after all, it's a Spanish restaurant, and Grigory wouldn't keep pointing to dishes if we were having a normal meal.

The waiter leaves, and I debate whether to start on the appetizers or wait for a go-ahead as Grigory tastes his wine attentively.

In any other situation, it would be normal—well, expected—that I started without permission. But *normal* isn't a good guideline when it comes to Grigory. Last weekend when he fed me pizza from his hand, I had to wait while the two men started eating, and it felt natural given the power dynamic. But tonight, I'm sitting at the table, on the same level as Grigory, and I don't know if he wants me to act submissively or like we're on a normal date.

A normal date with Grigory. That wouldn't be possible. I don't think I could ever behave like Grigory's equal in any given situation. It seems plain wrong. So I do what has worked for me before and listen to my gut, which tells me to wait.

It proves to be the right thing as Grigory dips a piece of bread in the aioli and holds it up to me. I glance at the bread between his fingers and gulp. I'm not comfortable eating from his hand in public. But at least it's not from a flat palm, and we're hidden behind the room divider, so I end up opening my mouth and taking it. His fingers brush my lips on the way, sending tingles into my nerve endings. I peek up at him through low eyelids and stop chewing as I meet his narrowed eyes, dark and focused on me.

Releasing me from the lock of his gaze, he breaks a piece of bread off for himself, and as I start chewing again, I realize how delicious the food is. I'm quick to accept the next piece of bread, and I want to moan at the silky texture of the aioli combined with the crunchy crust of the bread.

Grigory keeps alternating between feeding me and eating himself. There's something very sensual about receiving food from his hand. The fleeting touches of his fingers heat my lips, and the intensity of his eyes makes a tinge of red creep into my cheeks and stay there until all three dishes are empty.

The waiter conveniently appears when we have finished, and I can't help wondering if he saw how Grigory fed me. My eyes remain fixed on the table as he places small plates and bowls of colorful food in front of us. It looks delicious and exuberant, and there's way too much food for two people.

Grigory reaches across the table for my plate, and I stare after the white porcelain, thinking he's going to keep feeding me from his hand the whole night. But he only starts filling it with spoonfuls of the different dishes.

"Do you like shrimp?" he asks, casting a look at me as he takes the spoon in the bowl filled with shrimp covered in a delicious-looking sauce.

"Yes," I say, tugging my hair behind my ear and folding my hands in my lap. God, those eyes. I feel flustered just looking at them.

Setting the now full plate back in front of me, he starts filling his own, and once again, I'm in the dilemma of whether to begin or wait.

The full plate before me should probably be interpreted as a go-ahead, right?

I reach up for the fork, closing my fingers around the cold steel, but I quickly release it again and put my hand back in my lap.

My eyes dart up to Grigory and back to the plate, but he gives me no sign pointing in one or the other direction, and when he begins eating himself, my unease grows.

It shouldn't be possible to get this nervous from having a plate of food placed in front of you. It really shouldn't.

I reach up to tug my hair behind my ear even though no strand has strayed and stop mid-motion when I feel his eyes on me. Lifting my gaze, I look straight into the depth of a terrifying dark sea of black and brown. His pupils are huge, the brown color around them so dark the two seem to meld together. There's something triumphant in those deep pits. Something powerful. Like he's getting off on my nervousness? Or my submission?

"You may begin," he says, his voice a deep rasp as he asserts his dominance with three small words.

I stay frozen in place, unable to break away from those mesmerizing pits of will that call upon the deepest submission in me.

It's only when he makes a nod toward my plate, directly ordering me to let go, that I can break eye contact and pick up my fork to spear a square piece of meat.

The meat melts on my tongue, and I close my eyes, taking in

the spicy and sweet flavors exploding on my taste buds.

When I open my eyes again, Grigory is watching me. Smiling. "It's good, right?" His dark accent wraps around that submissive place inside me and pulls me deeper into it.

I nod, unable to find the words.

We don't say much for a long while as we keep eating. I'm too funny in the head and can't concentrate on more than one line of action—bringing food into my mouth, chewing, and soaking up the bursts of flavors erupting on my tongue.

My nervousness has waned to an almost pleasant simmer, and it's surprising how easy it is to just eat without any words. With most people, I would feel awkward about long stretches of silence, but with Grigory, it seems natural. Calm even.

Whenever my head starts to clear up, all I have to do is meet Grigory's blunt gaze and I fall right back into the woozy headspace, feeling small and vulnerable in the most delicious way.

Halfway through the meal, Grigory breaks into my hypnotic state. "What did you think about the show Friday night?"

I have to take a moment to gather my thoughts. Putting my fork down, I finish chewing and swallow. "It was very impressive. One of the best productions I have seen."

"What other shows is it up against?" His powerful authority has receded some, making him seem more approachable and friendly.

"Markus took me to Covent Garden to see *Aida* when I went to see him in London in the fall." My answer is even and open, and for once I almost feel at ease carrying a normal conversation with him.

He chuckles—a warm, deep sound—and smiles at me. "That's a hard one to beat, yes. *Aida* can be quite the spectacle in itself. But that production..." he gives a shake of his head, "it beat all others that season."

It was a huge production with majestic scenery, ornate costumes, and large crowds of people on the stage. I've never seen anything like it, and even though the *Tosca* show was in a league of its own, it couldn't compete with the grandeur of *Aida.*

"Did you see it?" I ask.

"No. I was busy putting together our new production of *Turandot* in Vienna at the time. But I heard more than enough about it. We were actually a bit nervous when it premiered since we hoped our *Turandot* would become the spectacle of the year. But Fabian and Covent Garden sure took the price."

"Oh. That's a shame." I pick up my fork to spear the last shrimp on my plate.

"Don't worry. I've won so many other times." He gives me a smug smile, a glimmer of humorous arrogance dancing in his eyes, and I can't help smiling myself.

"I didn't know opera houses competed like that."

"It's mostly a conductor thing. Fabian and I and a couple of the other conductors in the large houses have had this competition going for a long time. For a few years, we even had a bet going."

"Really?" I say, opening my eyes wide. Though on second thought, I'm not so surprised. I can clearly imagine Grigory taking part in such a bet, arrogant in his belief he'll win.

Taking the bowl of shrimp, Grigory lifts his brows in a silent question. I nod and smile when he spoons more shrimp onto my plate.

"Do you have a favorite opera?" I ask as I continue eating spicy seafood.

"I've always had an affinity for Puccini." He gathers the cutlery on his empty plate and leans back in his chair. "*Tosca, La Bohème, Madama Butterfly.* No one knows how to express love and loss as he does. But *Prince Igor* has become *my* opera. I'm always the one all the big houses want whenever they are doing it, and I have a hard time declining. It was the first opera I conducted, so it's special to me." He takes a sip of his wine. "It's becoming quite the bad habit. Last winter, I flew to Australia to do a revival of a production I'd conducted several times before. Twenty-four hours for something that barely got my creative wheels spinning...." He makes a flat line of his mouth and furrows his brows.

"But you must be used to traveling with the job you have?"

"I am. But twenty-four hours on a plane is long, even for the most hardened traveler. And I must say, I'm getting sick of all this back and forth." He waves his hand in a side-to-side motion. "I've worked on reducing it for some years now, but it takes time breaking a bad habit."

We keep talking for some time, and I find out that Grigory plans to focus most of his energy on his work with the opera here. Apparently, there's a lot of work that needs to be done, especially within the organization, to get everything to run smoothly. On top of that, he's going to stay on with the Vienna

State Opera as their principal guest conductor. I get a feeling Vienna and the opera there hold a special place in his heart.

"That's it," he says, cutting a hand through the air. "A few loose concerts here and there, but no more holding five large positions at once."

I don't get how he's done it. A lot of famous conductors are appointed chief conductor, guest conductor, musical director, and whatever else you call it, several places around the world at the same time.

"How did you ever find the time for anything but rehearsals, concerts, and traveling?" I ask.

"I didn't," he deadpans. "For a few years, I could barely make time for learning new music, and if I were lucky, I could squeeze in one hour by the piano in a day. It didn't work for me."

I feel like I'm getting to know more about him in one night than I have in six weeks. It's a huge change which makes butterflies flutter in my stomach. I really enjoy talking to him like this. But at the same time, it makes me sad because I want more of it, and in one week I'm going home.

I eat in silence for some time while he reclines in the chair, sipping his wine. When I've cleared my plate, I'm, for once, the one to break the silence. "I don't want this summer to end," I confess, turning my gaze to my folded hands in my lap.

When he doesn't respond, I glance at him beneath my lashes, surprised to find a tender mildness in his eyes—like he's touched by my confession.

It makes me dangerously hopeful. I'm not sure exactly what I'm hoping for, but the combination of his openness and the gentle expression makes me want to believe this might not be the end after all.

* * *

On our way back, I'm once again nestled against Grigory in the back of the car. I hate that we have to say goodbye, and I cling to him with an arm locked around his waist and a hand curled around the shirt under his jacket.

Our verbal communication may be underdeveloped, but I have no problem taking all the physical contact I can get if he just gives me the smallest invitation. I could never tell him how much I yearn for him, but the way I cling to him must say it better than words ever could.

I don't think it's just me who feels the impending separation sneaking up on us. His hard grip around me seems to mirror my anxious need to be close. I almost don't dare to believe it's reciprocated, but I can't find any other explanation as I sit here feeling closer to him than I've ever felt to anyone before.

Like on the ride to the restaurant, we don't speak. It's only when we turn down Markus's street that I again break the silence. "I hate that we have to say goodbye," I mutter into his suit jacket.

His large palm strokes the back of my head with startling tenderness, like I'm something fragile that will break if you press a little too hard. But then it stills, and I feel the growing tension in a frozen moment.

"I'm not sure I can do this, Clara." Grigory's voice is strained, like his shoulders and hand.

My heart suddenly pumps louder than the traffic outside. "What do you mean?" I say, trying to sound casual but failing miserably.

Grigory's other hand tightens around my upper arm, so much it hurts. But there's no answer.

"What do you mean?" I try to pull back to gain eye contact, but he won't let me.

"You and me, Clara. I don't think I can do it."

The car pulls up in front of Markus's building and a sudden urge to flee builds in my chest. We have just had a wonderful evening, and now he shuts off? Not sure if he wants this? We have just had sex a couple of days ago, for God's sake, and it was the best sex I've ever had. He's taken all I have to give, and *now* he tells me he can't do it?

Tears well up in my eyes even as rage simmers inside me. I try to slip my hands up to dry them away, but Grigory keeps me pressed to him, and my arms remain trapped between us, my head caught in his shoulder. It's like he doesn't want to let me go. It hurts so badly. Because why would he push me away if he wants me?

I start shaking with silent sobs, and he keeps holding me like he wants to comfort me even though he's the one inflicting the hurt.

"I'm sorry," he whispers into my hair, and my crying takes on desperate sounds. Everything with him is so hopeless. So meaningless.

I vaguely hear the chauffeur leave the car, and Grigory just holds me as my shoulders shake with violent sobs and my tears soak his jacket. I cling to him with all my might, like it could make him stay, but I know that the moment I leave this car—leave his embrace—a cold wall will shoot up between us.

"Is this goodbye?" I say between sobs.

"I don't know," he says, regret straining his voice. "I don't know." He kisses my hair, and I cry harder. I can't lose this. I just can't.

"Please," I say, pressing my fingers into him. "Please don't leave me."

There's no answer—nothing but his arms that still refuse to let me go.

So I finally force back the tears and pull away from him. This time, he lets me.

I don't look back as I slide across the seat and leave the car; I know it will only break me.

I run into the building and find a secluded nook behind the stairs, where I curl up shaking. There I sit for the next hour until I can convince myself it wasn't a last goodbye. He's just in doubt like he's been before. He just needs a few days, and then he'll hold me again.

I don't believe it, but I can't afford not to. So I force down the hurt and doubt as I take the elevator up to face Markus with the explanation that I feel overwhelmed by everything—which is a mild version of the truth.

— CHAPTER 24 —

"Come with me to the opera tonight," Markus says when we're eating late in the afternoon. He's going to the opera for another *Tosca* performance and is leaving in an hour.

I shrug and spear a piece of unappetizing defrosted pizza. I hate serving such poor food for him, but I haven't been able to muster the energy for more today.

"It will do you good to get out of the apartment and see something else," he says. When I don't answer, he continues. "I know you are overwhelmed by everything that's going on, but you can't just sit here wallowing. You usually like coming with me. You know people are always nice."

I swallow past the building lump in my throat as I stare into my plate.

"There's that sad look again, sweetie." Markus leans across the table to nudge my chin up. "Are you sure everything went okay last night?"

"Can we just not talk about it?" I say, hoping he doesn't notice the slight tremor in my voice. Several times during the day, I've considered telling Markus what happened last night, but whenever the idea pops into my head, my eyes prickle with tears, my chest constricting.

His eyes narrow. "The last time I let you stew for a few days, it turned out to be a really bad decision." He releases my chin and cuts into his pizza.

I bite my lip as I wait for an answer.

He finishes chewing and shoves his plate aside. "I'll make you a deal. If you come with me tonight, we'll postpone our talk until tomorrow."

"Thank you," I say, nodding my agreement. I'll do anything to avoid stirring up those feelings right now. I've already had enough crying this summer to last me an entire year.

* * *

There's a constant flurry of people coming and going in Markus's dressing room—make-up artists, technicians going over final details, colleagues wanting to chat. Markus is smiling and laughing, ever the charismatic charmer everyone loves—including me.

He was right. It's good to be here. I've made myself comfortable in the recliner opposite the door, laughing at the light banter and talking to all the people who want to know more about Markus's girlfriend.

Fifteen minutes before the show starts, everybody—including Markus—disappears, leaving the room pleasantly quiet. I take out my Kindle to read, and for the first time in days, I can get through a page without having to go back and reread. When Markus comes back in the first break, I've read more than I have in an entire week.

He is joined by a couple of make-up artists, and the tempo is high as he prepares for the next act. There's not much room for talking, but I enjoy being near him and observing the bustling life behind the scenes.

The second break is calmer since he doesn't have to change. He comes in alone and stalks up to me, caging me in with a hand on each armrest. "Are you feeling okay?"

I give him a drowsy smile and a nod. I'm so relaxed I could sleep right here, which would probably do me good since I haven't had a good night's sleep for several days.

"Do you need a nap?" He doesn't wait for my answer before going to the closet to retrieve his jacket. He drapes it over me and gives me a kiss, and then I'm alone again.

I'm already drifting off when the door opens a few minutes later. Looking up with a sleepy smile, I expect to see Markus. But my smile wilts when Grigory appears in the door.

He halts like he's gone wrong, and then he just stands there, eyes fixed on me with a burning intensity. Anger, irritation, lust? I can't read him. But something happens to him. He's no longer the composed man with an abundance of control and patience. His nostrils flare and his jaw tightens.

My heart races in my chest like it's trying to escape, but the rest of me is frozen. Grigory seems to be the same, and for a charged moment we just stare at each other, our eyes interlocked like neither of us wants to break away.

"Grigory," I finally say, a small plea for... something.

He makes a slight movement like he's about to step forward. Hope burns within me. But just as quickly as it came, Grigory crushes it, spinning on his heel and leaving.

He fucking turns around and leaves.

Fury is a tidal wave inside me, ripping everything apart as it goes. It's so strong I have to curl my fingers around the armrests to refrain from hurling my Kindle into the long row of mirrors.

Getting up, I pace the room with heavy steps, curling and uncurling my fists at my sides. I've never felt such anger before. I'm not the type of person to become destructive when my emotions spiral, but right now I imagine sweeping my arm over the make-up table to make all the things there fly, and I imagine the crackling sound of the mirrors if I were to hammer four legs of a chair into them.

It takes me all of forty-five minutes to calm myself down enough to sit still in the recliner.

Not long after I've gotten myself under control, Markus returns. "Did you get a nap?" His smile is wide and genuine, and I try to reciprocate, but it doesn't reach my eyes.

Before long, there's a constant commotion again. I keep my eyes trained on my Kindle, pretending to read the inconsequential words as people come and go, chattering on about the show and saying goodnight.

Lucia comes in while Markus is removing his stage make-up. "What a barbaric ending," she says with a dramatic intonation that makes me want to roll my eyes. "Has Grigory gone mad?" Suddenly, she's got all my attention. "It was way too fast." She fans her hand in front of her face and watches me as she exhales through rounded lips. "Never trust a conductor."

I give her a slight smile, like I'm not about to explode inside.

Markus turns to look at me, and even though I think I'm doing quite a good job of hiding my rage, I can tell from his assessing eyes he doesn't buy it.

Turning back to Lucia, he handles her outrage with the same calmness he handles everything else. "It wasn't that bad, and you did great as always."

"Have you seen him? I can't find him." She clearly isn't ready to let this go.

"Not since we left the stage," Markus says.

Grigory will surely get to hear her opinion about his speedy tempo. But the classical music world isn't known for its democracy. Grigory is heavily seated on the throne, and I'm sure an outraged diva will bother him as much as a buzzing fly. He's used to things going his way, and if he wants to conduct the last act faster than usual, he'll do so. And if he wants to ignore me after taking all I have and demanding my full and utter submission, he'll do that too.

There's absolutely nothing I can do to change any of this. I'm completely powerless, just like he wants it. If he wants to use me again, I don't have a living chance in hell to reject him. All sense and self-preservation evaporate in his presence. I'm driven by pure submissive instinct.

I feel so helpless, and Markus is the only reason I don't drown in all of this.

— CHAPTER 25 —

"What happened between Grigory and you last night?" Markus asks at breakfast the next day.

"Why do you think anything happened?" I poke at the pancakes on my plate.

"For God's sake." Frustration rises in his voice. "I'm not an idiot, Clara. You were fine when I left you, and when I came back, I could almost see the fumes rising from your head."

I must have been naïve for thinking I could cover up my fury. Being around Markus is like walking under a microscope; it's uncanny how much he sees. But what's worse is I feel horrible about trying to hide from him in the first place. Everything is spinning out of control, and I barely know what I'm doing half the time.

"And don't think I didn't notice how you almost sneered when Lucia mentioned Grigory," he continues. "It wasn't hard to put two and two together. You heard what she said about the last act."

"Was it really that bad?" I ask, hunching my shoulders in defeat.

"Lucia exaggerates. I don't think the audience noticed much.

But it *was* faster than usual." He brings more pancakes onto his plate and tops them off with a generous squeeze of syrup. Then he looks back at me with terrifying severity. "Grigory *never* loses tempo."

I stare into the air, unable to understand how our brief encounter could have affected him so much. It seems wholly absurd, and I want to laugh at the idea. But at the same time, the coincidence is too striking. Grigory looked all... I can't find the right word to describe it, but there definitely was a strong reaction.

"What happened?" Markus demands with a rumbling tone.

I press the heel of my hand to my forehead. My head is such chaos from all these mixed signals. "Grigory came in after you had been there. He seemed... almost agitated when he saw me. And then he left."

"What did he say?"

"Nothing. He just glared at me, then turned and left." I feel crazy as I recount what happened. How can such a small thing affect such a powerful man? There should be more to the story, but there isn't.

Markus slams his fork into the table. "That's it!"

I can't help my nervous startle. "Are you mad at him?" I've never seen Markus like this before.

"You bet your ass I am."

"I'm sorry," I say, running my hand over my forehead. I hate that I've come between the two men.

"It's not your fault." Markus reaches across the table to take my hand. "He's just a fool who fucks everything up when he's finally found something good."

What the hell does that mean?

I don't get a chance to ask before Markus takes the conversation in a different direction. "How did it go when he took you out to dinner?"

I open my mouth to answer, but Markus cuts me off with a stern warning.

"And don't just say *fine,* like all the other times I've asked."

I breathe a heavy sigh, feeling like a liar with all the things I've hidden from him lately. "It went well right until we were on our way back. Then everything changed when I said I didn't want to say goodbye. He seemed distant and said he didn't know if he could do this. It was like he was saying goodbye, yet he didn't want to let go." A stab of hurt spears my chest and tears prickle my eyes. It's so meaningless. If he wants me, then why does he keep pulling away?

"Come here." Markus pulls out from the table, and I go to kneel between his knees. He pulls my head into his lap and strokes my hair, and I wrap my arms around his legs and lean into him, shedding a few silent tears.

"He needs to figure out what he wants," Markus says, half to himself. "Until then, he can't see you."

I don't know what it is Grigory needs to figure out. Because what is there to figure out? I'm Markus's girlfriend, and I'm going home on Sunday. It's not like Grigory has to make some big decision about us.

It feels like a punishment that I can't see him, but I know Markus does it to protect me, and in the end I'm deeply grateful for it. I wouldn't be able to say no myself, and seeing Grigory right now would break me.

* * *

I start an arduous process of shutting down my hopes of seeing Grigory again. But it's like stopping an oncoming truck with your bare hands. What I do manage is to get my hopes down. Instead of hoping for more after I go home, I just hope to get a better ending. It hurts to think all the things we've shared will end with the cold rejection at the opera last night.

But it's no help at all. Because as the hope for something more dies, I realize this is the end with big fat capital letters. The knowledge hits me harder than anything else.

I've grown more attached to Grigory than I have dared to admit, and even though part of me knew it, it's only now I truly feel the depth of it. My response to him is so purely instinctive that I, on some level, feel like I belong to him.

It's wrong, I know. I belong to Markus. But I can't control it and I'm afraid how it will affect our relationship. These days, I just want to be alone, and I keep retreating to the piano room where I bury myself in melancholic thoughts whenever I can't concentrate on the piano—which is all the time.

The black and white keys remind me too much of the piano lessons with Grigory—his calm control and the punishing metal stick which somehow drove me both deeper into the music and deeper into submission. Whenever I think of it, I choke up and have to leave the instrument in a hurry.

Instead, I spend a lot of time on the oriental carpet, staring into the ceiling, trying to convince myself these feelings will fade with time and Markus and I can go back to the way things were before the summer.

I wish I could spend my last days here with Markus, especially now that he has a lot of free time after the premiere. But it's hard being around him. When I sit or lie in his arms, I wish it was Grigory holding me, and the guilt is terrible.

Two long days pass in this melancholic hole.

"This needs to stop," Markus says when he comes into the piano room Thursday at noon.

I drag my eyes from the ceiling to watch him tower over me.

"I know you're sad and hurt, but I won't accept that it ruins our last few days together." He pulls me up from the floor and gives me a shove toward the hall. "Go put on your shoes."

"I don't feel like going anywhere," I mutter.

Markus steps in front of me and grabs my shoulders, his jaw taut as he speaks in a stern tone. "This is not about you anymore. This is about me wanting a good end to a lovely summer with my girlfriend." He releases me and starts putting on shoes, and I'm too dumbfounded to move for a moment.

It hits me that I'm doing the exact same thing to him that Grigory does to me, and the realization jolts me into action. Within seconds, I'm dressed and ready to go, and Markus grabs me by the hand with a smile and pulls me out of the apartment.

* * *

Markus takes me on a river cruise on Spree. During the three months I've been here, I've done too little sightseeing in a city that has more than plenty to offer, and this is a good way to make up for it. We sail by a lot of the noteworthy buildings—Berliner Dom, the parliament building, and the Museum Island. Museums aren't my thing, so I'm pleased enough to see the beautiful buildings from the outside.

The weather is wonderful, and I remove my jacket to let the sun beat down on my skin. Markus has had the foresight to bring sunscreen, which he lathers on my white shoulders while we sit on the open deck.

We hold hands, kiss, and act like a real couple. It's nice and, not least of all, reassuring to know I can still feel this way about him. The heavy weight on my chest isn't gone, but it has eased enough that I only notice it for short moments at a time.

After the boat tour, he takes me to Tiergarten, where we sit in the grass and eat ice cream. We laugh from the pits of our stomachs when a playful Labrador makes a dog walker lose hold of three leashes.

The dogs run in all directions, creating chaos and joy around the park. Other dogs start barking, a small child gets a new friend, and a middle-aged woman, clearly afraid of dogs, gets a good scare. All the while, the young man runs around with his last two dogs, trying to catch the rest.

"We are so going to watch *The Secret Life of Pets* when we get home," I say with a bright smile.

Markus leans over me with dark hunger gleaming in his eyes until I lie flat on the grass. "No. I'm going to thrust my cock inside you until you scream." He crushes his lips to mine, and I wrap my arms around his neck as our tongues dance with each other. For the first time in weeks, I have a deep-seated need to feel him inside me.

The minute we enter the apartment, Markus starts ripping off my clothes. With his hands on my shoulders, he presses me to my knees and opens his pants. "Suck me off," he orders, and I eagerly lick up and down his hard length, taking it deep inside my mouth.

I don't get to keep control for long before he grabs my hair and pushes down my throat. It's only when I grab his thighs, desperate for air, that he pulls back, giving me a small reprieve before he repeats.

Moisture is trickling from my eyes when he finally throws me onto my back on the floor and grabs me by the neck. With a torturously slow movement, he pushes inside me. "You're so tight," he rasps and starts gliding in and out.

He picks up tempo and I give him a pleading look while small mewls creep up from my throat.

"Touch yourself," he demands.

I reach my fingers down between us and stroke my clit, bucking beneath him from the delicious feeling. It only takes seconds before his cock does a telltale twitch, and the moment he spurts inside me, I break into a long orgasm that has my back arching up over the floor and my feet curling in my shoes.

"God, Markus. I'm yours," I moan.

His response comes in a raspy sound, marked by two hard thrusts. "All. Mine."

— CHAPTER 26 —

My mood has been relatively stable since Markus took me sightseeing yesterday, and whenever sadness or worries creep up, I go to him and get a big hug. It's a much better strategy than retreating to the music room.

Markus is singing *Tosca* tonight, and since the show doesn't start until seven, I'm surprised when he's getting ready to leave in the early afternoon.

"Why are you leaving so early?" I ask, not happy about losing him. It doesn't take so long to apply stage make-up and change clothes.

"I need to talk to Grigory," he says with a tight expression.

I fidget with the buttons on his dark blue dress shirt. "Are you still mad at him?"

"Let's just say I'm not happy." His mouth flattens. "He fucked up. But I know he has his problems, and I need to know what's going on before I get worked up."

I could be disappointed that Markus doesn't take my side exclusively, but this is one of the things I love about him; the way he cares for the people around him. So I can't be mad at him for wanting to hear Grigory out.

"I want you in bed before I get home," he says. "You need to adjust your routine, so it won't be too hard getting up Sunday."

My flight takes off at the crack of dawn, so I have no problem seeing the sense in that, but I don't think I'll be able to fall asleep early. I don't think I'll be able to fall asleep at all, actually.

Markus's features take on a somber expression as he lifts his hand to my cheek. "I'm going to miss you, sweetie."

I know what he means. I'm feeling the imminent end of our summer closing in too. Placing my hands on his chest, I gaze up at him with sincerity deepening my gaze. "I'm gonna miss you too."

He pulls me into a big hug and presses a long, tender kiss to my lips.

After he's left, I begin to sink back into the dark hole that his presence has kept me out of. It's not just the prospect of going home; the thought of Markus talking things over with Grigory sets my wheels of worry turning. I'm convinced things are over for good between Grigory and me. I don't think their conversation will change that, but some small furtive part of me can't help hoping for something.

I slip into bed at ten, but when the bedroom door opens an hour later, I'm still wide awake.

Markus takes a seat on the edge of the bed and strokes my hair. "Do you need a sleeping pill?"

He all but forced me to go to the doctor and ask for sleeping pills when I had some stressful exams last winter. I only used them once when Markus threatened to spank my ass ten different shades of blue if I didn't. I have so much trouble sleeping I'm afraid it would become a bad habit if I found out they work.

So I shake my head.

He pulls the comforter aside and trails a hand over my naked body. "I just might know something else that will help."

Gripping me by the waist, he flips me onto my stomach. I hear the drawer in the nightstand open, and then he's circling gruff jute rope around my wrists. His hands move deftly as he pulls the rope between my wrists and around itself, creating two separate cuffs which he finishes with a knot. There's no way I'll get out of it. But just for the sake of it, I wriggle my hands, feeling the sweet resistance.

Markus knows being trapped and at his mercy calms me. It chases away my worries when I have no other choice but to submit.

Markus strips off his clothes and jumps up between my legs. With a hand on my lower back, he pins me to the mattress and slides a couple of fingers between my folds.

I'm already wet, and when he prods his cock against my entrance, he easily slides in. He could have speared me with one hard shove, but he opts for an agonizingly slow pace, pushing in increment by slow increment.

When he's all the way in, I'm whimpering and bucking my hips, my arms struggling against the rope. *I need more.*

"Please, Markus."

With a hand flat against my lower back, he holds me still as he pulls out just as slowly. And then he starts the torture all over again, slowly in, slowly out. He keeps going until my mind is about to split, overwrought with insane need.

I beg and plead for him to take me, and finally, he relents and shoves inside me, fucking me with a ferocity that has me moaning and groaning uncontrollably. Nudging a hand beneath me, he rubs my clit, and within seconds I'm coming apart around his cock, screaming from the intense orgasm. At the same moment, Markus makes a few telltale twitches, and my climax draws out as he pulses inside me, spilling his come.

Panting heavily, Markus lies down beside me, pulls the covers up to my waist, and caresses my back. He leaves the ropes in place. They keep me tethered, making sure my mind doesn't wander off to the land of worries, and I slip into a land of peaceful dreams.

— CHAPTER 27 —

The day before going home is hard. My imminent departure hangs heavy in the air, weighing down both Markus and me.

We try to tell funny stories when we go to the kitchen to prepare lunch together, but our laughter is strained, and soon gloomy silence descends.

I loop my arms around Markus, leaning against his back, when he checks on the pasta. "I wish I could stay."

He turns around and gathers me to him. "I know. I'm going to miss you too. The apartment will be so empty without you."

"Do you think we'll get to spend more than just a few days together again soon? I know it won't be three months, but just one or two weeks?"

"I really can't say. My schedule is hectic in the fall. My days off are few and scattered. Then it's Christmas and everything that comes with it..."

There's nothing more to say. It's going to be hard, and we can't do anything to change it. So we just hold each other until the pasta boils over.

Markus will do fine. He'll miss me, sure, but he gets so immersed in his work that it doesn't bother him to be apart for a few weeks at a time.

I, on the other hand, feel restless when we're apart and often miss him so terribly it's hard to focus on anything else. What's even worse is all the saying goodbyes. It tears at me every time.

We've done the back-and-forth routine before, but after this summer it's difficult to imagine how I'll be able to function in it again.

I have to. There's no other option.

Hopefully, it's just a matter of readjustment. One hard month, and then I'll find my balance.

It's a weak hope. If being away from Markus was the only change, I might have had a chance to settle back into the old routine. But it's not. So much has happened and my wounds from Grigory's constant pulling away are still gaping holes. The prospect of being alone with all that hurt stirs up a ton of anxiety.

I still wish I could get a better end, or at least a proper goodbye—anything to help the healing along. But with each passing hour, I'm more and more convinced I won't get it.

Markus hasn't mentioned anything about his conversation with Grigory yesterday, and it's driving me insane. I want to ask him about it, but merely thinking about Grigory makes my eyes well up, so I don't think talking about him is a good idea. What good would it do, anyway? If Grigory wanted to see me, Markus would surely have told me. He wouldn't torture me by keeping such information to himself.

I bounce back and forth between anger, sadness, and poor attempts at lightening the mood. Come late afternoon, I'm in a constant battle against the tears burning behind my eyes, and finally I can't hold them back anymore. I break down in Markus's arms and cry for what seems like an eternity while Markus tries, without much luck, to console me.

Markus orders in early in the evening, and we sit on the couch and watch TV while he eats and I poke at the food.

Markus keeps checking his phone in this restless way like he's waiting for something important. It's only now I realize he's been doing it all day.

I want to ask him about it, but his mood is as tense as mine, and judging from the frustrated way he handles his phone, I don't think the subject would do any good.

Suddenly, his phone rings, and his quick reaction confirms he was expecting it. I don't catch the name flashing on the screen before he grabs it and stalks to the bedroom.

Worry builds like snow in a blizzard while I wait. I have no idea what it might be about, but his taut expression has me concerned.

"What was it?" I ask when he returns.

"Something important that has fallen into place." He still looks grave, but the restlessness seems to have settled. His words don't explain anything, but I know better than to pry when he keeps his answers brief like this.

Despite barely having moved a finger all day, I'm exhausted after dinner. All the strain and worry must have sucked me dry. If I'm lucky, it means I'll be able to sleep tonight. Then all this tension won't be for nothing, at least.

I'm already considering heading to bed an hour after dinner. But I don't want to let go of Markus. I'm lying with a leg draped over him and my head on his chest, blinking my sleepy eyes. This will be the last time this summer we sit here together.

God, my chest aches at the realization.

The sound of the doorbell makes me groan. "Do you need to get that? It's probably just a pizza guy who has the wrong apartment number."

Markus gets up and places a pillow under my arm. It's a poor replacement, but I accept it anyway and settle in the new position with my eyes closed.

Low voices murmur in the hallway. Thinking Markus is about to send a delivery guy on his way, I startle when I hear two sets of footsteps enter the living room. My eyes flutter open, and I stare straight up at Grigory. He stands at the other end of the room with an expression I've never seen on him before. His eyes seem to hold tender care, worry, and uncertainty all at once. Every muscle in me tenses. I'm not sure if it's his expression or his mere presence that shocks me the most.

Snapping myself out of it, I push up to sit and force my eyes away. The whole day I've been hoping for this, but suddenly anger has my heart pounding and I want nothing to do with him.

"Go to the bedroom, sweetie," Markus says.

I scurry across the room without looking at Grigory—still clutching the pillow in my arms.

Anger burns white-hot inside me. I pace back and forth in the bedroom, my hands curled around the pillow as I try to contain the destructive energy surging through me. I don't remember ever being this mad. Maybe when I saw Grigory in Markus's dressing room a few nights ago—but besides that...

What the hell is he thinking, showing up after an entire week's silence? And at the very last moment, right before I leave.

He can't possibly think I want anything to do with him after the way he's treated me?

Maybe it has nothing to do with me? Maybe he just has some business with Markus he needs to talk over?

My stomach becomes a pit of searing rocks, and my hands clench painfully around the pillow.

No, it can't be. Markus wouldn't let him come here if not to see me. He knows it would only hurt to see him in passing like this.

Maybe Markus has made him come? It would make sense. He's done it several times before and it must have been Grigory he was on the phone with earlier.

The idea soothes the ache in my chest, but the relief only lasts a moment before the anger surges back.

Making Grigory come here this close to my departure is like rubbing salt in a wound. I might have obsessed about the idea of getting a good ending, but whether the end is good or bad isn't what truly matters. Markus should know that.

Suddenly, I'm furious with Markus too.

God, I can't control my feelings anymore.

And what does it matter why Grigory is here? I don't want to see him. Period. I can't think of any scenario in which it wouldn't cause more pain in an already painful situation.

I don't think I can hold onto this determination though. Because who am I kidding? I yearn to see him with my whole heart. It doesn't matter how much it will hurt in the end. I want to be near him—feel the warmth of his massive hands, his impossible power when he holds me.

I've ached for it for so many days, and now it's finally here within my reach. Right at the last moment.

A huge wave of sadness crashes against the anger boiling inside me. I want to smash something, rip out my own hair, scream and yell, cry and sob. I can't take it. I feel like I'm about to go insane and I need to get it out.

But when Markus comes in, I just stand there, frozen in place, my chest so tight I have to concentrate on getting air into my lungs.

"Grigory wants to see you. Come to the living room."

"I can't talk to him," I say, my voice weak as I shake my head.

"You don't have to. You just have to hear him out." Markus closes the distance between us with a few long steps and runs a hand over my arm in a soothing gesture.

"No! I don't want to fucking see him." I throw the pillow to the ground, my words coming out with a startling fury.

The rebuke in Markus's gaze is like a rush of icy water, sobering me immediately. I slam my palm over my mouth. I've never spoken to him like this and I didn't mean to at all.

He grabs me by the arm and hauls me into the living room, his patience clearly running low. "Have you considered that this might be hard on him too?"

I huff but keep back the mockery that wants to fly off my tongue. Grigory has had full control all the time; he could haul me around in this and that direction at any given moment. If something was hard, he could just shove me the other way—or walk away.

The man in question sits at the far end of the sofa. I try my best not to look at him as Markus releases me by the chaise lounge and takes a seat beside it, feet planted on the floor and arms crossed over his chest. He's in no mood for petulance. And I don't want to be petulant, but it's hard not to with Grigory here. So I perch on the edge of the chaise lounge, as far away from both men as I can get.

It isn't like me, acting out like this, but I can't stop myself. I cross my arms, staring into the wall, my anger on full display. I neither want to nor have the energy to hide it. Grigory deserves to see it. I've been meek and pliant for too long.

No one says anything for a while and it only makes me angrier. I bite my molars together. Why would Markus drag me in here if no one's going to say anything? To enjoy the infuriating silence?

Finally, Grigory speaks. "*Devochka*," he says to get my attention. Usually, it sounds caring and tender when he calls me the Russian word for little girl, but right now my angry ears only hear the belittlement. I refuse to meet his eyes, but he continues anyway. "I'm so sorry I've made you sad."

The regret in his voice tugs at something inside me—something that wants to quell the anger and make me face him. But I refuse to, and for once, my anger is strong enough to let me keep my determination.

"I would like to see you again if you'll allow it," he says.

What? He comes here and apologizes for having made me sad—which is the understatement of the year. And now he wants to see me after having kept a cold distance for a week? Like that isn't enough, he pretends I have a say in it. I can't believe him.

For the first time since I entered the living room, I lift my eyes, ready to sputter and let him feel the full force of my "sadness." But the moment I meet his gaze, I lose momentum. There's something vulnerable in the depth of his eyes that steals my breath—something open and honest I didn't expect to see from this man.

"I don't want to see you again." My voice is hoarse and unconvincing, and I shudder at the sound of it. Once more, I've fallen into his trap.

Grigory pulls in a deep breath, for once meant to level himself and not me. "Like your boyfriend so correctly pointed out, I've been a coward." He turns to Markus. "He's right, I'm afraid." Something unspoken passes between the two men before Grigory looks back at me. "You mean a lot to me, Clara, and I haven't dared to admit it. I've been pulling away even as I've been drawn to you. And because of my indecision, you've been hurt. I'm truly sorry for that."

His honesty hits me hard, and I just stare at him.

This wasn't what I expected. At all. I thought I was some plaything he could use however he liked without caring how I felt.

I've known I meant something to him on some or another level, but I guess I concluded he could turn it on and off and didn't truly care. How could I think anything else when he kept shutting me out?

To hear him say the words—hear that he actually feels what I so many times thought he did—it steals my breath and makes tears press behind my eyes.

"I've been afraid to admit how much I wanted you at my feet," he continues. "I tried to deny it, but every time you so sweetly submitted to me, it got harder."

I bite my lower lip. His confession goes straight to my soul, but at the same time, I can't believe it.

Why would he say it now that it's all over, anyway?

Frustration resurfaces. This changes nothing. I'm still going home tomorrow, and he's going on with his busy conductor's life. Even if I could see him again, then what would it change if he can't handle what's happening between us?

My anger spikes, and I direct it all at him with a sharp glare. "What does it help when you keep acting like I'm nothing?" *Fuck*, saying it out loud is like a knife to the chest and tears brim the corners of my eyes, the anger ebbing into a hurt so deep I can barely breathe.

Something shifts in Grigory. His features become somber, and for the first time while I've known him, he's the one to cast his eyes down. It's fleeting, but it's enough to cut deep inside me. I can't bear seeing him like this, and it takes all I have to suppress the urge to run to him and fall to the ground at his feet.

"For most of my life, my career has come first," he says. "I've had a lot of steady play partners, but it was always noncommittal relationships. When I finally started to want something more, it didn't go so great. I was too slow to claim the first woman I truly cared about, and the next one..." Grigory's mouth twists, and he shares a grave look with Markus before sighing and continuing.

"Magdalena was a very volatile woman. One moment she'd be deeply submissive and wanting to please me, the next she'd flip out about some trivial matter and fight me for control."

"I spent a long time trying to make it work." Grigory shakes his head and huffs like it was a really bad decision. "When things finally ended, I was drained and exhausted and couldn't stand the idea of having another sub. I guess I was afraid it would turn out to be the same nightmare. But then you came around, Clara, and reminded me how good it feels to have a sub at my foot."

He watches me with astounding honesty, and I suck in a loud breath as his eyes hone in on me with want and desire. It sparks the instinctive submission I've been trying to hold down tonight, and I feel myself slip into that space where I'm ready to obey any order he gives me.

Grigory smiles. "This, *devochka*, this sweet submission has caused me a lot of trouble during the last two months. You have no idea how much I've wanted to possess and protect you." His smile fades and his eyes fill with regret. "But I've been too scared to let you in. So I kept pushing you away, hoping the urge would die down. It was selfish and irresponsible, and I'm so sorry for the hurt I've caused you."

I stop breathing and stare into Grigory's sincere eyes, astounded by his confession. I barely register when Grigory turns to Markus and the two of them exchange a few words about who wants to say the next thing.

My eyes are unfocused and far off, my breaths shallow and small when Grigory calls my attention back to him.

"Clara," he says, and my eyes come back to life to focus on

him. "Markus has suggested I go home with you tomorrow, and I would very much like to do so." He pauses to let me take in his words. "But this will be your decision."

My mind reels with a staggering overload of information. His words barely register as I wind back mentally to process it all. A bad relationship that has ruined his ability to commit; protect *and* possess; go home with me tomorrow.

Go home with me tomorrow. I frown and shake my head. I have no idea what he's talking about. Markus hasn't mentioned any such thing. And if I'm not wrong, Grigory has left a choice up to me—a choice about him going with me to Denmark?

It can't be. I must have misheard.

I turn to Markus, hoping for some clarification.

"Shortly before the premiere, I opened up the idea of sharing you on a more permanent basis—" he says.

"I don't understand." I cut him off, too tired for all this new information. "You haven't said anything about this." I've always thought things would end after the summer.

"I planned to. But then things went south again, and I decided it would be better not to get your hopes up in case everything fell apart."

Markus keeps going when I'm too stunned to find my words. "I've suggested Grigory goes home with you, so you have some time together, just the two of you—to get over this mess. But Grigory and I agree this needs to be your choice. Neither of us wants to force anything like this upon you after all that's happened."

My head is working like heavy machinery. Only ten minutes

ago, I hated Grigory and thought everything was over. Now Grigory and Markus are talking about keeping up this threesome dynamic and Grigory going home with me *tomorrow.*

I can barely wrap my head around the idea. What will happen if Grigory comes to Denmark with me? How will I know he won't keep doing the same thing he's done all summer? If there's one thing, he's been consistent in, it's shutting me out.

My anger returns with a sudden burst. "And then what? He'll stay a few days, fuck me, and use me; then take off?" My eyes go wide with shock at my own crude accusation. I seem to have lost all control of myself tonight.

"Behave yourself!" Markus's words are a sharp reprimand, but all my attention is directed at the man at the other end of the sofa, who is now getting up and approaching me with determined steps.

Grigory crouches in front of me and takes my chin in a firm grip. His features are set in straight lines, eyes sharp and commanding. He's all control and authority again, and I shrink before him. I've never seen him angry, and I hope to God this isn't it.

"No, *devochka,*" he enunciates the words with cutting clarity. "Except for the remaining two *Tosca* shows, I've cleared my schedule for two weeks to be with you."

I blink moisture from my eyes and shake my head as much as I can in the grip of his hand. "You don't mean that." Tears start falling, sliding down my cheeks and dripping onto his hand.

He releases my chin and uses the pad of his thumb to wipe away my tears. Gently, he pushes my hair behind my ear and molds his palm around my cheek. I want to lean into his touch, soak up the warmth and tenderness, but the lingering anger stops me.

"It's taken me some time, but I've finally made a decision, and I'm not going back on it." Grigory's expression softens. "I want to be with you, and I'm not going to disappear on you again. I promise you that."

"Please don't do that for me," I say, my head stuck on his former statement. "You shouldn't cancel your concerts."

Two seconds ago, I was furious with him, and now I'm worrying about being an inconvenience to him. He breaks down my defenses so easily, and once more it's my need to submit to him that drives me. It doesn't make sense, but that's how he affects me.

"*That* is not up to you. The only thing you need to decide is whether you want me to come or not."

"But how do I know you won't back out? What's changed?"

"Clara," Markus interjects, and my head snaps in his direction. "When Grigory commits to something, he commits one-hundred percent. I wouldn't let him go home with you if I wasn't absolutely sure he was ready to take on this responsibility."

"But how can you be sure now? You were sure before too, right?"

Markus is quiet for a moment, and his grave expression tells me he might not have been so sure after all.

"Sweetie," he leans forward and takes my hand. "I've always trusted Grigory not to cross your boundaries. But I knew the more emotional part might be hard for him, and I saw the risk even as we kept going. I probably should have stopped it, but I guess I really wanted him to find this again—the fulfillment of having a sub to care for."

I frown and swallow hard, and I have to take a moment to process his words. Would Markus really use me like that for Grigory's benefit? "So you risked me getting hurt?"

I'm about to break eye-contact as heavy feelings bubble up in me, but Markus sees it and stops me with a hand on my cheek.

"I saw how much this meant to you. So I decided it was worth the risk to get here." He nods back and forth between Grigory and me, then continues. "If we do this, you might not have to be alone so much during the semester, and Grigory can help fulfill some of those submissive urges I can't take care of when we're apart."

"But, what if..." I stare into the space past his shoulder. "How do I..."

"*Devochka*," now it's Grigory's turn to call upon my attention, and Markus releases my chin to let me look at him. "We can only give you so many reassurances and promises. You need to feel in your gut whether this is right for you—whether you're willing to give this a shot."

"What if I don't?" I shake my head and look away once I say the words out loud. I can't bare those words. And in this moment, I have my answer. I'm not sure if it feels right, and it sure doesn't feel safe, but I know with all my heart I can't bear the alternative. So I shoot my eyes back to Grigory and blurt, "Yes."

An amused smile tugs at his lips, but he quickly schools his features. “If you agree to this, you’re not just agreeing to spend some time with me on and off during a couple of weeks. I’m not staying at a hotel nearby. I’m coming home with you to stay at your place for two weeks.”

The prospect has my heart beating wildly, and I’m not sure if it’s more dread or excitement. Nonetheless, my answer remains the same.

“Yes,” I say with conviction. “I want you to come home with me.”

This time Grigory lets his smile unfurl fully. He moves up to sit on the couch and takes me in his lap.

“I’m happy to hear.” He places a soft kiss on my hair and wraps his arms around me with a firmness that makes me think he’s relieved.

I press myself into him and feel a burst of relief of my own. It hits me so hard it knocks every last drop of energy straight out of me, making me sag in his arms. I’ve been running on fumes since he came—pure emotional adrenaline—and now there’s nothing left. I almost want to cry from sheer relief, but I don’t even have that in me.

Within seconds, I’m drifting off.

I hear Markus get up and feel his hand on my back. “Goodnight, sweetie,” he says, pressing a kiss to the top of my head. “I’ll see you in the morning.”

Strong arms—Grigory’s arms—carry me to bed and folds the comforter around me. Crouching beside me, Grigory caresses my forehead with the back of his hand, and I curl up on my side with closed eyes, reveling in the soothing feeling.

Two weeks with this stern, yet incredibly tender man. I can hardly believe it.

I blink my sleepy eyes open, needing to see that this is for real.

His eyes hold a profound tenderness that clashes with the perpetually stern set of his features. It never fails to astound me, seeing him like this, and it drags me deep under his spell. But it's not without a lingering worry. The tender care never seems to last long with Grigory.

"I'm scared," I confess.

Smoothing his hand over my hair and resting it on top of my head, he watches me with startling sincerity. "I promise I'll take better care of you this time, *devochka*."

I give a slow nod. "Thank you," I whisper.

"You're very important to me, Clara." He strokes my hair a final time. "Now go to sleep. I'll see you in about..." he looks up as he seems to count in his head, "six hours," he says with a warm smile.

He gets up to leave, and I want to beg him to stay. But I stop myself, remembering what he just said. *Six hours.* The lights go off and the door shuts. I quickly fall asleep to the reassuring knowledge that I'll see him again at the crack of dawn.

Dear reader

Thank you so much for reading! Please add a short review on Amazon and let me know what you thought!

If you'd like updates on the next book in this series, If I Were Yours, consider signing up for my newsletter and get exclusive excerpts and peeks into my other writing projects.

Ella

www.ellajacobs.com/newsletter

— ABOUT ELLA JACOBS —

Ella Jacobs writes steamy BDSM and dark romance. She loves exploring the emotional sides to Dom/sub relationships and subjecting her heroines to overbearing alphas with gray morals.

Besides writing, Ella loves music—classical, opera, pop, metal, rock. It inspires her to write, and when her characters are messing with her head, she sits down by the piano and plays Chopin and Liszt to regain her sanity.

Ella lives her own age gap romance with a gruff, loving alpha, who is always ready for some character analysis and rarely gets jealous when she falls in love with her fictive alphas.

You can read more about her own experiences with the BDSM lifestyle on her website.

www.ellajacobs.com

Printed in Great Britain
by Amazon

47267432R00202